MELISSA ADDEY

ON

BLOODIED GROUND

· THE COLOSSEUM SERIES ·

For Steven
You have been a constant reassuring presence as I wander
through the backstreets of Rome. Thank you.

Have you read the Moroccan Empire series? Pick up the first in the series FREE from my website www.MelissaAddey.com and join my Readers' Group, so you will be notified about new releases.

A gifted healer. An impossible vow. An empire's destiny.

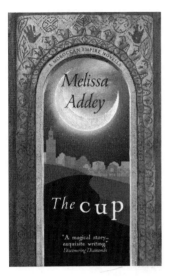

11th century North Africa. Hela has powers too strong for a child – both to feel the pain of those around her and to heal them. But when she is given a mysterious cup by a slave woman, its powers overtake her life, forcing her into a vow she cannot hope to keep.

Trapped by her vow, Hela loses one chance after another to love and be loved. Meanwhile, in her household, a child is born. Zaynab will one day become Morocco's queen and Hela's actions are already shaping her destiny.

Can a great healer ever heal her own wounds? Will Hela turn her back on her vow or follow it through to the bitter end? And will her choices forever warp the character of Morocco's greatest queen, and so shape the destiny of a future empire?

The Cup **is the magical prequel novella to the Moroccan Empire historical fiction series. If you enjoy exploring forgotten histories, the interwoven stories of women and emotional destinies then you will be gripped by this dramatic novella.**

Travel back to the beginnings of a legendary empire. Download your free copy of *The Cup* **today.**

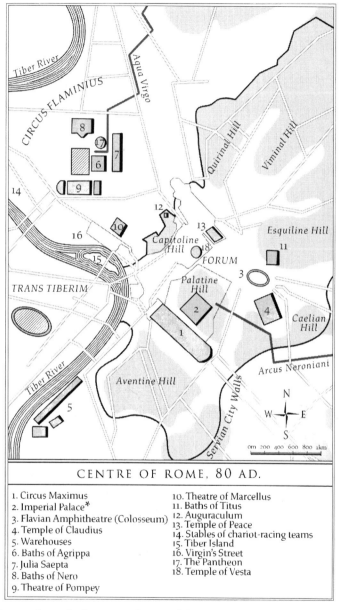

CENTRE OF ROME, 80 AD.

1. Circus Maximus
2. Imperial Palace*
3. Flavian Amphitheatre (Colosseum)
4. Temple of Claudius
5. Warehouses
6. Baths of Agrippa
7. Julia Saepta
8. Baths of Nero
9. Theatre of Pompey
10. Theatre of Marcellus
11. Baths of Titus
12. Auguraculum
13. Temple of Peace
14. Stables of chariot-racing teams
15. Tiber Island
16. Virgin's Street
17. The Pantheon
18. Temple of Vesta

*This map shows the locations of some of the places Domitian began building at this time, such as the Imperial Palace and the Stadium of Domitian, as well as the Ludus Magnus. The Ludus Matutinus would have been close to the Ludus Magnus.

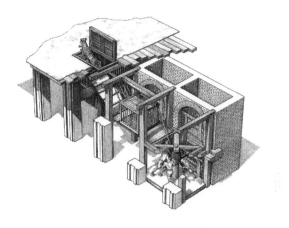

A section of the under-arena space (hypogeum),
with working lifts and trapdoors.

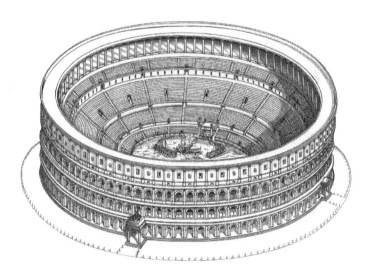

The Flavian Amphitheatre

HISTORICAL
BACKGROUND TO 81AD

I N 66AD THE ROMAN PROVINCE of Judea rebelled against Roman rule and drove the Romans out. Fearful that this might spark further rebellions in other provinces of the Empire, Emperor Nero recalled General Vespasian from exile (he had fallen asleep during a poetry reading by Nero) and sent Vespasian and his son Titus to quell the rebellion. This took four years, engaged one quarter of the entire Roman army and ended in Titus' troops looting and burning the Temple of Jerusalem in 70AD. Hundreds of thousands of Jews were killed or enslaved during this period.

Emperor Nero died in 68AD, the last emperor of the Julian-Claudian dynasty. His reign started well but his later years are mostly associated with extravagance and cruelty, which mainly affected the aristocracy. He remained popular among the lower classes which made up the majority of the population. He had a large area of central Rome cleared to create his Golden House, a vast palace complex with a lake. Rumours said the Great Fire of 64AD had been deliberately started by him to enable this project.

Following Nero's death came the Year of the Four Emperors, which culminated in Vespasian taking power in 69AD and founding the Flavian dynasty, which lasted twenty-seven years. He was the first emperor to come from the Equestrian rather than Senatorial rank and he set in motion a large number of building works, including the Flavian Amphitheatre, known to us as the Colosseum, which was located on Nero's now drained lake and largely paid for with loot from the Temple and the sale of Jewish slaves. Vespasian died in June 79AD and was succeeded by his son Titus. In October 79AD, Mount Vesuvius erupted, destroying multiple cities including Pompeii. In spring and summer of 80AD, Rome suffered first a "pestilence" (possibly malaria) in which 10,000 people died, and then a three-day fire. The Flavian Amphitheatre was inaugurated that summer, with 100 days of consecutive Games including water-based spectacles, for which they flooded the arena. Titus ruled for only two years, then died, possibly of a brain tumour. He was succeeded by his younger brother Domitian in September 81AD.

ROME, OCTOBER 81AD

BROKEN SHARDS

"LUCKY PECKER, DOMINA? VERY BEST quality, very affordable. Wood, bronze, even silver or gold if it takes your fancy. Lucky pecker, Dominus? Brings vigour in the bedroom, lots of sons, wealth in all your business transactions…"

"Morning Secundus." I say to the bustling man currently working the crowds in the Forum.

Caius Didius Secundus makes his living selling pendants in the popular shape of a phallus, a highly auspicious symbol found all over Rome. His merchandise is small and portable, which does make it prone to stealing, so he wears a normal tunic but also a cloak, even in summer, into which are stitched the many pendants he offers for sale. When a customer has chosen the one they like best and paid for it, Secundus will cut the thread and hand it over, along with an ongoing monologue about the many benefits it will bring his new customer in every possible aspect of their life.

"Virility of a gladiator, Dominus, I swear – Morning, Althea. You well?"

"Not bad."

"You're heading the wrong way. The Flavian Amphitheatre's

just there, if you hadn't noticed. The great big building at the end of the Forum?"

"Been summoned by Domitian," I say.

"The new Emperor? Already? He's barely got settled in."

"I know."

"Ooh. In trouble, are you?"

"Hope not."

"Tell him if he's feeling nervous about his sudden rise to power I can do him a very good price on a lucky pecker, get his time as emperor off to a good start."

I grin. "I will do."

I'm almost at the imperial palace, where Marcus will be waiting. We got the summons last night that Domitian wishes to see us. I left Marcus at dawn, cursing over the folds of his toga, Karbo trying to help him put it on elegantly. My own smartest tunic and headwrap feel overdressed, but you probably can't be too smart to meet an emperor. Titus used to just turn up at the amphitheatre if he felt like talking to any of us, which was alarming in its own way, but at least you couldn't fret about it in advance. This summons by Domitian feels far more formal and is frightening. I tug at the shoulders of my tunic and the brooches holding it in place, trying to make it feel more comfortable. I've sent word down to the warehouses by the docks to inform the cleaning team that they'll have to do without me this morning, instead appointing two supervisors to manage the work we had planned. The Games are over for the year, our workload therefore considerably reduced from the strain of producing vast daily spectacles to the simpler task of repairs and cleaning programmes. However Marcus and I are still supposed to be on site overseeing the end of season cleaning and refurbishment works; our absence will throw the teams into disarray, but then no-one would consider refusing an imperial summons.

The Forum is busy. I'm not sure I've ever seen it quiet in all my years in Rome. There's always something going on. Road-sweepers and carts at dawn followed by stallholders setting up for the day to sell everything from trinkets to street food, priests on their way to the temples. The drifting smoke above the Temple of Vesta assures all of Rome that the sacred flame is burning as it should, cared for by the six Vestal Virgins. The lawyers are setting up for the day, there's the odd tutor leading their pupils to find a good quiet spot in which to sit and carry out their learning for a few hours. Men hasten to attend the morning salutatio with their patron. Later there will be senators and other men of importance strolling together, having heated discussions or heading to the baths for a relaxing afternoon. And as the day goes on Rome's she-wolves will be on the prowl for rich customers. The Forum is always lively.

There's a cool breeze in the air, the desperate heat of the drought-dry summer washed away by the early October rains. It's been more than a month since I stood on our rooftop and laughed out loud with pleasure at the sensation of heavy rain falling on me, before I turned to see Marcus doing the same and...

And nothing.

I tug at the shoulder-brooches again as my stomach turns over. The feelings that rose up in me at that moment, the sudden realisation that I... that I am in love with Marcus... the dizziness and desire that swept over me... I have done nothing about them. In that moment of realisation I spoke his name out loud like a spell, an incantation that would bring him to me, but the thunder drowned me out, took the spell and threw it away in the wind. I stood there one moment longer, gazing at him as he, unknowing, looked out across the city, and all my certainty left me. I ducked back into my own roof hut just as Karbo woke and shrieked with glee at the rain, then ran out to play in it. I heard Marcus' laugh, Karbo's joyful yelps as they danced about the rooftop like madmen together, bare feet splashing in new-made puddles, while I sat drenched and shaking on my bed, trying to make sense of what I was feeling.

It took me two whole weeks to even look Marcus in the eye again when speaking to him, suddenly, ludicrously, shy in his presence. He asked more than once if I was well and I had to give hurried reassurances, heat rising up my neck and into my face.

"I knew it," was my friend Cassia's shrieked response when I finally broke and told her.

"Hush," I begged.

"I will not hush," she said, beaming. "I knew it! You two are made for one another. When's the wedding?"

"There is no wedding! He knows nothing about how I feel!"

"Tell him then."

"He might not... he..."

"Venus and Juno! He might not what? Want a lovely woman like you as his wife? Nonsense. Lucky to have you. You do everything together. He says you are his right-hand woman, that he could not do his job without you."

"That's *work*."

"Oh and he wouldn't like you in his arms? A pretty one like you? Snuggle into his bed one night, see if he asks you to leave."

"Cassia!"

She laughed, black curls bouncing. "Get on with it or someone else will. Handsome man like that." She grew serious for a brief moment. "A good man, too. He'd make a good husband, Althea."

"He's *been* a good husband," I said sadly. "He's still grieving for Livia."

"He'll grieve for her all his life. My father still misses my mother and that was many years ago. But that doesn't mean Marcus can't love a new wife. How long's it been?"

"Nearly two years."

"Tell him."

"I…"

"You want me to tell him?"

"No! Don't you dare!"

"Well, don't come crying to me when he comes back home with a new wife one day just because you didn't speak up."

The Praetorian Guards on duty nod without interest at the small scroll I present, which names me and allows me to enter the imposing building. I'm directed to a vast atrium where a tinkling fountain plays in the sunlight. There are marble benches set around the walls, where people, mostly men, are waiting to be called in. They must all have appointments, whether to see Domitian himself or one of the high-ranking senators and officials based here. I look around and spot Marcus, who, I'm glad to see, has successfully put on his toga. He doesn't look comfortable though.

"Hate wearing this," he mutters, rolling his shoulders.

"You look very smart," I say. *Handsome*, is what I want to say, but I can't bring myself to.

"Wish he'd just turned up on site."

"Do you think he's dissatisfied with something?"

"Who knows."

The large sundial near the fountain indicates that we ought

to be called for at any moment. Swallowing, I sit up straighter, the marble bench chilling my behind.

The sundial's shadow moves on and on. Marcus, who is reading through scrolls and occasionally huffing to himself, puts one foot up on the bench and leans against me, trying to find a more comfortable position. Once I would have leaned back against him, would have thought nothing of it. Now I sit stiffly, feeling the weight of him against my arm and shoulder. I am conscious of every part of our bodies and how they are touching. When I breathe in I can smell his scent, the fresh toga and his own clean sweat, a trace of horse from his visit to the Blues stables last night to collect Karbo from his work as a stable hand, the apple he was munching on when I arrived here.

I try to ignore the scent of him, roll my shoulders.

"Sorry," says Marcus, straightening up.

"I – don't mind," I say.

"Good," he says, slumping back against me, the warmth of him heavy, his arm pressed against mine, bare skin to bare skin. The hair on his forearm brushes against me as he lifts the scroll back up. "Mercury help me, what *is* this drivel? Can no-one explain themselves properly? All I asked for was a simple list of how many gladiators and of what type they have in the training school of Puteoli and what is this? A lot of nonsense about prices and suchlike. As if I don't know what a gladiator costs and as if the Emperor doesn't have the wherewithal to pay. Write back and tell them I just want a list."

"I already have," I say.

"I'm glad someone knows what they're doing."

Once, I would have smiled, pleased at the praise. Now I only wonder whether this is how he sees me: a comrade to be slumped against, his right-hand woman in the role he carries out as organiser of the Games. Nothing more. And yet there is so much more it could be, *we* could be. The warmth of him against me…

"I'm supposed to be overseeing the repairs to the lifts," he mutters. "The carpenters were due this morning. Jupiter knows what I'll find when I get back on site."

"Do you think they're going to call for us at all?"

"The gods only know." He fishes out another scroll. "Ah, you wrote to Funis. Has he replied?"

"No answer yet."

"We need to know by Saturnalia at the latest or we'll be left without a beast hunter and good luck to us if we have to start a new season of Games in March without one of those."

Funis, the beast hunter we met in Ostia last year when we needed water-based animals. His unusual clothing, the pattern of scars on his dark-skinned cheeks. The evil-eyed crocodiles he delivered to us when we took on the near-impossible task of flooding the amphitheatre for spectacular water-based Games. I shudder at what happened afterwards, the moment when I thought Marcus had drowned. But afterwards, when he held me while I wept… I should have said something then, should have touched his face…

Marcus is waiting for an answer. I clear my throat. "He said he wasn't fond of being in Rome; perhaps he doesn't want the role."

"Anyone with ambition would jump at the chance. Beast hunter to the Flavian Amphitheatre? Doesn't get more lucrative than that."

A Praetorian Guard is waving us over. "Marcus Aquillius Scaurus?"

We jump to our feet and follow him through a door and down a corridor. Halfway down is a lofty double door, this one flanked by more guards, who push it open at our approach.

We're shown into a large chamber, well-lit by windows down one side. In the centre of the room is a wooden table, at which are standing two men in togas, one of which is trimmed with purple. So this is Domitian. Thinner and taller than his brother Titus, a long face, short hair.

"Marcus Aquillius Scaurus, manager of the Flavian Amphitheatre, and his scribe, Althea Aquillius," announces the guard.

Domitian doesn't move. He's staring down at the table, on which is laid out a model of Rome, meticulously rendered in pottery.

The other man looks up at us. Slight of build, he is holding a quill in his right hand, while his left holds down on the table a partially unrolled scroll. There's something owl-like about him, with his large gold-hazel eyes and dishevelled brown hair sticking up like rumpled feathers. His skin is very pale, untouched by the sun. He stares at us for a moment, then looks to Domitian for guidance.

Domitian pays no attention. Very slowly, he squats down, bringing his eyes level with the table and the model, peering through the tiny streets of his toy Rome, gazing at something we cannot make out. He reaches out one finger and prods a building, straightening it up. I realise that each edifice on the table is a little block which can be moved about.

I glance at Marcus, who gives a miniscule shrug.

"Ahem."

The sound comes from another person in the room. A tall thin man, elegantly attired in a toga, standing unseen in a far corner. He has grey hair and, although he looks our way, he does not smile, only coughs again, a discreet sound.

"Ahem. Imperator."

Domitian looks up at the man, who flicks his eyes in our direction. Domitian follows his gaze to us and stands up.

"Who are you?"

Marcus inclines his head politely. "Marcus Aquillius Scaurus. Manager of the Flavian Amphitheatre, Imperator."

"Who's she?"

"Althea Aquillius. My scribe. You sent for us, Imperator."

Domitian doesn't offer any kind of welcome. Instead he sinks back into his squat. "Look."

We approach the table.

The model of Rome is exquisite. Every building I can think of, from the amphitheatre, Forum and great temples, down to the most insignificant and run-down insula, is represented, each made like a little toy house, moulded out of pottery, then painted in minute detail. The river Tiber has been painted onto the table, in a winding green-blue. I spot our own insula in Virgin's Street, close to the island in the middle of the river, which is occupied by the temple of Aesculapius, god of healing.

Domitian stands up again. "My architect Rabirius is preparing the designs for a large-scale programme of building."

The owl-man nods fervently and gestures towards the half-open scroll. Marcus and I shuffle closer, peer at what he is indicating.

The area around the amphitheatre is clearly marked out, but the arena floor is not shown as one smooth surface, but rather as some sort of odd maze-like structure. Outside the perimeter, four new buildings have been sketched. I frown, trying to make sense of what I'm looking at.

11

Marcus is looking from the model to the scroll. "You have… plans… for the amphitheatre's arena, Imperator?"

Domitian answers without looking up. "Yes. A brick-built hypogeum, two storeys high, sitting beneath the existing arena floor. It will be better than the current layout, which is really just a big empty area. It's a waste of space and doesn't allow for efficient management of lifts and so on. This will be better, more organised."

Marcus doesn't say anything but his eyebrows go up. "And these?" he asks, indicating the four new buildings on the scroll. One of them is quite large.

Domitian lays his finger on the drawing. "Gladiator schools. With barracks and arenas of their own, as required. This one," he points to the largest, "will be the Ludus Magnus, the Great School. Three storeys, one hundred and thirty-five rooms, a three-thousand-seater arena for practise so that the fans can watch the gladiators training. That one right next to it," he points to a smaller but similarly shaped building, "will be the Ludus Matutinus: the Morning School. For beast-hunters, venatores and the more exotic fighters, women and such, with a five-hundred-seater arena. Then two more schools in due course, the Ludus Dacius and the Ludus Gallicus, for the gladiators of those styles and provenances." He talks fast, but his facial expression remains strangely blank, though his eyes are bright with enthusiasm.

I look down at the model and then glance at Marcus who gives me a tiny nod, knowing what I'm going to say.

"The new gladiator barracks," I say tentatively, "according to the drawing they would need to be…" I gesture to the pottery model, which clearly shows that the designated area is already full of buildings, both large and small. There is certainly no space for four large new edifices to be constructed.

Domitian tilts his head. "Of course," he says. He reaches out with swift movements, picking up one tiny creation after another and letting them drop to the floor, where they smash, pottery shards skidding out across the marble floor, the noise echoing round the empty room. I gasp and step back, but Domitian, after breaking perhaps ten miniature buildings in this way, turns his head and gives me a sudden odd smile, teeth bared, which vanishes again in an instant. "I have these, you see."

He fumbles in the folds of his toga and pulls out four little pottery pieces, neat replicas of Rabirius' architectural drawings of the gladiatorial schools, then places each one into the new gaps on the model, tutting when he finds one more building that will need to make way for what he has in mind, casually dropping it as he did the others, one last crashing destruction.

"See?" he says, looking down at the revised model.

I steal a glance at the architect, who is staring down at the model, eyes wide.

"And there's so much more I want to build," says Domitian. "A new Circus, a villa for the Vestal Virgins near the Temple of Vesta, a new imperial palace here in Rome as well as one outside in the country. Temples. And, of course, there's all the reconstruction that needs completing after the fire in the Ninth Region. The Pantheon, Saepta Julia, Baths of Agrippa, the stage of Pompey's Theatre, the Diribitorium and the Theatre of Balbus." His words spill out so fast I can barely keep up, his finger moving above the model, indicating locations. Rabirius is nodding with enthusiasm at the catalogue of works, fumbling through a tub of scrolls as Domitian speaks, ready to produce drawings of everything being listed.

"Ahem." Again the quiet man in the corner.

Domitian looks his way.

"Your next appointment."

Domitian hesitates, then gives a reluctant shrug. "Very well." He looks at Marcus. "I would like to meet the animals."

"Imperator?"

"You have animals. For the Games."

"Yes, Imperator, they are delivered weekly, to the warehouses by the docks, but only during the Games season, they –"

"I would like to meet them. When shall I come?"

Marcus makes a quick recovery. "Were there particular animals you wished to see?"

"Antelope."

I was expecting something like lions or tigers, but Marcus smoothly agrees. "Next week, Imperator? I can send word of a good day for a visit to your secretary?"

Domitian waves a hand towards the quiet man's corner without looking at him. "You can let Stephanus know. He takes care of everything."

Marcus glances at the man, who gives a short nod.

"That was odd," I say, taking a deep breath as soon as we are outside and far enough away from the building that I can risk speaking out loud.

"Very," agrees Marcus. "All that building? That's how Nero started. It sounded like a good idea till he started behaving strangely."

I lower my voice. "He's already behaving strangely. Smashing those models? What was that about?"

A voice comes from behind us. "The Imperator has his own way of doing things."

I freeze, then slowly turn, as does Marcus. Behind us is the tall quiet man. Stephanus.

I swallow. "I didn't mean –"

The man waves away my untruthful protest. "The Imperator behaves... unusually sometimes. But he is not mad. You will come to know his ways, as I do."

We wait for him to continue.

"You will likely see a lot of him over the coming months. He is fond of the Games. He also has a passion for building and now that he has the power to do as he pleases, he will indulge it. He likes to manage things very closely and in person, he will not just give the command for the work to be done and walk away."

We nod.

The man gives a very small smile. "He also likes animals. As he has mentioned. He will be with you at the animal warehouse in six days' time, at midday. He rises late, since he has difficulty getting to sleep. I will see you then."

He turns and walks away briskly, without a farewell.

We look at each other, breathe out. My heart is still thudding.

"Find out who this Stephanus is," says Marcus. "I don't trust him. He's too quiet on his feet, for starters. And we've got to find a herd of antelope, off-season? With no beast-hunter?"

As I make my way back towards the insula that afternoon a man asks me for directions.

"Virgin's Street is just off Sand Street," I tell him.

"Full of virgins, is it?" says the man, winking.

"It's named for my landlady Julia," I say. "She served for thirty years as a Vestal Virgin."

The man swallows. "No offence intended to Lady Vesta," he says, making a sign to ward off the ire of the gods. He mutters thanks and hurries down the street when I indicate it to him while I turn into our insula's gate smiling to myself at his sudden respect.

Julia is pruning the vines that snake up the wooden courtyard staircase. Below her the children of the insula splash water from the fountain at one another and the adults gather after the evening meal, making the most of the last light of the day to chat between themselves. Among them are the tall gangly framed Fabius, physician to the amphitheatre and his dwarf daughter Fabia, one of my closest friends and physician to the second largest gladiatorial school in Rome. By the time I've got a plate of stew from Cassia's always-busy popina and eaten half of my meal, Marcus joins us, in time to hear me tell Fabia and Fabius about our morning's meeting with Domitian.

Fabia frowns at us. "He threw the pottery models on the floor? Do you think he's going to be trouble?"

Marcus shrugs, spooning up another mouthful of his own stew. "Not sure. He's strange, for sure. He seemed enthusiastic about public buildings for the good of Rome, but –"

Fabius chimes in to finish the sentence. "– but that's how Nero started."

"As long as he doesn't start raiding the temples to pay for them," says Julia from above, clipping away at the vine. "If he starts that, we'll know to be careful."

Karbo is following along behind Julia, picking up the fallen clippings. "If I put one in a pot, will it grow?" he asks.

"You want to grow a vine?" she asks.

"Yes. I want a garden on the rooftop."

"I'll help you. Marcus, you have a farmer on your hands. You need to buy back your family's farm so you can take him there with you."

Marcus laughs. "I could do with a strong boy," he agrees cheerfully, pouring more wine for Fabius. "The farm will be falling apart and overgrown, it's going to take some hard work when I return there, whenever that day finally comes."

I sit quietly, listening. Marcus speaking of leaving his life here as manager of the Games makes me anxious. Will he leave soon? And if he does, will he ask me to go with him, or simply leave me here? I imagine for a brief moment what it would feel like if Marcus were to turn to me and say that it is time to start the life he has always dreamed of; that he will buy back his family's long-lost farm and return to Puteoli to live there, but that he cannot think of doing so without me by his side, that he...

"Time for bed?" says Marcus.

I choke on my wine. "What?" I ask, spluttering.

Fabia pats my back ineffectually. Being a dwarf, her tiny frame is unable to put enough weight into the action and it takes me a few moments to recover.

"I need some sleep," says Marcus, standing up. "Tomorrow we need to request a copy of those drawings from Rabirius. I've had to put all the lift work on hold till we know what structure they'll need to fit into. I was hoping for a quiet winter. Why do we never get a chance to rest properly?"

I watch him making his way up the stairs.

Karbo appears at my side. "Can we have a cat?"

"What?"

"A cat. Domina has had kittens again. Can we bring one here? The little tabby one? I've called her Letitia. Can she live here with us? She would enjoy exploring the rooftops. Especially if I plant her a garden."

I set aside my own half-built daydream. "Very well. But she

17

is to be your pet, understood? You must save her scraps and feed her every day until she can hunt for herself. And right now it is time for bed."

I wake to a soft singing, which turns out to be Adah tending to the bees. She disdains protective clothing or smoke when caring for them, her gnarly wrinkled hands unafraid as she lifts up the wickerwork lids of the hives, shuffling from one to another through a cloud of buzzing with no apparent harm. Karbo and I keep a more wary distance.

"Can I try some, Adah? Please?" begs Karbo.

"In good time," murmurs Adah between snatches of song. I don't understand the words, it must be a song of her own Jewish people. She always sings to the bees, claiming that it makes them calmer than the usual burning of cow dung.

"It looks like a good harvest," I say, as she lifts out several chunks of heavy wax, dripping with golden honey and lays them carefully in a large platter.

"It is," she says. "Here, boy."

Karbo creeps up to her, crouching down in the vain hope the bees will not find him and sting him for stealing the fruits of their hard work. He takes the chunk of honeycomb from her and slips back to me, a couple of bees following the scent and weaving around our heads. Karbo breaks the chunk in two and honey drips down his fingers as he offers me some. We pop the honeycomb in our mouths and lick our fingers, while the bees continue to circle, wondering at the sudden disappearance of the honey they'd traced as far as us.

Karbo makes happy noises through his mouthful.

"It's delicious, Adah," I say and she smiles, satisfied.

"After this they can sleep for the winter," she says. "Rest and

18

be strong for the spring to come," she adds over each hive in what sounds like a blessing as she closes them up again.

"That's what we ought to be doing," I say. "Resting over the winter to be ready for spring and the next season of Games. But it doesn't sound like we're going to get much rest if Domitian has his way with all these building works he has planned. The amphitheatre's going to be one big building site."

Adah spits, not unexpectedly. "Cursed place," she says, referring to her long-held resentment over the amphitheatre built with money and slaves from the destruction of the Temple of Jerusalem, the most holy place of her people. "You should not work there any longer. Do something better with your life."

"Such as?"

"Get married and have children," she says promptly, a smile playing around her mouth.

"I'll think about it," I say, not wishing to develop this conversation any further in case she starts making suggestions of possible husbands for me to consider. "Karbo, you're supposed to be at the stables and I'm supposed to be at work. We'll see you later, Adah."

I can hear Adah chuckling to herself from the rooftop, before she drifts back to her beekeeping song. I run down the wooden stairs, only to be met by a dark figure standing in the gateway of the insula.

"Althea."

It takes me a moment to realise it is Funis, the beast hunter from Ostia. If anything he looks even more unusual here. By the docks his brown skin marked with facial tattoos, the armbands and the tiger tail he wears, as well as the Egyptian-looking top and skirt he favours fit in better, filled as the area was with people from across the Empire. Here, in our insula, he looks like a visitor from another world.

"Funis! You came to us after all. I thought your silence after my letter of invitation was a refusal."

He gives a chuckle. "It was. But then I thought better of my plans. Why deny myself Rome when she has called my name? My own prejudices towards her from the past should not cloud my judgement when looking to the future and what it may bring."

"I am glad to see you," I say. "And Marcus will be too. He was keen for you to join our team."

"I am at your service. I wondered if I could call on you to show me the amphitheatre?"

"Of course," I say. "I was about to go there. Do you need a place to stay? I can ask Julia if there are rooms free here in the insula."

He shakes his head. "I will be staying at the gladiatorial barracks run by Paternus," he says. "He's an old friend and has been good to me."

"Gladiatorial barracks are hardly luxurious," I say.

"I'm used to them from the old days. They make me feel at home."

We walk to the largest gladiatorial barracks, where Funis embraces the gladiator owner and trainer Paternus, leaves his travelling bag and promises to meet him at the baths later. Then onwards through the Forum and to the amphitheatre.

"Impressive," murmurs Funis, tilting his head back to look up at the third floor. "And you say Domitian has further building plans? I thought it was complete."

"He wants a different layout under the arena floor," I say. "I'll show you the plans."

We make our way to the arena floor, where Funis turns around on himself, looking up at the vast white expanse of seating. "Sixty thousand?"

"We can do. Usually about fifty thousand, but it's possible to squeeze more in."

He stands silent for a moment. "I can hear the roar of the crowd," he says at last. "It must be an extraordinary place in which to perform."

"You were a gladiator yourself, you told me."

"A long time ago. Beast-hunting is a lot safer as a career."

"Not tempted to take up gladiatorial combat again?"

He laughs. "No, thank you. Rome is dangerous enough, I don't need to add extra danger to my life."

I frown. "Is Rome a dangerous place for you specifically?"

"It is," he says, turning away to look at the Gate of Death, still locked up from the night.

"Why?"

"Oh, a very long story," he says.

"I'd like to hear it if you'd like to tell it."

He turns back to face me. "I will. One day."

"If you had misgivings about coming to Rome, what overcame them?"

He looks steadily at me for a moment, his brown eyes warm, a smile on his lips. "A letter."

My cheeks grow hot. "Being the beast-hunter for the Flavian Amphitheatre is a hard role to turn down," I say. "It's very prestigious. And lucrative of course," I add.

"Some things are worth pursuing, whatever your misgivings," he agrees. "Can you show me the space under the arena?"

We make our way through one of the hidden doors in the arena wall, through a stone tunnel and down a dark wooden staircase to the vast empty space underneath, the ceiling far above us. Tiny streams of daylight filter down between the arena's wooden boards, cutting up the area into tiny strips of light and dark, hard to see clearly in.

"Usually there's a lot more down here," I say. "The lifts which take the animals and gladiators into the arena, the physician's area, the morgue. If Domitian's plans are put into place, this whole area will be split into two storeys and lots of smaller spaces. Marcus doesn't much care for it."

"Does he still enjoy the role?"

"Yes. Although he gets frustrated when things are changed without warning, on the Emperor's whim."

"Understandable. Has he remarried?"

The sudden change of topic leaves me flustered. "N-no."

Funis looks directly at me. "And you?"

"Me?"

"Married?"

My cheeks are burning, I'm glad the light down here is so poor. "No," I say and then, my voice too loud, "Let me show you outside the amphitheatre. You can see where the new gladiatorial schools will be built."

I lead him back up to the exits, grateful to feel a cool breeze on my hot face as we come to the top outside but conscious of him walking right behind me up the stairs.

"You'll need to find us some antelope," I say, grateful to have thought of a matter of business to talk about. "Domitian wants to feed some animals and we don't have any in storage. We didn't get much warning."

"Of course," says Funis. "You have only to name the day and they will be there."

Two days later, a pale dawn wakes me. I could sleep in; our days in autumn and winter have far less work to do than when we have to provide the near-daily spectacle of the Games. But I'm too used to rising early and besides, I have news for Marcus. I wash and make my way to Cassia's popina, rubbing my bare arms. The summer warmth has well and truly gone. I'll need to air my winter cloak and Karbo's; they've been packed away for months.

"I'm making pancakes," Cassia says.

She knows me well. The fresh fruit that I am fond of in the summer is coming to an end, though there are still some late grapes. It's time to return to her griddled pancakes with date syrup, which both Karbo and I are fond of. "I'm going to need to get our cloaks out again soon. Although Karbo's boots will be too small, the way he's shooting up."

Cassia pours wine for two customers and flips my first pancake over. "It's the anniversary soon."

"Fifteen days." Fifteen days till the morning two years ago when ash fell softly over Rome and we found to our horror that Pompeii had been obliterated beneath its smothering weight, taking with it Marcus' wife and baby son.

"Has he said anything?"

"No. He didn't say anything last year either. He just disappeared all day and then went to see Julia." I glimpsed him sat at her table, head down, shoulders heaving.

Cassia serves me my pancakes and pours more batter onto the hissing griddle as she sees Karbo approaching. "It'll be easier to speak to him when the anniversary has passed."

The piece of pancake is too big in my mouth. I take my time chewing to avoid answering. By the time I've swallowed, Karbo is telling me in minute detail how he plans to take care of Letitia the kitten. I nod along without really listening until it's time to wave goodbye to Cassia and make our way to the amphitheatre.

Marcus interrogates me as soon as I arrive. "Tell me what you found out."

"His name is Gaius Petronius Stephanus. He's a cousin of Gaius Petronius Arbiter."

Marcus' eyes narrow. "Nero's 'arbiter of taste'? The one who people said wrote the *Satyricon* under a pen name?"

"Yes. But I don't think they were very close."

"Arbiter came to a sticky end anyway, didn't he? Can't imagine many in his family would have wanted to acknowledge him."

My notes say that Arbiter's preferential treatment eventually made the commander of Nero's guard jealous. Arbiter ended up being accused of treason and arrested for it at Cumae twenty years ago. He didn't wait to find out what his sentence would be, instead taking his own life. "How come his cousin's been hired then? If Arbiter ended in disgrace?"

"That whole clan are well in with the Flavians, they're not going to let one bad apple taint their chance of being cosy with the Emperor. What's Stephanus' actual job, did you find out? Is he Domitian's secretary?"

"No. Everyone was a bit vague about what exactly he does. Someone called him Domitian's 'handler', as if Domitian were a wild animal being trained up for the Games."

"He could do with some handling if he's going to be chucking pottery around and pulling apart half of Rome to add in the buildings he fancies." Marcus runs his hand over his hair and I have to stop myself imagining what it would feel like on my fingers. "Any luck getting the antelope?" he asks.

"Funis has sourced twelve. They'll be at the warehouse when he visits."

"As if we need Domitian treating our warehouse like a private zoo."

I shrug. "If it keeps him happy with us it's a small price to pay. It'll be easier once the season starts again in spring, then there'll always be animals down there for him to visit if that's what he likes to do."

"Funis is visiting us this morning," says Marcus. "Ah, there he is. We're glad to have you join us."

Funis offers a wide smile. "It's my pleasure to be here," he says. "Although I hear there's a building programme to get done before we can start a new season?"

Marcus tuts and strides over to the edge of the balustrade, waving down at the arena below us. "I've been sent a copy of Rabirius' drawings. This hypogeum he wants under the arena floor; it's like a labyrinth, two floors of it. Hardly any air flow, or light. So we'll need torches and lamps everywhere, which will turn it into Vulcan's furnace during the summer. And a fire hazard."

I offer Funis a copy of the drawings and he examines them with interest.

"It looks like a labyrinth," he comments. "Two floors of it?"

I nod.

"You don't look happy with it," Funis tells Marcus.

"I'm not. It's a waste of space. All those archways and corridors, they're only made possible with a lot of walls. Which means we lose space. And flexibility. We used to be able to put things wherever we wanted. Now the lifts will be fixed in place and you can't move a few out of the way when you need the space for something else. It's very elegantly designed but it's very rigid too. And complex. And it's… hidden."

"Hidden?"

"You can't see what's happening in another part of the hypogeum: everything's in tiny little spaces. So something could be going wrong somewhere and I won't know until someone gets a message by running to me, which will take time, or by signals like our whistles, which can interrupt music or the chorus." He looks worried and I want to rest my hand on his arm to reassure him.

"So remind me: did you like the design or not?" grins Funis.

"Will we still have the same number of lifts?" I ask, bringing matters back to practical considerations.

"Yes," Marcus acknowledges. "So that's good. Just less room overall and smaller, tighter spaces for everything."

I groan. Nothing is ever easy. "Right now I need to look over the merchandise the stallholders are preparing for next season. And it's time for the morning salutatio, you'll have people calling on you. Are you coming?"

Marcus shakes his head. "I'm heading to the Aedile's salutatio session to try and get some guidance out of him. But there's probably no arguing. The current Aedile doesn't stand up to the Emperor, anyway, never has done. So you'll have to run the salutatio here." He grins. "You do it so much better than me, anyway."

I laugh. The morning salutatio, when people who consider Marcus a valuable contact and patron visit him to proffer their greetings and mention what they may be able to do for him, or what they'd like him to do for them, is a regular part of Roman life for a man of means or, like Marcus, a man who can offer valuable opportunities. But Marcus finds the whole process tedious and manages to wriggle out of it most days, leaving the formalities of the process to me instead. His suppliers and other contacts found it peculiar to deal with a woman at first, but have given up trying to locate him, settling for me instead, knowing that their messages and presence (or lack thereof) will be duly noted and passed on. They find it odd, but then we're seen as a strange lot at the amphitheatre anyway, falling somewhere between the imperial power that funds us and the glamorous, but still lowest, dregs of society with whom we associate, from prostitutes and dancing girls to gladiators and wild beasts.

"I'll leave you to your work," says Funis. "I should get back to the gladiator barracks. There was a break-in last night, perhaps robbers looking to steal weapons. The entry guard was stabbed, but nothing was stolen as far as we can tell, perhaps they got disturbed. Patronus is in a bad mood and could do with a friend about the place."

We wave him off, the three of us going about our separate ways for the day.

When I reach the ground-floor corridor Secundus is hanging round with the other stallholders.

"I didn't know you wanted a stall next season, Secundus?"

"Oh, I don't, I prefer working the crowd while they're queuing. People buy on impulse when they're bored," he says, winking. "But I always like to see what everyone else will be offering."

I try to get some semblance of order out of the jostling crowd of men I need to get through. I point to the narrow table we've set up and take a seat behind it, Secundus hovering by my side like a keen assistant. I've got a scroll with stall spaces marked on it so that I can write in each name and where the stall will be when we re-open next season. Although the crowds can approach and enter the amphitheatre from all directions, there are certain favoured places for stalls. The imperial entrance of course, since some crowds gather just to watch the emperor arrive. The Baths of Titus, since some spectators will want to head straight there after a hot and dusty morning spent at the Games. Most popular is the area close to the meta sudans fountain, favoured by crowds and hawkers alike because of the way the waters cool the air during the heat of summer. These favoured spots go to the best traders, who have proven their wares are good quality and of interest to spectators, season after season.

"Right, let's start at this end, queue up in the order you arrived this morning and lay your wares out here on the table so I can see what you have in mind. What've you got for me on your second stall, Brocchus?"

Brocchus has more than one stall promised to him this year, having done a roaring trade last year. He specialises in models of gladiators which are always popular merchandise, but this new stall is something different. He unrolls a cloth wrap, carefully laying out the items inside it for me to look at. "Children's toys, Althea. Go down ever so well with the parents, especially if the children nag."

I look down at the clay and carved wooden or bone models of wild animals and gladiators, posed in fighting stances. Next to them sits a small green glass cup with a tiny spout. "What's that?"

"Ah, new for the season, very proud of this one, had the mould commissioned specially. It's a baby's bottle."

"With *gladiators* on it?"

"For the proud father who loves the Games."

"Brilliant," says Secundus. "They'll love that."

I hold up the little green glass cup. "I hope they do well for you. I don't need to see the other merchandise, I remember it from last year. I'll try and find you a good spot." I dismiss him and wave forward the next in line, a squat bald man, who is empty handed. "Calvus?"

"This is going to require a contract with Patronus from the gladiator school, but I'm thinking of a premium offering next year, not available to just anyone, but worth the price for the blessing it will provide to the happy couple."

"Which is?"

"Bloodied spears for weddings. Straight from the Flavian Amphitheatre itself, I mean you can't get more prestigious than that, can you?"

Secundus nods wisely. "Oh absolutely. Very good luck for the bride, that, having her hair parted by a gladiator's bloodied spear before they put on her veil."

I grimace. "I'm not sure I'd want that put through my hair."

"'Course you would. The blood will be dry by the time they actually use it, won't it?"

I shake my head. "Whatever the customer wants. But you'll have to talk to Patronus, or Labeo, if you want to get a bloodied spear. Normally all the armour gets sent straight back to the barracks at the gladiator schools, where they clean it up."

After a morning spent inspecting ever more outlandish ideas for Games merchandise, I send a messenger to find out if the antelope are safely installed and make my way to the Baths, where I meet Fabia for a well-earned soak.

"Labeo's beside himself at the idea of moving to a big new gladiatorial school right next to the amphitheatre," she tells me. "He can't wait. We'll be able to have a lot more gladiators once we have a large barracks like that."

"Will you be able to manage by yourself?" I ask. "Being physician to a big school like that was enough already. If they expand, will you be able to look after even more gladiators?"

"I'll get an apprentice," she says. "Or maybe even two. I could do with them."

The days pass quickly and down at the docks, at midday as promised, we're awaiting Domitian. The warehouse where we store animals is finally complete, having undergone significant repairs to the leaking roof. Once waterproof, it was cleaned and then laid out to enable us to receive deliveries of animals more easily and to keep them apart. Storing animals like antelope next to lions is always a poor idea. The antelope cringe in fear and end up not eating; the lions spend their time growling and swiping through the bars, maddened by the proximity of their natural prey. Instead we subdivided the giant space available so we can keep predators and prey separate. We built bigger and better pens too, and left corridors of space so that pens can be lifted straight onto carts to be taken to the amphitheatre. We will use the large pens for keeping the animals, then move them into much smaller, closed ones for transport. The heaviest ones have their own wheels mounted to the bottom so that they are simply hitched up to a cart and pulled through the streets to the arena.

Today the slaves stand to attention, as Marcus makes one final check. The warehouse looks ridiculously clean and neat; the floors have been washed for the occasion. Usually the air is thick with the smell of animals; today it smells fresh in a way I've never experienced before.

"We're ready," Marcus says finally, although with reluctance. "I don't know why he'd want to see the animals when they're not doing anything interesting. If he's keen on animals, why doesn't he just attend the Games in the mornings, when we do the hunts, come springtime?"

Only Funis is calm. "Who knows how great men think," he says.

Karbo dashes in. "They're here," he says.

"Keep out of the way," advises Marcus, hurrying out of the door to go and greet Domitian.

I expected a vast entourage: the Praetorian Guards, officials, hangers-on. But Domitian enters with only the tall shadowy figure of Stephanus behind him.

"Imperator," I say, bowing my head as Domitian strides past me.

He doesn't reply, though his eyes flicker towards me and away as he passes, intent on the cage of antelope ahead of him. Reaching it, he stops close by the bars, snaps his fingers and holds out his hand without looking behind him.

"Grass."

Marcus and I look at each other and both of us look to Funis, but Stephanus has already stepped forward and produces a clump of fresh grass from the folds of his toga, which he places in Domitian's outstretched palm.

Domitian pokes the grass through the bars of the cage, but the antelope huddle at the far side, uncertain of his intentions. They have been caught and made captive, brought to this frightening, echoing place. They can scent past predators who have been held here. Besides, they are no strangers to being seized by friendly hands offering just such temptations. Whatever trust they once had is long gone.

"What's wrong with them?" demands Domitian over his shoulder.

I stare at Marcus for help. He frowns but before he can speak, Stephanus smoothly intervenes.

"Timid, Imperator. You will have to show great patience."

Domitian sinks to the floor in a cross-legged position like a child about to receive tuition, arranging his toga folds so that he is comfortable. Once settled, he holds out the grass again and waits.

I glance at Stephanus, who is waiting in silence, hands behind his back. Catching my gaze, he gives a small nod, politely acknowledging a distant acquaintance, and returns his focus to Domitian.

Marcus looks at me and opens his eyes wider, a tiny comment on the absurd situation. Karbo peeps round a dividing wall at me, his face asking questions I am not at liberty to answer. I make a tiny gesture with my hand, a quick *go-away*. Karbo sticks out his tongue and disappears, no doubt to report to the rest of our hidden and curious team that something peculiar is going on.

It takes over an hour before the antelope trust Domitian and feed from his hand. Marcus, Funis, Stephanus and I stand in silence watching his back. He never speaks or moves in all that time, never sighs with irritation or moves his hand, only keeps the grass held out, resting his forearm on his knee to keep it steady. Eventually, a brave antelope moves forwards and reaches out its neck as far as it will go, its muzzle so close that its breath ruffles the grass. For a moment I wonder whether Domitian will grab at the animal, but he stays still and the antelope gathers its courage and eats. It is joined by another and when the grass is gone they retreat and Domitian stands up and turns to us, his previously blank expression lit up with a joyous expression which makes him look both younger and more handsome.

"They ate from my hand," he says. "I had to wait a long time but I knew they would come if I stayed still."

"Exemplary patience, Imperator," says Stephanus.

Domitian's smile broadens at the compliment, then turns to Marcus. "I will visit often," he says. Next time I would like to feed meat to lions."

Marcus opens his mouth to answer, but Domitian is not waiting for a response, he is already striding away, stepping out into the sunshine beyond the warehouse door, his shadow Stephanus following him.

We reach the door a few paces behind them and sure enough the entourage I had expected is gathered just outside, a few dozen bodyguards, officials and litter-bearers with a large litter, into which Domitian climbs, the drapes pulled around him for privacy, the whole group already moving away, curious bystanders scattering out of the way.

"Did he just sit there for the whole hour trying to feed the antelopes?" demands Karbo from behind us.

"Yes," says Funis smiling.

"Why?"

I look at Marcus. "I really don't know," I say, starting to laugh.

I'm eating at Cassia's the next morning when one of our slaves arrives from the barracks, white-faced and shaking with news that the slave who does the cooking for the amphitheatre's slaves has been killed. His body was found only paces from the barracks, throat cut, limbs stiff, blood congealing.

33

"It must have happened last night," they say. "Siro's body was found at dawn by a road sweeper."

"Siro?" I ask, horrified.

They nod, wringing their hands.

I try to wake up. "Karbo, run to Marcus and send him to the warehouses. I'll meet him there. You're not to come."

"But I –"

"No," I say and my tone makes it clear there is no room for argument. "Go. Cassia, I'll see you later." I'd promised to have dinner with her and Fabia. It's hardly an auspicious start to what I had hoped would be a quiet day with friends.

I follow the slave through the streets down to the docks. I know most of our slaves by sight, but Siro I knew by name. A Syrian, hence his allocated slave name, he was a lopingly graceful man, with two missing front teeth and a quiet disposition. That changed when I discovered he was a good cook and assigned him to the slave kitchen in their barracks situated in a large warehouse by the docks. Slowly he came out of his shell, singing to himself first quietly and then loudly in his own language as he turned out vast pots of vegetable porridge, loaves of bread, stews with scraps of meat from the amphitheatre. His fellow slaves, discovering his talent for cooking, would shyly request food from their own countries, food they were homesick for and he would try to recreate it from their descriptions with the few ingredients at his disposal. He used to call out to me when I inspected the barracks, offering to feed me along with the cleaning crews and other teams of slaves assigned to the amphitheatre.

There's not much to see. His throat is cut. Someone who knew what they were doing. A violent and bloody end. I shake my head, tell two of the women to clean him up, send a runner for the undertakers. Marcus arrives shortly after me.

"Why would anyone want to kill Siro?" I ask. "He's a cook. He looked after everyone."

"Unlikely to be anyone in our own team," says Marcus. "Rome is dangerous at night. He shouldn't have been out so late. What was he doing wandering round Rome at that time, anyway?"

It takes a while before a slave admits that Siro had fallen for a slave woman belonging to a family of merchants who live close to the docks and had sneaked out late to meet with her. We try to follow up on the information but no-one knows the merchant's name, so we can't find trace of them.

"Robbers. Street thugs," says Marcus. "They must have thought he had money on him and when he said he didn't they probably thought he was lying."

"Not the owner of the woman?"

"Cut Siro's throat? Doubt it. If they didn't want him around they'd have given him a thrashing or sent word to us. I'll send word to the Aedile so they can update their records."

The slaves we manage belong to the emperor, so it's his administrators that have to be notified, not that they will know or care who Siro was. He had no family here in Rome, so his only mourners will be his fellow slaves.

I promote Siro's assistant to our head cook and try to reassure the team as the undertakers take the body away. We're unlikely to find out any more information and meanwhile, a thousand slaves need feeding every day. I'm sad for Siro, but Rome's streets are treacherous at night. My own experience last year, when coming home alone at dusk threw me into Rullo's clutches has already taught me this lesson in no uncertain terms and Siro's fate has been a forcible reminder. I'm sorry for the unknown slave woman he has been courting and her confusion and sorrow when he no longer comes to see her, but there is no way of sending word to her.

After the unsettling events of the day, the familiarity of the insula and the surroundings of Cassia's warm popina are welcome. It's Cassia's night off, so the shutters are drawn close, but she invited Fabia and me to dinner and the popina has more room than her small apartment, so we agreed to gather there. Her father Cassius has already retired to his bed, so we will not disturb him with our chatter.

"It's your evening off and you're still cooking?" I say as I arrive.

Cassia grins. "Can't help it."

Fabia arrives with a gift of rich black grapes and adds it to my own offering of spiced apples baked into a rich pastry case. "You made that?" she asks, eyebrows raised.

"Less of the surprise," says Cassia. "I taught her well."

"Had to make it twice," I confess. "I burnt the first one in Maria's oven. Didn't stop Karbo from wolfing most of it and Marcus finished up the rest."

Cassia's eyes gleam. "And?"

"And?"

"Did you say something?"

I pretend not to know what she means. "About what?"

She huffs at Fabia. "Still hasn't told Marcus how she feels about him."

"It's impossible," I wail. "How do I even start a conversation like that?"

"Just tell him," says Cassia.

"Oh yes, that's excellent advice. Very detailed. Thank you.

'Marcus, you know how it's the anniversary of your wife and child dying? Well, how about you marry me? Because I've just realised I'm in love with you.' That sort of thing?"

"Yes," says Cassia, lifting out a tray of roasted pumpkin from the oven. "But without the reference to his dead wife. That will not set the right tone."

"Oh really? Hadn't realised that. Juno have pity on me."

"There's always that handsome man who turned up here asking for you."

"Handsome man?"

"Your new beast hunter."

"I'm not interested in him," I say.

"He couldn't stop looking at you."

"Never mind anyone else," I say. "I like – I love Marcus."

Fabia pours us all wine and adds water to the cups. "Maybe wait till the anniversary has passed," she says. "He will make an offering at the temple and pray for them, but it's been two years and perhaps the pain is no longer so sharp. You could..."

"Yes?"

"Spend some time with him?"

"I spend every day with him!"

"Not at work. Here. Invite him to dinner. Get Karbo out of the way. I'll have him at mine for the evening. Talk to Marcus about the future, about the family farm, see if he still thinks of going there one day. If he does, you can say how lovely you thought it was, how much you, too, would like to live in such a place. Plant the seed in his mind of going there with you."

"There you go," says Cassia approvingly. "There's a detailed plan for you. Venus herself couldn't do better. Now all you need to do is carry it out."

"I don't have the courage. My mouth goes dry when I think of saying... anything."

"Well, if you don't, someone else soon will. A handsome man like that doesn't stay a widower long. I'm surprised he's lasted two years. You better nab him quick, or you'll be coming weeping to me and Fabia when some woman who's not as shy as you steps up to the challenge."

"But what if he doesn't... if he doesn't like me in that way... it would be so awkward having to keep working together."

"Cross that bridge when you come to it."

"I suppose."

"No suppose about it. Get on with it."

"You're putting me off my food," I say. "It makes my stomach roll to think of him... of saying..."

"Ooh, she does have it bad." Fabia laughs. "You better start visiting Venus and Juno's temples and see if they can help your cause."

We settle round the table. Saltfish fritters and roast pumpkin are the main dishes, but Cassia has also laid out a collection of tiny bowls, filled with spiced chickpeas, little balls made of breadcrumbs flavoured with nuts and herbs, fried mushrooms and pickles. There is also fresh bread studded with olives, which is hard to stop eating.

"So good," says Fabia indistinctly through a mouthful, while I make noises of agreement, mouth too full to speak.

Cassia leans back against the wall behind her bench. "It's nice to sit down and eat," she says. "I'm usually eating with one hand and serving customers with the other."

There's a sound outside, beyond the courtyard's gate, a whimper which fades. We glance at each other, shrug. But it comes again.

"Baby," says Fabia.

There must be a woman and her baby somewhere in the street, passing by. Though it's getting dark. I hope they have someone to accompany them. A chill comes over me at the thought of Rullus last year, how he grabbed me in the darkness and how lucky I was to escape. Fabia sees me twitch and gently touches my arm.

"Anyway," says Fabia, "I meant to tell you. Father was saying that there will definitely be more physicians needed if the gladiator schools are to be extended and he knows a man who –"

The cry is louder this time, more indignant. There is a loud hammering on the popina's shutters.

Cassia frowns. "Who's there?" she calls out.

"Open up!" A man's voice.

Cassia stands on our side of the shutters, hesitant. "We're closed."

The hammering comes again. "Open up. Please!"

Fabia and I get to our feet.

"I said, who's there?" Cassia repeats.

"Quintus."

Cassia's frown deepens as she thinks. "From the fullery?" she asks at last.

"Yes. Let me in."

Cassia glances at us, but undoes the shutter and pulls it open. A young man takes a step forward, hesitating on the threshold. He's of average height, with black curls to rival Cassia's unruly mop and olive-toned skin that has been burnt dark brown by the long hot summer. I've seen him occasionally in the area; he's the local fuller's fifth son. Their fullery is a few streets down, easy to find by the stench of human urine used in the washing process

39

and the rhythmic sound of soaking clothes being stamped on by slaves to rid them of dirt and stains. Right now he looks anxious.

"I was hoping someone would be here."

"What do you want?" asks Cassia.

The man gestures to the shadows outside. "Have you seen it? I wasn't sure what to do."

"Seen what?"

"The baby."

Cassia stares into the gathering darkness. "Baby?" She glances over her shoulder at us. "We heard something, we thought someone was passing."

Quintus shakes his head, his expression anxious. The cry comes again, louder now that the shutters have been opened.

Cassia peers out into the dark. "Where is it?"

Quintus gestures. "Just there. On the ground."

"Pick it up," says Fabia.

Quintus hesitates but our expectant faces convince him. He steps into the darkness and returns a moment later, gingerly carrying a large woven basket. He holds it out at arm's length to Cassia.

"Put it there," she says, stepping back from him and indicating the countertop from which she serves her customers food and wine.

He places the basket down gently enough but the movement upsets its occupant. The baby cries again and this time it does not stop. Cassia and Quintus hover, but Fabia, ever practical, drags a stool over to the countertop and climbs onto it, which brings her up to our height. She looks into the basket.

"Hello, little one."

The wailing increases in volume. Fabia puts her hands into the basket and lifts out the wriggling bundle, pulls away the cloth wrapping it and reveals a furious, red-faced baby, who screams louder than ever.

"What's the matter with it?" asks Cassia.

Fabia gives her a look. "It's cold, hungry and its mother's nowhere to be seen?" she suggests. "Get some milk," she instructs. "Help me down," she adds to me.

I assist Fabia down from the stool. Still holding the baby, she sits and pulls away more of its wrap, nods. "A girl." She refastens the wrap in place.

Cassia is standing staring.

"Milk?" says Fabia again.

Cassia brings some goat's milk and Fabia uses a spoon to get it into the baby's mouth. She's eager, mouthing into the air and whimpering when the spoon is withdrawn, sucking frantically when it is put back in her mouth.

"Where did she come from?" asks Cassia.

Quintus shrugs. "How would I know? I was heading home and heard her, thought it was a kitten at first but then I made her out, wriggling in that basket. I didn't know what to do."

Cassia's eyes narrow. "Is she yours?" she asks bluntly.

"What? No!"

Cassia keeps her eyes on him. "Might be she's your baby but you don't want a baby. Or a girl. So you got the mother to leave her here so you get off without marrying her or a mouth to feed?"

Quintus raises his hands. "I'd never do such a thing. Bona Dea! What are you accusing me of? If it wasn't for me noticing her as I passed she might have died out there tonight."

"Why's she outside my popina?" asks Cassia to the room.

"You're known for feeding beggars," I say. "Maybe her mother thought you'd look out for her."

41

"I can't keep a baby! What will Father say? What will people think? They'll think she's mine. As if I haven't been shamed enough with a marriage falling through on the very day of the wedding!"

We all watch in silence as Fabia continues spooning milk into the baby. "We'll need a proper baby bottle," she says, calm and unflustered as ever.

"Are you *keeping* her?" asks Cassia.

"Are you throwing her out?" asks Fabia.

We all stand silent while the two women glare at each other, neither breaking eye contact.

"Julia," says Cassia at last, dropping her gaze. "I'll fetch Julia. She'll know what to do."

Moments later, Julia arrives and proves as practical as Fabia. "For now, we'll make sure she's fed and clean. Tomorrow we can decide what to do. Cassia, can you have her in your apartment? Fabia and Fabius will be out all day from dawn, your work means you'll be here all day."

Cassia splutters but Julia's calm request sounds like a command. Reluctantly, she acquiesces.

We all follow her back to her apartment, where her father Cassius has to be woken. Julia explains the situation as though it is entirely normal to bring an abandoned baby back to one's home after an evening with friends.

"Only for tonight," says Cassia more than once.

It is Fabia, still practical, who finds an old tunic, rips it up to create a clean wrap for the baby girl, spoons more milk into her and lays her gently on Cassia's bed. Cassia lies down, keeping a wary distance.

"Wouldn't it be better if she were with you?" she asks me. "You already have a child, you know what to do with them."

"Karbo came to me already a boy," I say. "I know as little as you do about babies. And tomorrow I have to go to work."

Cassia looks downtrodden but doesn't answer, only edges slightly further away from the baby, leaving her most of the bed.

I climb the stairs to the roof hut, where Karbo is already lightly snoring. It takes me a long time to fall asleep. Where is the baby from, and what is to be done with her? It's common enough for a baby to be left on the streets and found by strangers, when for some reason its family cannot care for it, or perhaps the head of a family has refused to welcome it into the family on the ninth day of its life, when it would be laid at their feet to be accepted and named. Sometimes a family without children of their own adopt such a child; sometimes, unfound or unwanted, they simply perish. This one has found its way to our insula and into Cassia's bed. Whatever is to become of her?

DUST AND RUBBLE

I CAN HEAR THE BABY CRYING as soon as Karbo and I approach the popina for breakfast the next morning.

"I can't keep feeding her with a spoon! It takes ages and she just cries," says Cassia, flustered by the crying baby in her arms and the curious, waiting customers. Some look annoyed with the delay in being served, others are asking questions about who the baby is or giving their conflicting opinions on how to quiet her.

I turn to Karbo. "Karbo, run to Brocchus. Tell him I need that baby bottle with the gladiators on it. Tell him his stall can be by the meta sudans fountain when we reopen next season if he'll send it straight back with you, no questions asked."

"Run!" begs Cassia as Karbo disappears down the street.

"I'll hold her," I say.

Cassia hands over the squirming angry bundle.

"She's wet," I say, holding her away from my clean tunic.

"I can't change her now, I've got customers!"

I take the wailing baby to our courtyard fountain. The cold water turns her scarlet with shock and outrage, but the sound of her cries brings the baker's wife out to investigate and, when she's done exclaiming over the story of how we found her, she goes into her apartment and returns with some strips of cloth.

"Mine are done with such things. Lucky I still had a few," she says.

She teaches me how to wrap the baby and I return to Cassia's where Karbo, panting, is holding the little green glass cup. Once filled with milk, the baby struggles for only a moment to understand what she must do, then sucks with desperate hunger, emptying the cup in moments, before making small grumbling noises which break out into a loud cry.

"*Now* what's wrong?" asks Cassia.

"I have to go to work," I tell her, passing the crying baby over the counter.

"Don't leave me with her!"

"How is she?" a voice asks from behind us.

We both turn to find Quintus standing outside the popina.

"Good, you're here," says Cassia. "Take her."

She hands the baby back over the counter and Quintus obediently moves forward and takes the little bundle. I expect him to drop her, but he looks surprisingly confident, holding her pressed against his shoulder. He pats her back a few times and she lets out a loud belch, then closes her eyes drowsily, letting her head rest on his chest.

"How did you do that?" asks Cassia.

Quintus grins with pride. "Got two younger siblings," he says. "You get the knack of these things."

"You're looking after her during the morning rush."

Quintus doesn't argue. "You might need to feed me breakfast, if I can't go home," he says.

Cassia pours half a cup of wine from the dregs of a jug and bangs down a plate with a piece of stale bread in front of him. "There you go."

"Thank you," he says politely.

"I'll leave you two to it," I say, grinning. "And someone needs to think of a name. We can't keep calling her 'she' and 'her'."

"Emilia," says Quintus.

"What?"

"I've named her Emilia. I thought about it last night."

"Are you keeping her?" asks Cassia.

"I'm not going to dump her back on the street," he says indignantly.

"Is she going to live with you?"

"I thought she could live here, but I'll help out."

"Oh you did, did you?" starts Cassia, outraged.

"I'm late," I say, grabbing Karbo by the tunic and pulling him with me. "See you later."

Karbo trails behind me. "What will happen to her?"

"I don't know."

"Can't you adopt her? You adopted me."

"And you're a handful," I say, smiling. "I couldn't even if I wanted to. That took special dispensation from Titus before he died. I don't see Domitian being so easy to get favours from. Women can't adopt children. It has to be a man."

"Will Quintus adopt her?"

"I don't know," I say. "Perhaps. But his family's big enough as it is, I'm not sure his parents would want to take in a foundling, with eight grandchildren of their own."

When we get to the amphitheatre Marcus has a face like thunder. "He actually wants the hypogeum built before March. *Before* our new season starts."

"He? Domitian?"

"Yes."

Four months is not long to build a two-storey brick building, complete with lifts that fit within the structure, trapdoors and so on. "Can't it wait till next year?"

"Do you want to ask him that?"

"No thank you. So they'll build the hypogeum this year and build the gladiatorial schools next year?"

"No. All of us together."

"What?"

Marcus expands. "The amphitheatre first, to complete before the season opens in March, while they rip down the buildings to allow them to build the two largest gladiatorial schools by summer, the Matutinus because it's smaller first. The Magnus will probably take a bit longer as it's so big. But he's not holding back. Practically every builder in Rome has been hired for this and he's talking about bringing in building teams from further afield, or even drafting in soldiers for extra labour. He's not being patient about it."

It's a huge workload, but the imperial purse is deep and it looks like Domitian is a decisive person, not given to delays when he wants something. He's a great fan of the Games as well as chariot racing. No doubt the stables will also get some imperial attention soon enough.

"And what is the theme for next year's Games? Have you decided yet?"

Marcus shakes his head. "I was trying to spend some time planning before all this got thrown at us." He shrugs. "I'll think of something. Let me know if you had something in mind."

Later I find Funis, busy inspecting the mechanism of the lifts and taking measurements so that he can work out how many differing animals each one can hold.

"Time for the baths," he says. "Want to come, Althea?"

Although I've happily bathed with most of our team on one occasion or another, something about the idea of bathing with Funis is too intimate. "I promised Cassia I'd give her some help with the baby," I say.

Funis smiles. "I heard. Not every day a baby is dropped on your doorstep. Would you like children of your own one day?"

Once again, he has steered the conversation towards me and my future and again, I find myself flustered by his interest, his attention. He has a knack for asking about the very things I long for but cannot see a way towards. "I have Karbo, the gods know he keeps me busy enough," I say with a laugh that sounds false, even to me.

"Sounds like you and your friend Cassia both have kind hearts," says Funis smiling, and turns back to his measurements, calling out the numbers to his assistant, a young slave boy.

I'm rocking a sleepy baby Emilia for Cassia during the supper rush while Marcus sits at a table nearby. It should be a quiet evening in the insula's courtyard, but Karbo and his friends are engaged in a game that involves a lot of roaring from one boy in the middle of the group and much swordplay and elaborate death scenes from everyone else.

"Be quiet!" bellows Marcus after a while. "Trying to think!"

"They're playing at Theseus and the Minotaur," I say.

"They need packing off to bed," he grumbles. He has scraps of papyrus and a couple of empty scrolls in front of him, as well as a quill pen and ink waiting for ideas which, clearly, are not forthcoming. "All I've got so far is we need to showcase Carpophorus," he says. "He's been one of the finest bestiarii Rome's ever seen and now he's retiring, it's his final season and he'll be a huge draw to the crowd, everyone will want to say they saw him fight. But all he likes doing is stomping about killing animals. He's not all that for gladiatorial bouts, not his specialism." He crumples up another scrap of papyrus, dissatisfied.

"Karbo," I call. "Too much noise. Shall I tell you the story of the Minotaur instead?"

"NO," says Karbo, still dashing about an invisible labyrinth.

"It's that or bedtime," says Marcus firmly.

Reluctantly, the children gather at my feet.

"Long ago on the island of Crete," I begin, "the king died. As he was childless, his stepson Minos declared himself as the next ruler. He called upon the king of the seas, Poseidon, to send him a bull from the sea, which would prove his claim to the throne was looked upon with favour by the gods. If such a bull were sent, he declared, he would sacrifice it to Poseidon, to honour and thank him for his favour.

And a bull did come from the sea. It was huge and white and perfect and at this sign of favour from the gods, Minos was acknowledged and crowned King of Crete. But he did not stand true to his word. Instead he sacrificed a lesser bull and Poseidon, angered at this slight, made Minos' wife, Queen Pasiphae, fall in love with the white bull, feel lust as she might for a man. So besotted was she that she went to the palace inventor Daedalus and asked him to make for her a wooden cow, in which she could conceal herself and thus mate with the bull."

I grimace. Marcus grimaces back at me.

"Go on!" says Karbo.

"Months passed by and Pasiphae bore a terrible creature, which had the body of a man with the head of a bull, and which she named Asterius. Ashamed, King Minos ordered Daedalus to design a labyrinth in which to conceal the beast forever and there it grew up into a vicious monster, the Minotaur. It had a taste for human flesh. Afraid of not fulfilling its dark desires, King Minos ordered that Athens, his vassal state, should send each year fourteen youths, seven men and seven women, to be thrown into the labyrinth and torn to pieces by the Minotaur. Three Twice the terrible orders were given and twice a ship with funereal black sails set sail from Athens to Crete, carrying with it the sacrificial victims who perished at the hands of the grisly monster.

"But Athens had a hero warrior as its prince. Theseus, son of King Aegeus of Athens, had already proven himself time and again against many terrible dangers and had even gone with other heroes on their adventures, such as Jason in his quest for the Golden Fleece, and Hercules to conquer the Queen of the Amazons and had always been victorious. He told his father that the next time the sacrifice was to be made, he would join the youths and maidens selected. He would enter the labyrinth, slay the dreaded Minotaur, and –"

"That's it!" says Marcus.

"What?" I ask, startled.

"We'll take the story of Theseus and the Minotaur as our theme for the Games next year. We'll work our way through the whole story at key events during the season. We can have demonstrations of bull-leaping for the Minoans and some of Theseus' first heroic deeds, like fighting alongside Hercules against the Queen of the Amazons. Then we can have the Minotaur killing the sacrificial victims and finally the moment when Theseus kills the Minotaur. Perfect."

I nod. It will give us a strong theme for the season, which will help us develop more spectacular events in all the Games we put on. It will allow us to draw on legendary feats and stories with which the audience is already familiar and which will lend themselves well to the gladiatorial battles and animal hunts we need to provide. Having a story running throughout the season makes people want to come back over and over again, keeping the amphitheatre full and the Emperor happy.

"Good choice," I say, and Marcus grins back, his previous grumpiness erased.

"I'll make some notes about the different elements," he says, pulling a scroll, quill and ink towards him with more enthusiasm.

"Only," I add, "the bit with Pasiphae and the bull… it really has been done in the arena before, but…"

"We'll fake it," he says.

"Go ON!" says Karbo, bored with our sudden enthusiasm for planning the Games when he and his friends want to hear the rest of the story.

"Yes! Go on!" cry the others, tugging at my tunic. Emilia startles, hiccups and then, as I hush the other children, she grows softer in my arms, slowly falling asleep.

I try to remember where I was and speak more gently so as not to wake her. "Umm, so… so, Theseus' father, King Aegeus of Athens, afraid for his son's safety, begged him not to go. But Theseus was adamant and when the time came he took his place aboard the tribute ship with black sails, together with seven maidens and six other Athenian youths. As they set sail, he promised his father that he would return in a ship with white sails, to signify his victory over the beast. And so they reached Crete. There were many rituals to be undertaken before the sacrifice was made and in the days that followed, Princess Ariadne, daughter of King Minos, fell in love with Theseus. She went to him in secret one night and told him that she would help him defeat the Minotaur if, in return, he would take her with him back to Athens as his wife, and this Theseus agreed to do."

I imagine myself as Ariadne, whispering with a Theseus-Marcus, our heads close together. Perhaps they sealed their bargain with a kiss, although I'm well aware their romance does not end well...

"AND?" demands Karbo.

"And," I say hastily, "Ariadne, being very clever, gave to Theseus a ball of red thread she had spun with her own hands and told him to tie one end to the entrance of the Labyrinth, so that he would not get lost inside its maze of corridors. The next morning, the fourteen Athenians were taken with much ceremony to the opening of the Labyrinth, and sealed up inside it. The others were terrified, of course, fearing that at any moment, around one corner or another of the impossible maze, they would be found and eaten alive by the monster that dwelt within. But Theseus used the ball of red thread given to him by Ariadne, tied it to the entrance and made his way to the centre of the Labyrinth, where he found the Minotaur. In the desperate battle that followed, Theseus was at last victorious and returned safely to the door to the outside world, where his fellow countrymen and women stood huddled together, waiting for him to return a hero or for the beast to find and kill them. When they emerged in triumph, Ariadne joined Theseus and the whole company set sail for Athens. But alas, Theseus did not honour his promise. Instead he abandoned Princess Ariadne on the island of Naxos, where she married the god Dionysus. But Theseus was punished for this deed, when, in his haste to return home, he forgot to...?" I pause, to let the children complete the story.

"Change the black sails for white!" they yell back at me.

"Indeed. And so his father, seeing the ship returning with black sails, and despairing at the thought of his own son being dead, jumped into the sea and drowned. And so Theseus lost his own father, even as he returned victorious."

"Couldn't be better," Marcus mutters to himself, still scribbling. "Battles with Amazonian women and centaurs, Golden Fleece adventure, culminating on the last night of the Games with the Minotaur. Carpophorus can be Theseus. Perfect end to his public career." He looks up, beaming at me. "Well done, Althea. It's a perfect theme. We can work so much around it. Tomorrow we'll start proper planning."

But as the days grow cooler and the anniversary of Pompeii's destruction approaches, Marcus grows noticeably more irritable, disappearing for long stretches of time, muttering every time he sees anything to do with the new plans, even snapping at head of the under-arena area, Strabo, who lets it wash over him, unbothered.

"I'm sorry he got cross," I say, when Marcus has stamped away over some minor misunderstanding about where the props will be stored overwinter, since the whole of the under-arena space now has to be fully cleared for the builders to move in.

"He didn't mean it," Strabo says, lumbering over to a group of slaves and indicating which items are to be taken to the warehouse at the docks we have secured. "Hard time coming up. He'll be better afterwards."

I nod, glad of Strabo's calm understanding.

Funis watches the exchange. "I was going to ask Marcus about some of these animals I need to source," he says. "But perhaps it would be better if I spoke with you, for now?"

"Yes," I say. "What did you need?"

"The overall theme is Theseus and the Minotaur. What other elements are you including?"

"We've had a fantastic helmet with horns made for the Minotaur and we'll do a few shows of the beast's conception, birth, early years, the festivals and culture of Crete, the maze itself of course and the Minotaur killing anyone who enters. Theseus will go on some adventures: with Jason for the Golden Fleece, with Hercules to battle the Queen of the Amazons. There's a hint of romance with the Queen and also with Princess Ariadne because Carpophorous is a bit of a favourite with the ladies in the audience."

"So I've heard. Is he a favourite of yours, too?"

"He's a great bestiarius, but not really my idea of a handsome man."

"And what is your idea of a handsome man?"

"So," I say firmly, refusing to answer and feeling my cheeks grow hot, "the grand finale will be Theseus against the Minotaur. That's when he will kill the monster. Last day of the Games for the season."

Funis looks amused at my refusal to answer, but takes the hint to keep the conversation focused on business matters. "I've met Carpophorus. He's an impressive bestiarius. He'll be bored when he retires. He may be getting too old to fight but he says he would consider being a beast hunter. I might need a man like him, perhaps we can work together. How many times will you run each element of the story?"

"Hard to tell. Once for each of them at least, but if something is really successful, it'll get run several times. The Golden Fleece quest and the battle with the Amazons will be popular."

"And the bull-leaping of Crete."

"Yes. Not many people will have seen that, but I've heard it's spectacular."

Funis nods. "It is. It requires extraordinary skill not to get hurt. I better start training bulls and round up a larger team of bull-leapers."

"I've never seen bull leaping," I say.

"It's what it sounds like. Men and women, although the crowd usually prefers women. In the arena with bulls. A bull comes running at you, you leap towards it, grab its horns, vault over the back of it and land unharmed. Acrobatic."

"Sounds dangerous."

"It is. One moment you're safe, the next you could be dead. The crowd loves it."

Quintus is always carving when I see him, finding small bits of scrap wood and turning them into toys. He gives tiny wooden horses, cats, pigs and sheep to the children of our insula and a horned bull to Karbo when he hears about our theme for this year. He is ready with a smile for everyone he sees and will lend a hand with whatever anyone is doing. He has quickly come to feel like part of our community and it's strange when he speaks of "home" and means somewhere else.

"Does your father mind that you spend so much time here?" I ask.

"There's enough people to run the fullery, that's mostly what he worries about, so I can slip away if it's quiet," says Quintus. "My mother frets more. She wants me married off and giving her more grandchildren, though you'd think with eight already born that would keep her busy."

"What does she make of Emilia?"

"Thinks I'm mad, picking up some unwanted baby off the street." He looks down at the gurgling baby, who is currently examining her toes with great interest. "But we could hardly put her back there, could we?"

I shake my head. "But she'll have to be adopted one day," I say.

"I'll find a way."

"Good lad," says Maria from above us. As usual, she's been listening to anything that goes on. Ever since I've lived in this insula, Maria has been at her self-allotted post every day, sat on the walkway just outside her own room, vast bosom resting on a cushion to make the balustrade more comfortable. From there she can watch everything that goes on in our courtyard and the inhabitants' lives, commenting as she sees fit.

I twist to look up at her. "But who is she supposed to belong to as she grows up?" I ask. "No-one's formally adopted her."

"All in good time," says Maria. "And you're doing a fine job, young man."

Quintus picks up Emilia. "Looks like I have more work to do," he says. "This one is wet."

He leaves the courtyard to change her and Maria smiles at me. "Don't fret, Althea," she says. "Bona Dea looks out for babies. She has a plan."

"Does she?"

"Oh yes," says Maria with satisfaction. She winks and adjusts her bosom on the cushion. "You'll see. Let fortune run its course."

The twenty-fourth of October comes and I wake very early, uneasy memories of the past dragging me from sleep even though it is not yet dawn. The day when, two years ago, the sky darkened across Rome and grey ash fell all around us in the amphitheatre, silent and soft. Delicate and, as we came to find out, deadly. I lie awake for a while, then slip out of my bed and walk out onto the roof terrace, my feet cold. Marcus is already there. He is standing close to my roof hut, looking out across still-dark Rome to the south, where, far away, a lost city he once called home is buried under a smothering blanket of ash and lava and where, somewhere within that dark embrace, lie the bodies of his wife and baby son.

I want to creep back to bed, want to avoid the awkwardness of grief, but this only made me feel worse last year, when Marcus avoided me all day, even though only we two shared the horror of the aftermath, when we returned to Pompeii and he dug through the ash in desperation while I prayed to every god I could think of and none of them heard my call, trapped as we were in the realm of Hades. Seeing him turn last year to Julia instead shamed me. I take a deep breath and make my way to him, stand by his side. My sorrow at what happened is made harder because he is mourning his lost love and, if I could have my own desire, it would be to take her place as his wife. But now is not the time for those feelings. Above all else, Marcus and I have been friends. We have stood by one another through horrors such as others can only imagine. I think of the short hours when I knew his family, try to recall what I saw of them, how they looked, how they behaved.

"He looked so like you," I say. "But with her hair."

He nods, does not turn to face me. But his right arm wraps around my shoulders, he lets it rest heavy on me, sharing his burden.

"You must see them always in your dreams," I say, my voice shaky.

He is quiet. I have overstepped our moment of confiding, I have said something foolish, starkly set against the grim reality of their fate and his loss. I try to think what I can say to take back such nonsense, am about to open my mouth, but he speaks.

"Their faces are fading," he says, voice low and hoarse, and his shoulders heave. "I cannot see them clearly anymore when I try."

He sweeps me into his arms. His head lies heavy on my shoulder as he sobs and sobs, his tears rolling down my skin. It takes all my strength to stand upright against him. My arms meet tentatively around his broad back and tighten to hold him as he weeps. My tears fall, not for the darkness that crushed Pompeii but for the guilt crippling Marcus because he can no longer recall the exact outlines of his wife and son's face. This man who would know the scent of them, the touch of them, their voices, in an instant, is broken by the loss of their faces, fading from his memory despite his enduring love for them. He has no portraits of them, only the tiny dolls made of wood and wool that stand on his household shrine, made with kindness by Balbus the toymaker, a skilled man who never saw the woman and child whose likenesses he tried to craft.

Marcus pulls back, though I would have held him forever, wipes his eyes and nose, looks down at my wet face. He brushes away the tears on my cheeks.

"I'm sorry," he says, clearing his throat when his voice croaks. "It is not your grief to bear. Though you have helped me bear it all this time."

I want to say something important in return, but I do not know what.

He takes a shuddering breath in and blows it out in a rush. "Did you make Myrtis' spiced honey cakes to remember her by?" he asks.

"Not yet."

"We should," he says. "Wake Karbo and we'll go to Cassia, beg her for some kitchen space this morning. I'll mix, if you'll tell me what the ingredients are."

"And work?"

"Never mind work today," he says. "This is more important. Wake Karbo."

When I've woken Karbo Marcus takes his hand and leads the way to Cassia's. She is waiting for us, a basin and little bowls already laid out, filled with ingredients.

"You remembered," I say.

"How could I forget?"

"Emilia?"

"Still asleep," she says, laying a finger to her lips. "Try and be quiet. That girl can cry to wake the gods."

And so we spend the hour before dawn and the arrival of customers in the dimly-lit popina, mixing up Myrtis' spiced honey cakes, with the addition of pepper which made hers different from every other cook's. I tell Karbo and Marcus how I used to sit with her in the kitchen in Pompeii when we were both slaves together in a rich merchant's household, how we'd eat cakes and chatter together before the rest of the day's work faced us. We eat the warm cakes straight from the oven and share them with the first customers and passers-by, before taking some to the little shrine at the end of the road in gratitude for having been spared, in sorrow for those who were lost.

"I'll be out most of the day, but I'll make a sacrifice at the Temple of Jupiter later," says Marcus. His eyes are still red-rimmed but he manages a smile of sorts, gives me a crushing one-armed embrace around the shoulders before striding away, leaving me alone, my fingers still sticky-sweet from the cakes, wishing I could run after him and slip my hand into his, follow him everywhere.

"I'll keep an eye on him," says Fabius when I pass him in the courtyard. "He said we'd meet at the baths later."

"Thank you," I say. "It's a hard day for him." I'm grateful to Fabius and his long friendship with Marcus, his calm knowing that today his friend will need him, to sit in silence or talk of the past, to laugh or perhaps even to cry.

Later I will find Marcus again and sit with him on the roof, in the dusk, let him talk about Livia and Amantius, as I am the only one left who knew them when they were alive. And perhaps that shared bond we have will strengthen further, will lead to something more, to...

But it goes as it always does. Fabius and Marcus go to the baths and to dinner. They come home late and another moment that I have half-planned slips away and I am left to dream again, dreams that fade away before I can make them real.

Rome is agog when the news is finally released about Domitian's ambitious building programme, not least because of the speed at which he is putting it into action. There's uproar in the neighbourhood surrounding the amphitheatre when the plans are displayed in public. More than ten large buildings will be pulled down to make way for the first two gladiator schools, as well as the odd smaller building, a roadside shrine that will have to be moved, a few decrepit shops, tatty enough but whose owners and proprietors have enjoyed the benefits of heavy footfall and passing trade that comes with being situated so close to the Forum and the Flavian Amphitheatre. Shopkeepers and landlords alike are outraged at the idea. The landlords are soon silenced when the imperial purse turns out to be more generous than expected, but the people living or working in the buildings are resentful at the sudden change. No-one dares to challenge Domitian, of course, at least not in public.

"What in Hades is this?" Marcus roars when we arrive in a cold dawn light a few weeks after the announcement.

The pristine white stone of the amphitheatre around the Emperor's entrance has been daubed in mud... or possibly something worse, as there are also several cartloads of manure dumped in front of it, blocking the way in.

"Looks like the locals aren't happy," I say. "Karbo, get down to the docks. I'm going to need a bigger cleaning team this morning. I need thirty extra slaves, with brooms and shovels. Tell them to bring the mules and the cart. Run."

He darts away while Marcus and I survey the mess, the anger of those whose buildings will be knocked down having spilled out against the towering symbol of the Games rather than their imperial patron.

"They must have worked through the night," mutters Marcus. "Good thing we were here early."

When the Games aren't on we don't come here every day, and often arrive late in the morning, rather than our usual dawn arrivals when the season is in full operation. But today we had arranged to meet our aquarius to shut off most of the water supplies for the building overwinter, leaving only the ground floor water system working. The work planned for the day included wrapping some of the spouts and pipes in cork and wool lagging to avoid any freezing during the coldest parts of the winter. But this silent, stinking protest is unacceptable; placed right in full view of the Forum, it must be made to disappear immediately and preferably before word gets back to Domitian. Should word get back to anyone, there should be no trace of what happened by the time he or anyone important comes to check on the amphitheatre.

The team of our slaves gathered by Karbo arrives and within

an hour, as the late autumn sun slowly rises and the Forum begins to grow busy, the worst is gone; there only remains the daubing on the walls. We use the water fountains inside to fill buckets, which half the team pour down the sides from the first floor, while below the other half of our crew use brooms tied onto poles to reach the offending splatters and scrub the wall back to its pristine white, a task which thankfully soon looks as though we are simply carrying out normal cleaning routines, rather than an emergency correction. Marcus has stomped off somewhere muttering about night-time guards being required from now on, while I oversee that the work is done to a high standard. The Emperor's personal entrance cannot be anything but perfect. The odd person passing glances up at our work, but I'm glad that no gawping crowds have gathered, as they would surely have done had we arrived later in the morning. The aquarius and his team arrive but I tell them they will have to start the lagging on the upper floor while we maintain the water supply down below until the job is finished. They look bemused but make their way up to the third floor.

"Handled with aplomb, as expected."

I startle. Stephanus is standing just behind me. Does the man have Mercury's wings on his feet, to always creep up so quietly?

"Word came to you already?" I say by way of greeting. There's no point pretending he doesn't know what happened, I'd lay a large sum of money he knows every detail already. I can only hope he can see that we have worked very hard to keep the matter as little gossiped about as possible.

"I find it is better to let the populace express themselves in unimportant but symbolic ways and feel that they have had their say, won a small victory, than let resentment build too high, don't you think? Especially when one is confident that any such 'expression' will be taken care of discreetly."

I blink in confusion. Is he really suggesting that he allowed this protest to happen, maybe even encouraged it? Or perhaps actually arranged for it to happen? Surely not. "Did you –" I begin, but I don't even know how to complete the sentence.

He looks amused. "The common people will feel they have had their say. The more exalted will barely know it happened. The Emperor is still asleep. Your team are very reliable. I commend you for your excellent management of the situation."

"We might not even have been here," I protest, still appalled by what he's suggesting. "It's not Games season, we're not here at dawn every day."

"Your aquarius was keen on an early start," he says.

"How did you even know he was due –"

"It's been a pleasure speaking with you," he cuts me off. "Until another time."

I open my mouth to say something else, to ask another question, but he has already turned away, striding past the giant golden Colossus Sol statue glinting in the early rays of the sun, making his way back through the Forum, no doubt returning to Domitian's service before he even awakes.

"I'll have to have a guard on here every night from now on," calls Marcus, appearing through the now-immaculate imperial entrance. "What a waste of a morning this was. Anyway the aquarius is here now and the cork lagging is ready for the lower pipes. We've wasted enough time today. Keep the extra cleaning crew, they can help us catch up. We need this job done before we get a hard frost. Come on."

I stand thinking for a moment. Did Stephanus actually arrange the "protest" himself, to make the locals feel that they'd had their say... without having protested at all? Did he set everything up, even our arrival here early this morning so that everything would be taken care of, allowing just enough protest to be effective? Here and gone again, to be whispered about with satisfaction by those who are angry without causing real offence? I shake my head. It's too early and too much has already gone on this morning. But Stephanus is a wily one, that I am increasingly sure of. "Coming," I call back to Marcus.

If I thought last year's demolition and rebuilding work in the insula and around us in the Ninth Region was noisy, dusty and impossible to escape, it's nothing compared to what is happening now. It's extraordinary what an emperor can command. Whole buildings tower above us one day and come crashing to the ground the next, curses and bricks flying though the dust-filled air as vast teams of builders, recruited not just from the whole of Rome but all the surrounding areas, descend on the shops, apartments and other edifices that Domitian has indicated must make way for his first two gladiatorial schools. I watch from the upper levels of the amphitheatre as the buildings are swiftly demolished, echoing the tiny pottery counterparts that Domitian smashed on the marble floor of his palace. The air is barely breathable, I have to hold my hairwrap in front of my mouth and Karbo refuses to accompany me after the first few days. But it is mesmerising work, one moment a building whole and complete, within a few hours standing without its roof, its walls rapidly shrinking downwards, pulled by unseen hands (or rather, more accurately, by the giant sledgehammers the builders wield without mercy) until it reaches the ground and meanwhile endless carts take away the ensuing rubble. Some will be reused, such as the roof tiles, which will top the gladiatorial schools.

Others, such as the broken-up bricks still clinging stubbornly to the concrete, will be broken up still further for use in the construction of roads, or ground down to make a waterproof plaster to help repair the many fountains, aqueducts and baths in the city. The endless noise grows wearying to all, people trying to hold conversations in the Forum scowling and leaning closer to one another to hear better, before rapidly deserting the area, if they are able to go elsewhere.

"It's ruining trade," says Secundus. "Customers don't buy trinkets if all they can hear is hammering and their clothes are gathering dust. Especially the richer women, they worry about dust in their hair... or hairpieces, I should say."

"They'll start the building work soon, I hope," I say.

"Hardly going to be quieter, is it?"

"A bit, perhaps?" I say hopefully.

"Now you'll like this story, Althea," Secundus says, grinning. "Sold a lady one of my peckers last year, finest quality bronze. Week later, she comes back and says she's lost it, wants to buy another. I say, Domina, I assure you, it'll still be working its wonders on you, even if you've lost it. No, no, she says, I must have another, I want to conceive a child, a son. Well, I'm not going to refuse the sale, am I? So I sell her another. Don't see her for almost a year. Yesterday she comes to find me in person. Secundus, she says, I've borne twin sons, my husband is delighted with me!"

I laugh. "You're going to be telling that story all over Rome now, aren't you?"

"Of course. I've already sold ten peckers off the back of that, three of them to the same lady for her sisters and cousins. Might you be in the market for a lucky pecker or even two, should you be wanting twins?"

"Need a husband first," I say.

"Got one in mind?"

I shake my head.

"Ah, now, you're blushing, Althea, I can always tell when a woman has her eye on a man. My lucky pecker will get him to look your way, you know?"

I push him lightly away on the shoulder. "You're incorrigible, Secundus."

Karbo's tiny kitten Letitia arrives in our lives. The amphitheatre's cat, Domina, is growing weary of her new brood, who have grown large and now pounce on her out of the shadows to chew her tail and ears, learning to hunt and fight using her as their training ground. She swipes at them from time to time or hisses, brings them dead lizards and half alive mice to encourage their killing instincts and show them the way towards independence. Karbo swoops in to choose his favourite kitten and take her away to a new life in our insula, hurrying her through the ever-busy courtyard and up the wooden staircase to our rooftop world. He makes a space for her on his bed and watches over her like a mother as she explores her new surroundings, first our hut and then further afield. Named for the goddess of gaiety, she lives up to her name, bounding around the rooftop and playing with anything that moves, from her own tail, which has Karbo in fits of giggles, to the discarded feathers of doves or even a wisp of straw carried to us on the wind. At night, she sleeps on Karbo's bed with him, as close to his face as she can, while he curls a sleeping arm around her, protective even in his sleep. She chases pigeons and shadows, sleepy lizards and even ants, when she finds a column of them busy about their own affairs.

"You'll have to hold her or this will never get done," I tell Karbo. I'm trying to sweep the rooftop clean, but Letitia is certain that this is a game invented for her alone, and so follows me around, pouncing on the broom, tumbling over when she tries to ride on it.

Karbo clutches Letitia to himself, cooing over her, while I briskly finish sweeping the rooftop which is heavy with leaves that have twirled across the rooftops of Rome throughout the autumn and found their resting place here. "There, that should be the last of them, the trees are all bare now," I say.

We mainly stay away as the building works proper begin. Carpenters swarm across the arena and rip out most of the wooden flooring, leaving a gaping hole in the centre of the space. They're followed by the builders, whose work demands that carts full of bricks arrive daily.

On a rare visit to the amphitheatre I stand with Marcus in the imperial box, looking down into the vast dark hole from where red brick dust and curses rise, together with endless scraping sounds as mortar is laid and the first floor of the hypogeum begins to take shape, the maze-like pattern from Rabirius' meticulous scrolls turning into reality, our simple open space now shaped into something different.

"Don't like it," Marcus mutters. "It's going to cause trouble."

"How?"

He shrugs. "I don't know,' he admits unwillingly. "I just feel it."

"We're going to number all the lifts and all the rooms and cages," I try to reassure him. "We've worked out a system of signals as well, both with the whistles and with bells which can be rung on a different floor if there's a really big problem."

"I know."

"What else can we do?"

"Nothing."

"It'll be alright," I try again. I touch his hand lightly, wanting to clasp it but not daring. "We'll get used to it." I watch his face, brown eyes moving and forehead furrowing as he looks around the whole amphitheatre, then back at the dark hole that will become the hypogeum. For a moment my heart beats faster when I realise he has not moved his hand from under mine. Perhaps he will clasp my hand in his now, perhaps he will say he is tired of this life and…

"Getting used to things isn't the same as them being right," says Marcus and he turns to leave, his warm hand gone from under my fingers, leaving them cold.

We barely see Funis during November. Occasionally a messenger boy will run to me with a note checking something: the space available, whether the bulls can be penned in somewhere within the amphitheatre or will have to wait outside, what animals we're likely to need in the first week of the season when we open. Evidently he is busy, but he does not respond to invitations to join Marcus and me at the insula for a more relaxed meal or at the amphitheatre to see how the hypogeum is shaping up. I wonder sometimes, with an odd flutter in my stomach, whether he would come if I alone invited him, but that is not a path I want to venture down, when I have eyes only for Marcus. It would feel like teasing and I do not want to do that.

We are all growing used to both Emilia and Quintus becoming part of the insula's community. At first Quintus comes by only in the mornings, to feed and rock Emilia while Cassia serves customers, then he returns to his own home, where he works alongside his brothers and sisters in his father's fullery, managing the business of keeping the clothes of the Ninth Region's citizens clean. Sometimes he will return in the evening, to pace our courtyard with Emilia in his arms until she falls asleep. But, as time goes by, he returns more often in the evening and even sometimes, when he can get away, in the afternoons when she is often restless, carving a small wooden horse and singing old songs to her. Cassia mostly ignores him, but I catch her glancing his way once or twice, when he is rocking Emilia or speaking softly to her.

"He's kind," I say quietly, watching him one evening.

"And what am I?" bristles Cassia, chopping vegetables for the next day's savoury porridge. "Taking in a baby I know nothing about, and not even married?"

I laugh. "I already know you're kind-hearted," I say. "Everyone knows it round here. It's probably why Emilia was left outside your popina." I lower my voice so Quintus can't hear us as he pauses by the steps where Julia bids him goodnight. "But Quintus could have told us about her and not looked back."

Cassia shrugs, but her eyes rest a moment longer on Quintus when he lays Emilia down at her feet in the wooden cradle the baker's family donated when it was decided Emilia would be staying. He straightens up slowly as the baby snuffles and turns, her eyelids fluttering at the change of position. He keeps one hand on her belly until the last moment, a comforting touch, and after a moment, she subsides and moves deeper into sleep.

"Long day?" I ask.

He nods, brushing back his dark curls and straightening out his back. "Fullery's hard work," he says. "I'd rather have my own trade but it's not easy to move away from the family business."

"What would you like to do?" I ask curiously.

"Make toys like Balbus does," he says without hesitation. "I asked to be apprenticed to him when I was younger but my father said he needed all his children in the business. Of course now several of my siblings are married and even have half-grown children, so there are plenty of us. He could easily do without me, but I'm too old for an apprenticeship, so I'm stuck in the fullery." He gives a warm smile with a hint of sadness to it.

"I'm sorry," I say.

"Ah, it was only a dream," he says. "And now I have a better doll than any that could be carved from wood or made on the potter's wheel." He gestures down at the sleeping Emilia. "I must go. My mother will not be pleased if I'm not there for the evening meal."

"I'll have your breakfast waiting," says Cassia without looking at him.

"I'll be here," he says. "Goodnight, Cassia. Goodnight, Althea."

"Goodnight, Quintus," I say.

"'Night," says Cassia, chopping another carrot at ferocious speed.

"He likes you," I say, when he has disappeared through the gateway to the darkening street outside. "He's been here every day since Emilia was found."

"Nonsense," says Cassia, but her knife slips and she cuts her thumb.

"I won't say anything else," I tease. "Wouldn't want you to be bleeding over him."

"Get to bed," says Cassia, chopping faster than ever. "And stop with your nonsense. Man doesn't even have a trade. That fullery will go to his eldest brother when his father dies. It would cost a lot to set up one of his own and he doesn't even like the business."

"Oh, so you have thought about the practicalities?"

"Don't know what you're talking about," says Cassia, bringing the knife down too hard. A carrot slips and rolls away.

"Just promise me you'll still have all ten of your fingers when I see you tomorrow," I say, giggling. I bend to stroke Emilia's tiny head, covered in silken black hair and start up the staircase. "Goodnight, Cassia."

"Umph," is all the response I get.

THE BULL-LEAPERS

ATURNALIA ROLLS AROUND AGAIN AND we decorate the courtyard and our rooms with branches of greenery and dangling ribbons in bright colours. I buy all of Adah's stock of beeswax candles, wrap little scrolls around pairs of them with jokes and riddles I have spent a few evenings writing out in my best hand. I wrap each one with red leather strips and Karbo and two of his playmates deliver them to our friends, suppliers and acquaintances all over Rome. They spend the rest of their time begging for festive cakes and biscuits from Cassia or wistfully mentioning certain gifts they might like to be given, should I be feeling generous.

Marcus gives Karbo a finely tooled belt, which he swaggers around with, and I give him a blue cloak in honour of the Blues racing team. His old cloak is too short for him, he's grown so much this past year. I spent some time cutting and resewing the good woollen fabric, adding an embroidered sun to the centre, turning it into a cosy blanket to lay over Emilia's cradle, a shining reminder of the warm summer days to come after the dark of winter. She clutches at it, having only recently discovered her own hands and what they are capable of, pulls it right up to her face, mouths at it with interest.

"You funny girl," I say to her. "It's been a strange entry to the world for you, hasn't it? But the gods smiled on you when they saved you from the streets."

Quintus brings her a life-size wooden mouse he has carved, nibbling on an acorn, which she in turn chews on with enthusiasm. It fits neatly in her small hands.

"You're very skilled," I tell him and he ducks his head at the compliment.

"She deserves good things," he says, mimicking her earnest expression.

Later I notice a wooden brooch Cassia has taken to wearing, a flower with twining tendrils and leaves. "Where did that come from?"

"Quintus," she says, face turned away.

"He's a wonderful craftsman," I say.

"He's alright, I suppose," she says.

I grin at Fabia, who winks at me.

"Did you give him a gift for Saturnalia?" she asks Cassia.

Cassia shrugs. "Just a basket of biscuits for his family," she says. "Nothing special. Sent out lots of them to acquaintances, thought he might as well have one too."

We nod, lips pursed together so as not to laugh.

"What?" she demands, looking at our pinched mouths and shaking shoulders.

"Nothing," we chorus.

"Better be nothing," she warns. "You're in my way, be off with the pair of you."

"How are we in your way when we're on the other side of the counter?" asks Fabia.

"You're being noisy," amends Cassia.

"Barely said a word," says Fabia.

I'm half asleep on the first day of the festive season. The cold mornings are not conducive to early rising or quick wits, but even I notice that when Quintus arrives and Cassia feeds him breakfast, it's no longer stale bread, but rather a freshly baked fruit bun from the bakery and, this morning, a hot spiced wine to warm him. I raise my own cup to him in festive salutation.

"Io, Saturnalia!"

"Io, Saturnalia!" he replies cheerfully, bouncing Emilia on his knee and tearing off a chunk of his bun to give her. She gums it with interest, dropping most of it on the ground and beaming at him as she rubs some of the mush into his tunic.

"She will need to be adopted one day," I say.

"I intend to, but I need my father's permission and he wants me to marry first. My mother says a new bride won't want some foundling given to her to bring up."

I glance at Cassia, who is pouring wine and apparently listening to some endless anecdote by one of her customers. "And do you have a wife in mind, Quintus?"

"Oh, I don't know," he says. "These things are tricky, aren't they? Finding the right wife? How does one know you're suited? How do you know whether you just like a girl for her good looks and then it will turn out she's ill-tempered or... or something?"

But his neck has flushed and he is very carefully looking anywhere but at Cassia.

I give him an encouraging smile. "A good start is probably someone you already know, someone you see every day and work happily with on... something." I stroke Emilia's hair. She reaches out for my hand and chews on my knuckles, dribbling enthusiastically.

Quintus risks a quick glance at Cassia. "I'd want to set up by myself," he says. "There are enough of my siblings and their families working at the fullery. I'd like my own work, my own place. But I'll have to find a trade of my own and I've always worked in my father's business, I'm not sure what else I'd be good at."

Fabia, Cassia and I go shopping together on one of Cassia's rare days off and exchange gifts of embroidery threads, shells and beads, so that we can all sit together and update our tunics and headwraps with new decorations.

We receive gifts from friends and from our own team, including candles and gaming dice as well as foodstuffs; beautiful red pomegranates and little honey cakes, small sacks of lentils and jars of olives. Our suppliers send more lavish items, especially to Marcus, keen to impress and maintain our lucrative Games business over the next season. We are sent glass cups decorated with gladiators from Patronus and perfume in little glass vials from Labeo. Gilded dates still on the stem, Syrian figs, the best garum sauce and smoked cheese, as well as truffles and honeyed mulsum wine, arrive in large quantities. More toiletries than we can think what to do with, from elegant strigils and tiny ear scoops to soaps and oils. Marcus keeps the odd item, such as a drinking flask and a new strigil, but mostly distributes the goods onwards to me and Karbo, as well as other people in the insula. Lamps and candles are popular gifts and well-received. Secundus, who is fond of Karbo, sends him a tiny collar and a feather-filled leather ball for his cat Letitia, who is annoyed with the collar but delighted with the little ball, chasing it so wildly that I insist she must only play with it in the courtyard, I am afraid that if she plays with it on the rooftop it will one day be thrown too far and too fast and Letitia will follow it over the wall and fall down onto the street, four storeys below, a leap I'm not sure even a cat can walk away from unscathed.

Karbo brings me a bracelet he has woven himself, made from long horsehair strands, interspersed with blue beads. "From the Blues team's four best horses," he tells me proudly. He is still as devoted as ever to his work at the stables, still a natural, by all accounts, at looking after the fastest and most highly strung horses in Rome, used in the Circus Maximus' chariot racing events. Thinking of last year's races that we attended together, I can hardly hold back a grimace at how close the charioteers come to death every time they drive the chariots.

"I don't want to think about how you managed not to get kicked when you gathered these," I say, embracing him. "But thank you."

He has made a matching one for Marcus and we raise our hands in a kind of salute when we spot them on one another's wrists.

"He's growing up fast," sighs Marcus, examining the beads. "Has he asked you if he can be a charioteer yet?"

I grimace at the thought. "No."

"You know he will do soon," says Marcus. "As soon as he thinks he stands a chance at being chosen for a trial drive."

"The answer is no," I say.

Marcus raises an eyebrow. "Are you ready for his tears and fury when you tell him that?"

"Are you ready to watch him die on the racetrack?" I ask.

"It's a risk. But he does have an affinity for horses."

"Good, then he can carry on being a stable hand," I say. "They don't get killed. Or a trainer," I add, grasping at any possible ways out of the dilemma coming closer every day.

"They don't earn glory and vast sums of money either."

"There's no glory in dying," I say.

"Better start practising your refusal speech," he says. "He's going to take some persuading out of it."

It's strange to have conversations suited to the parents of a child and yet not be a couple. I want to lay my hand on Marcus' arm, to beg him to help me persuade Karbo against the life of a chariot racer, and a year ago I would have done just that, but now touching him is too intimate, I cannot bring myself to do it, to move closer, to plead while gazing up into his eyes. The very thought of it makes me awkward. "I'll expect you to back me up when the time comes," I say, overly brisk. "You don't want harm to come to him any more than I do."

He gives me a rueful smile. "This is for you, before I forget." He holds out a cloth bundle and when I open it there is a new wooden writing tablet, intricately carved.

"I asked Quintus to work it for you."

"It's beautiful," I say, delighted. My old one is battered and stained, having been clutched to me every day for years now around animals, dust, food and drink. It has also been dropped more than once, so that one leaf was developing a worrying crack down the side. I trace the delicately tooled and polished lines which depict a trailing vine covered in flowers, like the one Julia has in our courtyard. "I shall think of you when I use it," I add, shyly.

Marcus laughs. "All the time then?" he asks. "You're hardly ever without a tablet in your hand. I'll never be out of your thoughts."

I laugh but my stomach turns over. *Yes. Yes, I will think of you that much. I do think of you all the time. You are never out of my thoughts.* "This is for you," I say, holding out my gift to him.

He opens the little pottery jar and looks at the contents. "Raisins?"

"A special kind," I say.

He tastes them and his eyes brighten at once. "Strawberry grapes? You found raisins made from strawberry grapes?"

I smile, pleased that he can taste the difference from the usual raisins one finds in Rome. "I ordered them specially from the Puteoli region," I say. "To remind you of the ones that grow on your family's farm."

"They make me homesick," he says shaking his head. "I thought I'd have left Rome by now, be done with the Games. And yet, here we still are."

I cling to that *we*, take a deep breath, thinking I might say something, though I'm unsure of what exactly, perhaps something about what I remember of the farm, keep him talking about it, see if he will mention his plans and whether they might include me. "I –"

"Here," he interrupts me, holding out some of the raisins pinched between his fingers towards my lips, expecting me to open my mouth.

Heat rushes up my chest and into my neck, my cheeks, as his fingers brush my open lips and I bite down on sweetness, catching his fingers in my mouth.

"Careful!" He laughs. "You nearly bit me!"

About to choke on a raisin, I turn my face away and duck my head to stop a coughing fit. Julia appears in the courtyard and Marcus offers her some of the raisins, which she accepts.

"Althea remembers your family farm as fondly as you do, Marcus," she says smiling over at me as I recover from coughing. "She will retire there herself if you do not make haste."

For a breathless moment I wonder if she can see into my

heart. I stare at her but she raises her gaze up to where Maria is sitting on her balcony. "Have you tried these raisins, Maria? You must, they are wonderful. Marcus will bring some up to you."

Marcus climbs the stairs, offers the jar to Maria, who tastes them suspiciously but then takes another few. "Good," she pronounces. "You should grow a vine like that here, Julia."

"Marcus will have to promise me a rootstock when he finally retires. Which will be when?"

I hold my breath.

"Ah Julia, I don't know," says Marcus. "Every time I think I might be able to leave the amphitheatre complete and in good hands, some other crisis comes up, some other demand, some other project. I'll be glad when this building nonsense is over, it might mean a chance to leave."

I glance at Julia to see how she has taken this idea. She gives her usual calm nod.

"You never meant this to be a long-term job," she reminds him. "One day the memory of the farm will draw you home." As she turns to go back to her apartment she catches my eye and in her smile I see her knowledge of what I long for. Perhaps it is her decades as a priestess that has given her knowledge of what people want, what they pray for when they go to temples, or perhaps Julia knows me too well to not see how I look at Marcus. Which makes me wonder why he cannot see it for himself and with that comes the fear that perhaps he does not want to see it.

I send a standard gift of honey cakes and the traditional candles with riddles to Funis, and he appears in our insula one day with gifts for everyone, from little model animals for the children to jars of spiced figs in honey for the adults.

"Something for you, Althea," he says.

79

I look down, expecting a jar like the ones he has been handing out to Julia, Maria, Cassia and others in our insula. But instead it is a little cloth bag and when I open it, there is a bronze bracelet in a twisted design. At one end is a bull's head, opposite it the mid-vault body of a bull-leaper, so that it appears the space between them which will allow it to fit onto my wrist is part of the flying body's journey which will lead it over the bull's head. It is beautifully and intricately made, I have never seen such a design.

"A commemoration of this coming season and our work together," he smiles.

"This – this is too much," I stammer.

"Nonsense," he says firmly. "It gave me pleasure to see how the jeweller created what I asked for. And I wanted to invite you to come and see the bull-leapers. They will be arriving in a few weeks and I want them to try out the arena space."

"I want to come!" says Karbo, jumping up and down at my side.

There's a tiny flicker of disappointment in Funis' eyes and I can tell he wanted this to be a private outing, time for us to be alone together watching the spectacle he is arranging. But he is too good natured to deny Karbo.

"Of course," he says with a smile. "I will send word when they are ready."

I make my way to the amphitheatre every few days, drawn to watch as the intricate outline of a maze of passageways and pens, rooms and lift-shafts, begins to take shape, only a few bricks high. The chief builder waves when he sees me, his leathered brown face creasing still further as he consults the complex drawings sent by Rabirius, ensuring they are re-created in the real world.

"I'm not giving the order to build higher till we're sure this is right," he says in passing. "Picky bugger, he is."

"Rabirius?"

He gives me a look and lowers his voice. "Domitian."

"Did he brief you himself?"

"Oh yes. And turned up at my actual house, three nights in a row, because he couldn't sleep for worrying that some minor detail wasn't right. Made me come and look at it, right away."

"Here?"

"Yes. A hammering on my door in the middle of the night and me and him down here in the dark, surrounded by flaming torches held by the Praetorian Guard. Can you imagine? My wife thought I wouldn't come home alive. Fretting over the exact measurements. I'd have liked to tell him I've been building for longer than he's been alive, but I wasn't sure that would go down well. There's something odd about him. Middle of the night and that's what he's thinking about? Why isn't he asleep like the rest of us?"

I shrug. "Who knows."

The builder looks around, lowers his voice even further, so that I have to lean forward to hear him. "D'you think he's dangerous?"

I think back to his calm patience with the antelope. "I'm not sure," I say. "He certainly gives all his attention to things he's interested in."

"You can say that again. My wife was worried sick."

He walks away, skirting a pile of bricks that have been delivered from the brickyards. On top of the pile is a freshly-made brick with the imprint of a child's foot in it, which makes me smile. The thought of a brick-maker's son, barely half Karbo's height, running about the yard, chosen to place his foot on this brick as a symbol of good luck for his family having secured a huge order, for an imperial building no less, the brick arriving here to be built into the hypogeum of Rome's greatest public edifice, is touching in an odd way. I wonder how many hands, how many people, have been involved in the making of this vast space, from the Jewish prisoners of war brought back here by Titus after the Judean rebellion, to the slaves, builders, the now-dead architect who planned its original structure, followed by Rabirius and his labyrinthian designs to be added into its existing structure, and even this unknown child, whose small foot has nevertheless set its mark on the amphitheatre for all eternity.

"Morning, Cassia," I say. "The usual, please. Morning, Quintus."

Quintus waves with one hand while shaking the rattle for Emilia with the other, who stares up at it, amazed. But he looks serious today, there's no bright smile or warm greeting. His sturdy shoulders are slumped and his dark curls are dishevelled.

Cassia ignores my order and leans on the counter, bringing her face close to mine. She, too, looks pale, anxious. "Have you heard?"

"Heard what?"

"The Vestal Virgins."

"Did the fire go out?" Very occasionally the sacred fire that the Vestal Virgins tend goes out, which is supposed to signify the end of Rome itself, so it's a terrible omen and the Emperor himself is supposed to whip whichever Vestal was responsible. Although it's happened a few times and Rome is still standing, which suggests it can't be as ominous an event as everyone makes out.

Cassia's eyes are wide. "No. Worse."

"Worse?"

"They were caught."

"Caught doing what?"

"With a man."

This is much worse. Above all, a Vestal Virgin is a virgin. Pure, untouched. They are absolutely not allowed to lie with a man. "Which one?"

"Two of them."

"*Two?* With – with the same man?"

"No. Each one with a different man. Once one was discovered, she told on the other. They were sisters."

The punishment for a Vestal Virgin who is found to have been with a man is death. And the death enshrined in Roman law for them is very cruel: they are locked alive in a small underground chamber and left to die from starvation or, more likely, a lack of air. It is forbidden to harm one of the Vestals, so they are put into the chamber with food and water and sealed up, so that it can be said no-one harmed them, everyone's conscience clear.

"Will they be entombed alive?"

"I suppose so."

"Wine and bread over here, Cassia!" a customer calls.

"I've got to serve customers," says Cassia hurriedly. "Will you go and see if Julia is alright? She will have heard already. She may have served alongside them. Here," she adds, thrusting a plate at me with small plum pastries on it. "Take this to her. You can share it for your breakfast."

I take the plate and make my way back into the courtyard. Marcus will be waiting at the arena but this is more important. I hesitate outside Julia's door but gather up my confidence and knock.

"Enter."

Julia is standing in front of her household lararium, deep in prayer. I stand in the doorway, awkwardly holding the pastries, a foolish offering given the seriousness of what has happened.

She lowers her hands. "Althea."

"I heard – I'm sorry…"

She must have prayed all night, there are dark shadows under her eyes. "Thank you."

"The pastries are from Cassia," I say, not wishing to claim the kindness as my own.

She nods. "Sit."

I sit down. She pours me a cup of watered wine and pushes the pastries towards me. "I cannot eat just now. Eat on my behalf, keep me company for a while."

I don't think I've ever heard Julia express a need for company, for comfort. I take a small bite of the plum pastry, find it hard to chew and swallow, harder still to speak. "The Vestals that have been found… did you know them?"

"One of them. She was twelve when I left. A new woman and only just understanding what already was lost to her. The other had not yet joined us. She is still very young. They covered for one another, a dangerous game. And sure enough they have not been able to keep their secrets."

"One told on the other when she herself was found out?"

Julia sighs. "It was too late. The first moment, a first glance, even allowing themselves to daydream of such a thing and they were already lost. You cannot keep secrets in the House of the Vestals, it is impossible. There are servants everywhere. You are accompanied wherever you go." She gives an involuntary shudder. "I thank the gods I was never tempted during my years of service. Once you are tempted, it is already too late." She sighs. "But *two* of them."

"What will happen now?"

"Domitian will give the order for them to be executed."

"By the – in the burial chamber?"

"That is the law."

We sit silently for a while after that. There is nothing else to say. I finish the pastry when urged, though it tastes of nothing in my mouth. In the end Julia touches my hand and says that Marcus will be waiting for me. I nod and get to my feet, still sombre.

Julia embraces me before I leave. "Thank you for coming," she says. She has maintained her upright posture and her level voice, but when I look back one time through the half-open door she has returned to the lararium, palms up, ready to pray again for her sister Vestals.

Perhaps her prayers worked. By the end of the day, Rome is both shocked and relieved. The Vestal Virgins must be executed. Everyone expects this, though they shuddered at the method demanded by law, the Vestals to be entombed alive. But Domitian has surprised everyone. He has said that the two culprits may choose the manner of their deaths, they will be able to pick something a great deal quicker than a long slow starvation or suffocation, alone and underground.

"Looks like he's not a bad sort," I hear one of Cassia's customers say. "New Emperor. With that sulky face on him I was expecting worse. But he's been generous, allowing them a choice like that."

Domitian's reputation, at least, has done reasonably well out of the incident. Coming so early in his reign, it has allowed him to appear sternly wedded to the law and an upholder of Roman values, but surprisingly merciful in carrying it out.

Julia's face remains white and still. She spends her days in prayer for the two women but she is relieved that they will meet a quick death. When the day comes there is a subdued atmosphere, not just in our insula, but across Rome. The streets are quieter and few people attend any public events. Today is the day the two Vestals will be taken privately somewhere and killed by whatever method they have chosen, for it has not been made public knowledge, nor will the execution fall to us to carry out. We put to death many criminals as part of the Games, public executions serve as a warning to the common people of what will befall them should they ever break the law. Even when disgraced, the Vestals are treated with greater care than common criminals. Despite this, their names will be chiselled away from their statues, they will not be remembered, only taken away and disposed of somewhere secretly, nameless, lost to future memories. New girls will be chosen to serve Vesta; Rome's divine flame will burn on in their shamed absence.

Today the arena is empty, as is the amphitheatre. The endless dust from the works all around us and in the hypogeum below hangs in the chilly air. I wrap my cloak tighter about me. Funis sent a message yesterday, carefully naming both Karbo and me, asking us to come and see the bull-leapers try out the arena. Although a small part of the arena floor is still open for the building works, most of it is slowly being put back in place. So there is more than enough space for the bull-leapers to test out their routines.

"Are the bull-leapers here?" asks Karbo.

I point across the arena to the Gate of Death. "They're going to come out of there."

"Wrong gate," says Karbo automatically.

"The Gate of Triumph is blocked by rubble this morning," I remind him.

Karbo shivers.

"I told you to wear your cloak."

"Didn't want to."

"Regretting it now?"

"No."

"You're shivering."

"N-not."

"You silly," I say. I wrap part of my own cloak around him and he huddles closer to me. He feels large, solid, nothing like the scrawny child he once was. "How are the stables treating you?"

"They work me like a dog," he says, delighted. "I cleaned out five stalls yesterday. Five! All by myself. Feel my muscles."

I squeeze his proffered arm. "Hercules, that's what you are."

"*And* I polished eight saddles. Then they let me saddle up a horse and said I did it really well. I did up the harness, then I poked the horse in the belly so it would breathe out and tightened it up again. That's what you have to do, else it's too loose, you see, the horses try to fool you, but now I know what to do." He is bursting with pride at his new skills and knowledge.

"Excellent," I murmur, trying to sound admiring rather than worried about Karbo poking a temperamental racing horse in the belly.

"Ready?" Funis has arrived behind us without our noticing. His dark skin has grown lighter in these cold winter months without much sun, but he still favours his foreign clothing, although today he has conceded to the weather and is wearing a thick woollen cloak in a dark green. He pats Karbo on the shoulder, who returns his warm smile with a grin, before turning his attention back to the arena. "Now you'll see something special," Funis promises me. "Watch."

I look where he indicates, though I am aware even as I do so that Funis is not following my gaze but rather watching my face, his whole attention on me. I feel awkward knowing I am so closely scrutinised, but as soon as I turn to him his attention is elsewhere, on the team of ten men and ten women that make up the bull-leapers.

They stand in the chilly dawn air, huddled in long cloaks, talking amongst themselves. The women have their hair worked into tiny tight braids plaited flat against their heads, pulled back from their faces, then twisting into one thicker plait. Around their heads, keeping any loose strands of wayward hair away from their faces, are colourful bands of cloth.

"Can't risk hair getting in your eyes when a bull is coming at you," says Funis, looking them over.

The bull-leapers shed their cloaks, both women and men bare-chested, wearing only tight-fitting loincloths in bright colours that match their headbands. The women's thick plaits are tucked into the back of their loincloths, so that they will not swing loose and cause a distraction.

"They work in teams," says Funis.

The leapers begin to run around the arena floor, first slowly, growing faster and faster, swinging their arms as they go. First one, then another and another throw themselves forwards, performing handsprings and cartwheels, with their hands on the floor or sometimes without using their hands at all. Some even go backwards.

"They're like spring lambs!" says Karbo and he's right, their legs have a bounce no human normally possesses. "Won't they get tired out?" he adds.

"They need to be warmed up before they leap the bulls," points out Funis. "If they fall while they are warming up, there is no harm done. If they miss their timing when there is a bull present… they could lose their lives."

"Does it happen?" asks Karbo.

"Occasionally. And it's why the crowd watch, really," says Funis with a small sigh. "It's not the beauty or the skill of the leaping they are here to admire so much, as the possibility that they'll see someone gouged to death. The crowds are always bloodthirsty," he adds, making his way over to the team. He speaks with them for a few moments, returns to us and raises his hand in a signal to Strabo.

The Gate of Death slowly opens.

I find myself clutching Funis' arm without thinking. The bull standing in the gateway is huge, the largest I have ever seen. Dark brown, with horns as long as Karbo's arms, it stands silhouetted for a moment, then steps forwards, unafraid of the group of humans it faces.

"Is it good-tempered?" I whisper to Funis.

"He's finished off two men and one woman in his time," says Funis.

I gape up at him. "And they didn't kill him?"

"He'd be hard to replace. He makes it look even more dramatic. They make sure to tell the audience he's a killer."

"I wouldn't have the courage to face him," I say.

But the bull-leapers have already moved into their positions. The first woman runs towards the beast. Karbo is on his feet. I am still clutching at Funis' arm and he puts his hand over mine, warm and confident.

The woman leaps as the bull turns towards her. Her hands clench around his horns and he, annoyed, tosses his head – and the woman – backwards, but her hands have released him, her body turns on itself, her feet touch lightly on his rump but already her knees have bent to allow her to push away from him and down to the ground, landing safely. The bull turns, angered at this taunting use of his body and his horns graze her skin as she bends her back impossibly in an arch that saves her. His prey is gone, skipping to one side like one of our dancing girls, risking nothing but her modesty. I take in a gasp of air, I had forgotten to breathe in watching this extraordinary demonstration of skill and fearlessness.

The bull snorts, looks this way and that, turns about on itself. It spots a man in a bold yellow loincloth, who waves his arms. The bull does not hesitate. It charges wildly, Karbo shouts and the man twists backwards and to one side but not far enough, the tip of the bull's left horn scrapes against the man's ribcage, a line of blood showing at once, while the rest of the team immediately move to draw attention to themselves. The man moves out of the way, one hand to his side, blood seeping through his knuckles but already two more women have leapt through the air, one man has dodged and dodged again the searching horns and all are unscathed.

"Is he alright?" I ask Funis.

"He is well," he says with confidence. "That is a common injury, there is not one member of their team that has not been caught in that manner more than once."

"Too dangerous," I say. "Karbo, you are never, ever to take that up," I add, for his eyes have a gleam to them that usually only comes when he talks of horses.

He gives a shrug, half relieved, half regretful. "But the thrill of it..." he says, his voice trailing off with uncertain longing.

"No," I say more firmly.

"See?" He grins at me, "Chariot racing not so dangerous now?"

"Why must you like anything that's dangerous?" I give him a little push. "Get out of here, back to the stables or you'll be late for work."

"Ah, the cry of all mothers," says Funis. "Why can their sons not choose a quiet life?" He strokes my hand with a gentleness that reminds me that I am still clutching his arm and I pull away, blushing.

"Your mother can't have liked you being a gladiator," I say, hoping to move on to a story from the past rather than our present closeness.

"She thought it might be a way out of slavery, and that was all that mattered to her," he says, looking away.

"And she was right."

He makes a gesture that is neither a nod nor a shake of the head, something oddly in-between, unreadable. "For me. Not for herself."

"She stayed a slave till she died?"

His jaw goes hard at the memory. "I tried to buy her out as soon as I began making money."

"Her master wouldn't let her go?"

He shakes his head, abruptly walks away from me, across the arena floor to speak with a member of the team. I watch him go, wondering what happened. Most masters are not averse to a slave having their freedom bought by a family member, even by the slave themselves if they have saved enough money, a difficult but not impossible task. Rome is full of freedmen who were once slaves. It would take a master with a grudge against a slave, or a stubborn mind, to insist on a man or woman staying enslaved even when offered their full value. And it is unlike Funis to break

91

off a conversation with me, he is usually more than willing to seek me out, to engage me in conversation. This memory, of his mother being enslaved and he unable to free her, despite his success as a gladiator, must be both distressing and something he does not wish to divulge further details of, at least for now. I'm curious, but I won't probe further. Past memories can be painful.

The cold days of the new year come upon us and we wrap up warm in thick cloaks, wear boots against the cold wet streets. Married women all but disappear under their winter-weight palla shawls, draped about them and pulled up over their heads for warmth and protection against the unpleasant weather. Not having a palla, I layer up my headwraps, sometimes wearing one on top of another to keep my head warmer.

"The horses were behaving oddly today," says Karbo one evening. "One of them nearly kicked me, and he never kicks. And when we locked them up for the night in their stables they kept whinnying, two of them even struck out with their front hooves at the gates, they wanted to be let out."

I frown. "Did the trainers say anything about it?"

"They'd gone for the night, it was just us stable boys."

I shrug. "Maybe they just get grumpy where it isn't peak racing season. Fewer races might mean they don't get as much exercise and it's what they've been bred for, isn't it?"

Karbo nods, rolling the tiny leather ball for his cat, who ignores it for a moment and then pounces, not at the ball, but at Karbo's hand, and bites.

"Ow!" he yelps, swatting the cat away. She hisses back at him, baring her tiny teeth. "You bad cat!"

"Looks like all the animals are grumpy," I say. "I'd be nervous about earthquakes but it's hardly the time of year for them.

Spring and autumn, I'd be more worried. Maybe the windy day has just annoyed them all. Let's go and eat some dinner. Cassia's made a really good vegetable porridge, I could smell it on the way past earlier today." I shiver. "I could do with something hot. I wish spring would come faster."

"When spring comes we'll be working again," says Karbo, following me down the stairwell.

"I'd rather have the Games start again and some warmth to go with them," I say. "I'm bored of winter."

It's dark when I'm shaken awake.

"Too early," I mutter, but the shaking continues and when Karbo shrieks I'm awake in an instant. I reach out to him, find a flailing arm in the dark, realise the shaking is going on without anyone's hands on me. It is the floor swaying under us, the walls creak. Something smashes outside.

"Earthquake!" I scream and yank Karbo to the door. We run out into the first glimpse of dawn. A roof tile crashes at our feet, one shard hitting my bare calf. We both scream as Marcus' door bursts open. He runs across the roof towards us and as he does so the tremor stops, the lurching from under us gone.

"Earthquake," I gasp again as he embraces us both.

"Downstairs and out," he says. "There's likely to be another tremor."

We follow him down the wooden staircase, which creaks under the weight of all the inhabitants who have hurried out of their rooms and apartments, children crying in fear or asking endless questions which their parents ignore as they call out to one another – is everyone safe? Anyone injured? Is everyone out?

We gather outside the insula's courtyard, as far away from buildings as we can get, standing in the middle of Sand Street, shifting from one space to another, our feet uncertain of finding any stability. The insula has survived well enough, since it was only strengthened and rebuilt recently. There are a few roof tiles in the street, smashed terracotta shards here and there. Julia, calm as ever, is doing a headcount, ensuring everyone is safely out of the building. There are clouds of rising dust to the east and west so she sends Karbo and one of the baker's children in the two directions to find out what's fallen. They run back in a few moments to say that a small insula has collapsed, although it was a crumbling wreck anyway and no-one has been hurt. The other cloud of dust was a group of three little shops, which had been poorly built. One man has received a blow to the head and a woman has broken a finger when she reached out to grab something and was hit by a falling tile, but otherwise the area has been lucky.

"Thanks be to Neptune," murmurs Julia when she hears the children's reports. "We will sacrifice to him."

"That's why the horses and the cat were behaving strangely!" says Karbo.

"You're right," I say. "We should have trusted our instincts. And theirs."

Marcus looks anxious. "The gods only know what will have happened to the foundations of the hypogeum," he says. "They've only just started building. We need to go and inspect it."

He sets out with Karbo and I trotting after him, he is walking so fast.

"Slow down a bit," I beg after a few streets.

"Sorry," he says, briefly slowing his pace before speeding up again two streets later, as we come to the Forum and he has a wide-open space to stride through.

"Why are we rushing?" complains Karbo.

"Be all we need if there's damage and they have to slow down the works," Marcus mutters.

We circle the building on the outside, but cannot see cracks or any other signs of damage. Inside, we dash down the steps leading to the lowest level of the hypogeum. The head builder is there, also inspecting the building and looking pleased.

"Works every time," he says with satisfaction.

"What does?" I ask, grimacing as I catch my breath, Karbo and I both clutching at our aching sides.

"Trade secret," he says, winking.

"Tell us!" begs Karbo.

The builder grins, leans in confidentially. ""When you build a really big structure, something important like this amphitheatre, you don't want it falling apart next time there's an earthquake, do you?"

"But you can't stop earthquakes," says Karbo, confused.

"What happens when you throw a stone in the water?" asks the builder.

"It sinks."

The builder laughs. "What happens to the surface of the water?"

Karbo frowns. "You get ripples. What's that got to do with earthquakes?"

"Earthquakes are the same," says the builder. "The tremors are ripples but in the earth instead of in the water and each one that comes, rocks the building a little more, a little more, till it can't stand against it, and it starts to crack. Now, look about you, and tell me, can you see any cracks?"

Karbo looks closely. "No."

"So what we do when we have a large building, is you build in holes."

"Holes?"

"Gaps in the building. Like the big arches of the amphitheatre that you can see above ground, we do the same kind of thing below the ground. And when a ripple comes, a tremor, there's nothing for it to pass on to. It can't keep pushing, it just loses its power. Of course some of the ripples get through, but not all of them, so the earthquake *loses its power*." He speaks the last sentence very quietly, avoiding Neptune himself hearing and being offended at a mere mortal, a common builder, having found a way to outwit his divine wrath.

Marcus' shoulders have come back to their usual resting place and he's smiling. "I hoped it would work," he says. "But you never know."

The builder grins. "It always works," he says confidently.

"But an insula fell down near us," objects Karbo.

"You can't do it for smaller buildings," says the builder. "There's not as much room to build like that. You need big buildings, so that there's space to have the holes as well as the foundations. We always do it for amphitheatres. You don't want them falling apart, they're a big job to fix and they're a lot more dangerous if they fall down. You don't want fifty thousand people running screaming during an earthquake and some of those big arches coming crashing down on them, do you?"

Karbo is wide-eyed. "Who invented it?"

"Ah, who knows? But we pass it down, builder to builder. And now I've told you, you'll have to be an honorary builder and swear yourself to Vulcan, eh?"

Marcus grimaces. In his mind, Vulcan is the god who crushed Pompeii, who stole his wife and son. He might not demean the god out loud, for that would be foolish, but I doubt he sacrifices to him or speaks his name with praise.

We spend the rest of the morning at the insula, cautiously awaiting further tremors, but there is only one more, very light and quick, a fleeting moment. Karbo and Marcus visit the stables in the afternoon and find a priest conducting a hastily arranged sacrifice and blessing. Neptune rules horses as well as earthquakes, so the stables are concerned that he is in some way offended with them and think it wise to sacrifice to him so that he will be appeased. Horses panic during earthquakes, they try to kick down their stable doors and can damage themselves in the process, which is highly undesirable when they are the finest racehorses in Rome, perhaps in the Empire. Marcus takes the opportunity of this visit to the stables to look over his own two horses. They are certainly not the finest racehorses in Rome, just ordinary beasts that receive free stabling in return for use in more prosaic jobs like pulling cartloads of straw or hay or feed about the place, as well as spare harnesses and saddles to the races. He returns satisfied that they are well and calm enough, perhaps happier for being stabled together. Few of the racehorses benefit from this. Each is kept in its own stable, to discourage fights between them, high-spirited as they are.

"We had to take each horse out and let it run in the training ground," Karbo reports back. "So they'd calm down after the earthquake."

"I hope you were careful," I say, worried by the thought of Karbo around powerful, frightened horses.

"They trust me," he says simply.

"They do," chimes in Marcus, patting Karbo's hair. "He must be blessed by Neptune. Like kittens with him, they are."

"Letitia!" says Karbo, reminded of his cat and running

upstairs to find her. He comes back down with her purring in his arms, all forgiven.

But when Fabius comes home in the evening he has brought Funis with him, his head heavily bandaged.

"Funis! What happened?"

"Roof tile," he winces. "Caught me good and proper."

"In your barracks?"

"Not even during the earthquake," he says, accepting a cup of hot wine from Cassia. "Happened this afternoon."

"But there weren't any aftershocks,"

"It came loose on the roof during the quake, fell off later in the day."

"Lucky not to have been killed," says Fabius. "It caught him on the side of the head, if it had come down straight on top of his head…" he grimaces. "He's staying the night in my apartment so I can keep an eye on him."

After the earthquake, the building of the hypogeum proceeds at pace. With its foundations in place and a team of builders, the first storey is rapidly completed. Standing above it on the arena floor, all I can see below is a curved grid of brick passageways, with walls rising upwards, and many small chambers. Some will be fitted with wooden lifts that will rise through two storeys, other lifts will only rise one floor before delivering their occupants, be they human or beasts. There will be space for Fabius, our physician, as well as a morgue where dead gladiators will be stripped of armour before being taken back to their respective barracks. Executed criminals will also be stripped of any armour or weapons, blunt or otherwise, with which we have seen fit to provide them. Their bodies will not be returned to grieving fellow gladiators, to be treated with comradely honour, but instead will be dragged away with metal-hooked poles by our undertakers, who will dispose of their bodies in a mass burial pit as instructed.

Meanwhile the endless rubble around us swiftly disappears, cartload after cartload loaded up and taken away for sorting and cleaning, while more valuable items like rooftiles have been neatly stacked for reuse. Piles of earth appear as the foundations are dug, the workmen slowly disappearing underground as they dig deeper and deeper, spadefuls of earth lifted by buckets. The more senior builders stand over the slaves who are doing most of the hard labour, occasionally lecturing their apprentices on important building tips, mostly admonishing them for being too soft to do a proper hard day's work, which, the builders claim, they did much better in their own younger days, making audacious claims for how high a wall they could build in one day. The apprentices roll their eyes when their masters aren't looking or make sly comments and laugh between themselves. The slaves keep their mouths shut, knowing better than to talk when they're being worked so hard, a useless waste of energy.

Day by day the outlines of the two new schools grow clearer as the foundations are laid and they begin to rise up from the ground.

TUNNELS

THE HYPOGEUM IS TAKING SHAPE well, the first floor is almost complete, only one more to go and the final sections of the arena floor will be re-laid. Marcus begins to relax, assuming that we are on schedule for the opening of the new season's Games. But one morning I find him staring wide-eyed at a new set of drawings, being held for inspection by the owl-like Rabirius.

"Good morning," I say, joining them. I'm huddled in my cloak, the damp days of February are cold and I'm looking forward to some sign of spring weather to come soon.

"Tunnels," says Marcus, without greeting me. He rubs his eyes, looking tired.

"Tunnels?"

"Domitian wants to have tunnels joining up the schools and the amphitheatre," says Marcus.

"What for?"

"So that the gladiators can arrive from their schools straight into the hypogeum of the amphitheatre without being seen." Marcus gives me a brittle smile, eyes indicating Rabirius. Presumably we are not at liberty to comment unfavourably on this new element of the plan, in case our lack of enthusiasm is reported back to Domitian.

I turn to Rabirius and try to emulate Marcus' smile. "Why?"

Rabirius shakes his head without commenting.

"Thank you for letting us know," I say politely to Rabirius, now packing away his scrolls, leaving me with a copy of the diagrams.

"I'll be over the road briefing the builders," he says, and sets off.

I turn back to Marcus. "We don't know Domitian's reason for it?"

Marcus shrugs. "Probably thinks it's more efficient or something. Or more dramatic that you don't see the performers until it's time for the Games? Or fewer opportunities for armed gladiators to revolt while they cross the road?" He sighs. "I don't pretend to read the mind of emperors. They don't think like ordinary people."

Our own builders will have to accommodate the tunnels, and there's a fair amount of cursing when they hear about it. The entrance points will come in on the lower floor of our hypogeum and so digging starts all over again, this time creating two large tunnels between each school and the amphitheatre. A whole new building team is assigned to this job, as our own team flatly refuses to take it on and Marcus backs them up with some force. If they don't continue with the hypogeum we won't be opening the season on time, and that's not something he can allow.

"So this year there's no flooding of the arena required?" I ask Marcus, teasing. "Blue cloth for a sea, as usual? Sure you don't want some real water like last year?"

"Don't even joke about it," he says.

Vast strips of blue-dyed cloth ripple across the length and breadth of the arena, pulled up and down by dozens of our slave team to create the illusion of water as three half-scale ships are wheeled in, bearing the doomed tributes to the Minotaur. Later in the season the heroic Theseus will also make his arrival in them. We practise hoisting the sails, which make the ships look more realistic. I stand back and consider the black sails against the blue ripples. The effect is good, it brings the sea voyage to life. I'm glad there is no real water demanded this year, in this regard Domitian has been easier to work with than his deceased brother Titus.

I've taken it upon myself to appoint Celer as the amphitheatre's chief chariot driver and manager for horses. He drinks less when he has something to occupy him, and his old skills as a charioteer come back to him. He recruits other retirees, those who escaped the racing arena with their lives and bodies sufficiently intact. We have developed our own chariots for shows; they are plain wood with easy to change decorations made of flag-like cloths, so that designs can be applied and removed. This season the chariots will be primarily used for the Amazon scenes, and the set designers are busy creating colourful patterns which will be used when the fearsome women warriors meet Hercules and Theseus in battle.

Now that we have our theme and it looks like the arena will be ready in time for the opening, it's time to begin choosing our performers for the season. Patronus is busy dealing with the building of the new Ludus Magnus and transferring from his old barracks to the new ones, while maintaining a strict schedule of training for the gladiators performing at the Games in a month's time, so he puts us off as long as possible.

"Let's visit our new neighbour Labeo," suggests Marcus one morning, looking out from an archway on the middle floor across to the gleaming new gladiator schools. "Have a look round his Ludus Matutinus, see how it's shaping up. We can start discussing what we need and what he has available."

The Morning Gladiator School has been so named because it will include the training of animals, which are usually showcased in the mornings, but it will also house and train the speciality acts that Labeo has always provided for us: the bestiarii who fight animals, the venatores who hunt them, as well as those gladiators who require special training not always available in a regular school: women, dwarfs, giants and other such unusual performers. There will be some space provided at the larger school if required for training with larger animals than usual or particularly impressive hunt scenes, but most of these acts will be managed under Labeo.

The Ludus Matutinus, being significantly smaller than the Ludus Magnus, is already close to being finished; the main structure is in place and now it's only a matter of completing the interiors and paintwork. Its inhabitants have moved into the new accommodation and the gladiators are already training even though they are surrounded by plasterers and painters, who are spending a lot of their time watching the training bouts rather than getting on with the work in hand.

Owner of the school, Labeo, laden with gold rings, neck chains and bracelets as usual, greets us as old friends. "Marcus! Althea! I was thinking, do they even *know* what I have in store for the Games this year? You wouldn't credit some of the women I have. And dwarves of course, giants, always got them in stock," he adds affably, as though speaking of items in a shop rather than people. "But my women are the best, as I don't even need to tell you. Alyssa has been training them all winter, they're fighting fit and gorgeous. I've had a new set of hair pieces bought in last week. We like our gladiatrices with long tresses, don't we? I hope you have a wonderful theme for us this year?"

"The Minotaur and Theseus," I say.

Labeo has a quick think. "*Tell* me you're going to include the Amazons?"

"Of course."

"The gods above, you cannot even imagine what my girls will be like. Bare-breasted of course, long hair, perhaps some face paint? Tattoos. Properly savage."

"Won't they need some armour, if they're fighting?" I ask, wincing at the thought of the women going into battle scenes bare-breasted, no matter how accurate to history the look is.

"Some, yes," says Labeo casually. "But not too much, not in the wrong places, eh?"

We make our way into the central yard, which is shaped around a miniature amphitheatre that can seat five hundred spectators. It's surrounded on all four sides by the barracks, containing the usual armouries, a medical centre, sleeping quarters, kitchens, toilets, a large room for eating and other such amenities.

"Dreadful, isn't it?" says Labeo. He indicates the team of plasterers working their way from cell to cell in the sleeping quarters of the barracks, joking and whistling as they go about their work. In other areas there are painters daubing the building inside and out with whitewash, while a deep red trim is being added around the edges of the yard and the amphitheatre. "Can barely hear ourselves think. Not that most of that lot need to think," he adds, waving disdainfully at a group of ten gladiatrices, who are engaged in learning sword fighting. They look new and inexperienced, their moves clumsy. Two of them are already tired out, not displaying the kind of stamina necessary for long-term success in the arena.

"You've got a fantastic building though," I say to Labeo.

He strokes the gold chains round his neck and gives a pleased shrug. "Unbearable, having all these builders about," he says, but I can see he's delighted really. He has a magnificent new school to house his wares, right by the amphitheatre, built by imperial command. His school is even going to be completed before the supposedly more important Ludus Magnus. For now, he is relishing being the centre of attention. "There's two more schools going to be built on the other side of the amphitheatre," he says. "Dacian and Gallic apparently, but they're not going to get round to those right away, they're too busy with these first two plus the tunnels and special ramps so Domitian can arrive from his palace underground and all sorts." He's proud to have one of the two larger schools, for his contributions to our spectacles to have been noted and rewarded in this way.

"And now you have your own amphitheatre," I say.

"It makes the fans happy," he says. "And whatever pleases them pleases me."

The seats of the tiny amphitheatre are half occupied with fans of the Games, the rest of the space is taken up with she-wolves on the prowl and vendors of food and drink. The women who have already found their targets lounge in the laps of their customers or lean against them as they watch the women training, whispering filthy jokes and sharing sweet or savoury snacks they order from the vendors, their clients paying for whatever they order: wine, olives, bread and garum sauce to dip it in, spiced roasted chickpeas, dried figs, nuts, small honey-cakes. The she-wolves take the opportunity of the men being distracted to ensure they get a solid meal inside themselves, ready for their own performance later. The men watch the gladiatrices with hungry eyes, rubbing the thighs of the women sat next to them, squeezing their waists tighter. They drink more wine than they can handle, some of them lurching to their feet when it comes time to leave, unsteady but certain that they are going to have a good time with their chosen companion.

"They won't be able to perform," scoffs Labeo. "They shouldn't pay for services up front, but the women know better than to let them get away with that. More fool them."

"Not tempted?" I ask him. "Considering how many of them hang about here?"

"Oh, I'm tempted by other goods," says Labeo with an easy smile. His eyes drift over the crowd to a young man who waves back at him. "My assistant. A good lad."

I nod. Clearly the assistant's role goes beyond the standard tasks required in running a gladiatorial school.

"So," Marcus begins, when we have settled down with drinks and cakes, "the theme this year is the legend of the Minotaur and we'll be focusing on Carpophorus as Theseus, as it's his final year."

"Such a shame," laments Labeo. "Best bestiarius Rome's ever seen. Martial even writes poems about him, you know. *Had the ages of yore, Caesar, given birth to Carpophorus, barbarian lands would not have boasted of their monsters.* That's one of them. I'd have kept him going a few more years but he says he wants to retire from the arena and be a beast hunter instead, supply animals to amphitheatres. I blame that Funis of yours for putting ideas in his head."

"Funis?" asks Marcus.

"Oh they spend all their time together. Carpophorus follows

106

him about like a lost puppy, I'm surprised he doesn't sacrifice to him."

"And he wants to be a beast hunter?"

"Apparently they're planning to go into business together. Funis wants a good man to work with, and there's no-one better than Carpophorus when it comes to animals, we all know that. Can hunt them, train them, kill them if needed. Brave, I'll give him that. Not much on the brains front, but I expect Funis will make up for him in that regard. They've already got a pretty lucrative contract supplying you lot at the amphitheatre, it'll easily keep two men in business."

"We'll make the most of Carpophorus while we still have him," says Marcus. "Keep him in good condition, Labeo."

"Always, of course. He's one of my best performers. No barracks for him, he has his own villa. Though he's not proud. Trains with the rest of the men here in the school, hangs around here even when he's finished. He's used to the camaraderie. His wife tries to put ideas in his head but he's a simple creature, bit like the animals he spends all his time with."

"I'll go and have a word with him," says Marcus. "Althea will talk you through what we need for the rest of the season." He makes his way out of the seating, heading towards the barracks in search of Carpophorus.

We sit in silence for a moment, watching the women training. I spot expert gladiatrix Alyssa adjusting the shooting pose of one of the women who is learning to fire arrows. When she catches my eye she raises her hand to me in a kind of salute and the sunlight glints off the bronze it is made of. I still shiver at how Alyssa lost her own hand to a pack of slavering hounds in the arena, but I also swell with pride at Fabia's expertise in saving her life, how calm she stayed in the panic that ensued. When Alyssa's fighting spirit was lost along with her hand, Fabia found the solution, the bronze prosthetic hand allowing Alyssa to handle a bow again. Fabia herself, I see, is busy inspecting a fellow dwarf's ankle, crouching to look at it more closely, turning the foot this way and that while the gladiator tries not to grimace with the pain. She straightens up, gives directions. The gladiator tries to argue with her but her firm shake of the head means he will be out of action for a while at least.

"Knows what she's about," says Labeo, watching my gaze. "Softy though, I'd make them perform even if they are in pain. No-one said being a gladiator was going to be an easy life, did they?"

"I'd be grateful to have a physician as good as her for your school," I say.

"Oh I am," says Labeo. "I wouldn't be rid of her. Though she'd rather be the chief physician at the Flavian Amphitheatre." He winks. "She'll make it one day, you mark my words. Never known a woman with such ambition."

I acknowledge a brief wave from Fabia who has noticed my visit. "Did you find her an assistant?"

"Ooof, the trouble we've had on that front."

"Why?"

He shrugs. "She's a woman and a dwarf. The ones that don't mind one thing object to the other. She's had assistants and apprentices come and go for weeks. They start all humble and turn disrespectful to her in a matter of days. She won't have it. Sacks them right away." He grins. "Told you, ambitious. She won't let anyone stand in her way. Least of all some jumped-up assistant or know-it-all apprentice. Anyway, these last two have worked out. Her father sent for an apprentice from Egypt. And the assistant is a slave girl, but she shows some aptitude for herbs, apparently. Knows a good chance in life when she sees it. Here comes Fabia. I need to have a word with one of the trainers. I'll leave you to have a chat with her." He rises and makes his way towards the training area.

Fabia is followed by two people. A young girl, her dark hair neatly plaited, her skin still winter-pale, and a tall young man with golden-brown skin and black hair arranged in the Egyptian style. He hovers behind Fabia, attentive to her every move. As they reach us Fabia directs the girl elsewhere and she hurries away.

"Watch out for arrows," says Fabia as Labeo crosses paths with her. "They're supposed to stick to their own target area but you never know, some of them are new and aren't very good at hitting the target. But Alyssa will sort them out."

"She looks happy," I say, rising to greet Fabia.

She beams. "She is. She can still shoot faster than any recruit and as well as most of the venatores. And she makes a good trainer."

We embrace each other.

"Was that your new assistant?" I ask, pointing at the girl in the distance.

"Yes. Decima," says Fabia. "A good girl, very careful with preparing remedies. And this is Sadiki, my new apprentice," she adds gesturing upwards at the young man standing behind her. "This is Althea, you've heard me speak of her."

He bows. "My honour to meet a friend of the Physician."

I smile at hearing Fabia spoken of so formally. "Good to meet you," I reply. "You're from Egypt?"

Sadiki nods. "I trained there under my father, he is a physician also."

"An old friend of Father's," says Fabia. "Sadiki wanted to

come to Rome as an apprentice and Father wrote and said that I was looking for one." She notices one of the women clasping her hand after a mis-timed blow with a wooden sword, her face twisted up in pain. "Excuse me, I need to check on her."

Left alone with Sadiki I can't help asking the question that came to mind. Or at least part of it. He's attentive to Fabia, as well as deeply respectful in the way he speaks of her, but I can't help wondering how he feels about being apprenticed to a woman, and not just a woman but a dwarf, given Labeo's earlier comments. "You were happy to be apprenticed to a woman?"

He turns his attention back to me from watching Fabia crossing the yard. "I was unsure at first," he says. "I did want to be a physician to gladiators, so of course I was interested in the opportunity. It was odd to be apprenticed to a woman. But my mother had always worshipped Bes. She gave me her figurine of him before she died last year, so I thought it a sign from her."

"Bes?"

He pulls out a little figurine. It's a model of a dwarf, with a large head and bowed legs, wide eyes and a protruding tongue. His head is crowned with a feathered headdress. "He is the god who protects mothers and children. We place him on the outside of birthing houses to drive away evil spirits and protect those within. And because he drives away evil he also symbolises the good things in life – music, dance… umm," he blushes slightly, "…sex." He clears his throat. "Anyway. My mother was a midwife and in Egypt many dwarf women are midwives, it is considered good luck. So I am… accustomed, my mother had several colleagues who are dwarves. Although I had not yet met one who is a physician to gladiators," he adds.

"Fabia is special," I say, laughing.

"She is," he says solemnly, watching her tend to the injured gladiatrix. "She is one the best physicians I have ever met."

Labeo arrives back. He waves Sadiki away, who bows to me and makes his way back to Fabia's side. "Now," he says, settling back. "Tell me everything."

I begin to describe the season's plans.

"No, no," says Labeo, cutting me short. "The Emperor. Is he mad?"

"Labeo!" I hiss.

"Oh, everyone's wondering. Funny old fish. Face like he's been slapped and can't do anything about it; annoyed but hasn't worked out how he's going to punish you yet. He likes the Games though, thank the gods."

"He's odd," I agree. "But not dangerous… I don't think."

"Not dangerous *yet*," says Labeo. "You can't trust them. They go funny in the end, most of them."

I don't answer, instead take a sip of my wine and turn the conversation back to safer topics.

"So first of all, we need a lot of gladiatrices for the Amazons."

"Done," says Labeo. "Easy. Do you want one of them dressed up as Queen Hippolyta?"

"Patronus is supplying the queen."

"A gladiatrix? Why does he have a woman? *I* do the women."

"He just has the one," I say. "She's pretty special, he says, or he wouldn't have taken her. A Briton. Name of Billica. She was sold as a potential gladiatrix because when they attacked her village she killed three armed men, despite only being sixteen."

"No-one offered her to me," says Labeo. "What colour's her hair?"

"I don't know."

"Red," he says. "Only good colour for a Briton woman. Dye

it if it isn't, add some extra if it's a bit thin. You have to build her up, make a name for her if you want her to do well, have a long career. She has to be recognisable in the arena even at a distance, sexy, get a reputation as a savage so men like the idea of taming her in the bedroom. Patronus doesn't know how to manage a gladiatrix. He's going to under-sell her."

"Apparently hardly anyone can manage her," I say. "She's kept locked in her sleeping quarters unless she's in the training ground and no-one gives her real weapons till she's about to fight, they don't trust her. But Patronus says she's fierce when she's let loose in the arena."

"See, that sort of information ought to be all over Rome by now, it'll make the crowd keen to see her. Should have been mine," says Labeo, sulking. "But tell Patronus, I'll help prepare her for the Amazon scenes. Can't have her letting down the side when my girls will look spectacular."

"I'll tell him. Now what I really need is something more difficult. An outstanding *damnato a munera* gladiator. Actually I'll need several who've been given that sentence. Patronus has a few and I need them all, but none of them are really special. I need a leading man to set against Carpophorus. Do you have anyone?"

Damnato a munera. Damned to the Games. It means a criminal who has been condemned to die in the arena, but will be fighting as a gladiator before their end comes. Some must die at once, others are given a specific sentence to serve, during which they will be trained as a gladiator and fight in formal bouts. But all the time they fight, time is running out, for they must die within a certain period, also set by a judge. It can be up to a year, but no longer.

I've caught Labeo's interest. "For what?"

"First of all there are two rounds of Athenians being fed to the Minotaur," I say. "We need men and women who will fight, but they need to die. They can't give in to the Minotaur, but they can't win against it either."

"How many?"

I make a face. "I need fourteen women from you. Seven for one event, the first time the Athenians send tribute to Crete, then a second group of seven. The matching men will come from Patronus' school."

"Don't have that many," he says. "I think I've got nine. You'll have to share them into the two groups. But you can chuck some criminals in there with blunt swords. They'll swing at the Minotaur if they get desperate, it'll do. The other ones will make up for them, they'll fight harder. But we can blunt their weapons too. And a female gladiator with a few months of training behind her is not going to make it against a man with years behind him. Who's your Minotaur?"

"I don't have one yet," I say. "That's why I need someone special. He needs to be *damnato*, because he'll be the Minotaur through the whole season and have to fight properly all the way to the end. Then in the closing Games Carpophorus-as-Theseus will kill the Minotaur. It'll be the big finale."

Labeo lights up. "Oh, I have just the man. Wait till you see him. *Damnato*. Really good with a sword and a fierce fighter, makes an excellent gladiator, you wouldn't credit it. He should have been a gladiator from his first days as a slave, then he wouldn't be condemned to death, he'd be one of Rome's favourites, raking in the money with girls falling at his feet."

"What did he do?"

"He killed his master, said he tormented all the slaves in their house, men and women, beat them, starved them. A poor sort of master. But you can't have slaves going round killing their masters, whatever they've done. He's handy with a sword, so they gave him to me. He has to die by the end of the year, which will coincide with the end of the season of Games."

"He can't earn his freedom if he fights well?"

"No. Has to be dead by the end of the season. You'd think he wouldn't bother fighting, but he says it's about honour, showing that he isn't a coward."

"If he can be relied on to do as he's told he could be the Minotaur."

Labeo is enthusiastic. "He'd be excellent for that. Happy to kill other people if needed, but he's also mindful of the referees during a proper bout, no silly stuff behind your back or anything underhand like that. And he's young, good looking. The ladies are fond of him already, wait till they find out he's going to die at the end of the season and they'll be swarming all over his barracks of a night-time. Nothing a noble lady of Rome likes more than a gladiator who's going to die soon. Tragically romantic. And more importantly, can't tell tales to your husband if he's dead, can he? Or anyone else. No nasty gossip to ruin a lady's reputation."

"They won't be able to see his face much," I point out. "He'll be wearing the Minotaur's mask any time he's on the arena floor."

"I don't think they're that bothered about his face," says Labeo, making an obscene gesture. "It's other parts of him that'll put a smile on their face, won't it?"

"If you say so," I say.

"Ah, don't fret about him. He's got his pick of the ladies, he's being trained by the best in the business and has a full belly every night. He's killed the man that did him wrong and he's still alive to tell the tale."

"For a few months."

"Better than being killed off straightaway, isn't it?"

"I suppose."

"Carpophorus has taken him under his wing anyway, looking out for him, showing him the ropes. He'll do you proud. I swear."

"What's his name?"

"Felix. That's him. Second from the right."

The man he's indicating is talking with Marcus and Carpophorus. He's nothing special to look at, decently broad-chested and a good height, shorter than Carpophorus, but that will be easily remedied with a spectacular horned helmet.

Felix. *Happy.* A common name for a slave, the sort of name handed out by a master who likes the idea of their slaves being cheerful and well-disposed. Poorly named, in this case. But there it is. One season of glory, fighting for his honour, then killed as required by his sentence. By the time Marcus has re-joined us, the deal has been struck and Felix is now damned to this season of Games and the dark role of a monster.

When we visit Patronus a week later, the Ludus Magnus, the Great Gladiatorial School, is supposed to be complete. There's to be an opening day for it shortly, which Domitian himself will attend. Patronus has asked Marcus to help him design a suitable theme and programme for the day.

In reality, the wooden amphitheatre and its arena are in place but the barracks are still being built all around it, the builders laying roof tiles while carpenters work on gates and windows. There's dust everywhere, the plasterers haven't even started and the painters won't be able to get near the place for weeks. Patronus looks weary, I'm sure his hair is whiter than last year.

"Marcus," he says with some relief. "Thank you for your help with this."

They've settled on the twelve tasks of Hercules, with a different gladiator taking on the role for each of the twelve feats. In this way Patronus can showcase his very best fighters, gladiators whose names are known by everyone in Rome, giving each one a chance to shine.

"Most of Hercules' tasks involve killing animals," comments Labeo, who has joined us to look round. Despite his own impressive new school, he knows full well that it's seen as secondary to this one. "That's venatores' work. *My* school's speciality. Why's he using that as a theme?"

"The animals are all being portrayed by gladiators or criminals," I tell him. "The nine-headed hydra is going to be one gladiator against nine criminals, and we're giving them real swords. Not that they've been trained," I add. "Patronus is having spectacular helmets commissioned for the event. Snakes, lion, boar, stag... the drawings look beautiful. The armourers are working on them already. And it crosses over nicely with our theme at the Flavian Amphitheatre. We've got Hercules trying to steal the Minoan Bull, the father of the Minotaur, as well as Hercules and Theseus fighting the Amazons, so we'll repeat a section of that show here. And if today's programme goes well, we might show it off again during the season."

The amphitheatre that holds the Great School's training ground is impressive. Seating three thousand spectators, it would not disgrace a small town and right now the arena is noisy with the thunk thunk thunk of wooden training swords hitting each other or stumps of wood. Here the audience is markedly different, fewer she-wolves are prowling, most of the seats are taken by die-hard fans who are earnestly watching as their favoured gladiators practise their moves, muttering to one another about technique or past glories. The most ardent supporters have already made it their habit to stop off on their way to or from the baths to watch their favourites. The street food and wine vendors have added the venue to their regular trade, wandering up and down the seating offering everything from cheese buns and pickles to dried figs stuffed with a honey-nut paste and cups of hot spiced wine on colder days. Patronus takes a cut of their profits and everyone's happy.

Also evident are the bookies, who are taking notes, jotting down in inscrutable shorthand their views on the form of each gladiator and adding odd symbols of their own invention: are they getting a bit old for this game? Are they hungry enough for the win? How are they looking physically? A good gladiator needs muscles, yes, but also, preferably, a bit of fat here and there, which will protect them from the lighter cuts they receive and make the heavier wounds easier to bear. A younger gladiator will have better speed, probably less fat on them, but also less cunning. They do not have years of knowledge on their side. A gladiator who has won many battles over the years may have put on a bit of weight, may be less fleet of foot, but they also know every trick possible in a bout. They can see a younger man's ideas before he even enacts them, dodge blows that would have landed on someone less experienced. They can afford to wear out a younger, hungrier competitor, before delivering a blow that might well prove fatal in the arena. The older men also know how to put on a show. Most of their movements are larger than they need to be, the sword arcs wider so that they can be seen from the back of a sixty-thousand-seater amphitheatre like our own. When a retiarius, a 'fisherman' gladiator, catches his opponent in his net, he does not hesitate to show off his capture, forcing the secutor or 'fish' gladiator to his knees to humiliate him further, so that the crowd has time to applaud and jeer.

A small group of new recruits have been gathered together and now they are led into the arena. They will take their oath as gladiators in public, adding a bit of showmanship to the moment. The fans lean forward, casting their judgement on the newcomers. They would like to say that they were here the day a future star was sworn into the gladiatorial life.

They repeat the time-honoured words, their voices, a mix of accents from across the Empire and tones, from bravado masking as confidence to resentment and terror. "I will endure to be burned, to be bound, to be beaten, and to be killed by the sword."

Marcus and Patronus appear at my side, Marcus looking weary. "Domitian's sending me notes again about the Games."

"For the battle with the Amazons?"

Marcus rolls his eyes. "Yes. He sent a note to ensure they would definitely be bare-breasted. I'm not running a brothel."

Patronus chuckles. "Labeo wouldn't care. I'm pretty sure he pimps them out willingly, don't you?"

"Certainly. Good money in it," says Labeo.

Marcus shakes his head. "That's your business. How many are fighting in the Amazons' battle, Althea?"

"Two hundred for the biggest scene. About one hundred and fifty proper gladiatrices who will take part in the fight. The other fifty, some of them are dancers, some of them will ride in the chariots. They won't fight but they add to the numbers, make it look more impressive during the fight. We've colour-coordinated their outfits, anyone in blue isn't actually fighting, the men won't engage with them. Everyone else is fair game. Twenty criminals marked out with a red dot on their foreheads, they've got blunt weapons, they're for killing."

"Who's playing Queen Hippolyta?"

"Billica."

Marcus shakes his head. "Don't know her."

Patronus gestures at the barracks. "She's a Briton. A mad crazed bitch. Kills anyone you put in front of her. Won't take orders. We're going to have to put in a group of male criminals so she has someone to kill. But she's sensational in the arena. She's tall too, she'll look even taller if you put her in a chariot." He nods to Labeo, one trainer to another. "I had your Fabia and Alyssa come and look her over to see if she needed training in anything."

Labeo snorts. "They said she was terrifying. Spat at them and tried to bite Fabia. Didn't dare unchain her. You have to sort out her hair though. That mousey colour isn't impressive. If you've got an advertised Briton as your lead gladiatrix people will expect blonde or red, and red's more impressive."

Patronus raises his eyebrows. "What would you do with it?"

"Dye it red and add some extra hairpieces."

"She'll bite anyone who tries that."

Labeo shrugs. "Keep her chained while you do it."

"Why's she so wild?" I ask. It may be common for gladiators to kick up a fuss at first, but they usually get punished for bad behaviour and learn not to resist their fate.

"They slaughtered her whole village, as I heard it," says Patronus. "She hid and came out fighting, killed three Romans in full armour before they caught her. Hardly ever talks, but I've got another Briton and he says she just wants to kill Romans. Which she does, very ably. But keep her away from your prize fighters, because she's a savage."

Marcus frowns. "She wouldn't have a chance against Carpophorus or any of your best gladiators."

"You say that, but they listen to the referee and also, they'd rather not die. She doesn't care if she lives or dies. Makes you fearsome in the arena, if you don't care about living."

119

THE LABYRINTH

I T'S EARLY MARCH, ONLY A couple of weeks to go till the opening Games of the season, when Rome will watch the creation of a monster and the birth of a hero. Everything should be ready, but I am anxious and sometimes I have to force myself to leave the amphitheatre rather than staying later and later. I retreat to the rooftop of the insula with Karbo, carrying bread, cheese, olives and fruit, and enjoy the delicate return of spring warmth.

The roof terrace is changing. It was bare when the builders finished last year, save for the two rooftop huts, one belonging to Marcus, one to Karbo and me, which were then joined by Adah's beehives. Now it is a garden.

I started with the lower half of a broken amphora, filling it with earth and planted seeds in it, offered by Julia, who has an abundant supply from her many years of gardening. They grew well and now I have pale yellow primroses to welcome the returning sun. Karbo spent time poking at them, before asking to grow other things. Between us we made a rough structure from old planks of wood, taken from the offcuts as they replaced the arena floor at the amphitheatre. It is raised up off the rooftop like a bed on little legs, filled with earth, most of it carried bucket by bucket back from the loose soil on the riverbanks of the Tiber. Karbo found an old bucket with a hole in it and a cracked cooking pot Cassia was going to throw away. He is using them as tubs for peas, finding the odd branch to stick in the pots for them to twine up and poking the little shrivelled green seeds down into the ground. I doubt I will actually get to eat any of the peas when they are grown, for Karbo is very fond of them.

Our main vegetable bed contains broad beans sown last autumn and their strong shoots are already reaching up for sunlight. We should be able to harvest the beans in early May. They are considered a delicacy, eaten fresh from the pod with strong salty sheep's cheese.

I close my eyes to enjoy the last rays of sunshine. The beans are Ripe and I invite Marcus to eat with us. We sit in the golden May sun and eat fresh beans and cheese, with warm bread from the bakery and good wine. Karbo eats with us and then wanders away to play with Letitia.

Marcus makes a joke about Karbo and me evidently being born to be farmers, if we can grow such good crops even here, on a rooftop in Rome.

I ask about the farm, just lightly, wonder out loud whether he still intends to return there one day, and Marcus' voice changes, it becomes husky as it does when he feels something strongly and he turns his face away and mutters something. I have to ask what he said and he turns his eyes on me, his direct gaze making heat rise up my neck and he says that he will only return there if he can take me with him, as his wife... and I...

"Your farm is coming along well," says Marcus.

I open my eyes to find him standing over me, smiling.

"I – I didn't hear you coming up the stairs," I say, flustered by his sudden appearance and blinded by the low sun's fading rays. I stumble to my feet, awkwardly resting one hand in the soft earth of the bed and then having to brush the earth off my hands.

"I want a fruit tree," Karbo announces. "Can we grow one? And a vine for grapes?"

Marcus laughs. "A fruit tree might break through the roof into the rooms below," he says. "But perhaps a vine. It'll be a long time till it's too heavy for the roof and then it can be moved elsewhere. You should grow the strawberry grapes from my family's farm, they were delicious."

"Do you still intend to go back there one day?" I ask, clutching at the remnants of my daydream, trying to make the moment that I was lingering over happen in real life.

Marcus shrugs. "Who knows," he says, with little emotion. "I can barely think through the next two weeks. Ask me again some other time, when this season is properly underway. For now all I can imagine is some catastrophe on the opening day. And all I can hear is scraping from the tunnel digging or hammering from the arena floor finally going back into place. My whole future comes down to a matter of days, not years ahead. Have you eaten? I'm famished."

I mutter that we have already eaten. He pats Karbo's shoulder and strides away, clattering down the staircase towards Cassia's and a hot meal.

"A vine!" says Karbo. "He said we could grow a vine."

I try to show enthusiasm for Karbo's gardening plans, which moments ago had been a pathway for my desire and are now nothing but mud and fading light.

The road sweepers have either grown lazy or have deliberately allowed straw and dung to build up in the immediate vicinity to the amphitheatre, perhaps paid to 'forget' by those who are still angry about the buildings that have been torn down to make way for Domitian's vision. I send out a team of our own cleaners to sweep up, while making a comment to one of the official sweepers, currently leaning on his broom, about how I'll be meeting with Domitian personally very soon and how very particular he is about cleanliness. I've no idea if that's true but note to my satisfaction that the official sweeper is taking his role more seriously the next day.

Interspersed throughout our ongoing story of Theseus and his many adventures, we will also be weaving in the story of Ariadne. Princess of Crete, daughter of Minos, sister to the doomed Minotaur, she will help our hero Theseus escape, having fallen in love with him. For this role we've chosen a dancer who goes by the show name of Luna, famous throughout Rome as a performer at the best private villas, a rarefied she-wolf available for more intimate encounters, if the (very high) price is right. She has black hair that falls well below her knees, possibly with the assistance of bought hair from previously shorn slaves. She is not very tall, but she moves like a snake, leaving onlookers wondering whether she actually possesses bones in her spine, so far backwards can she bend her body when dancing. Her costume for this season is a magnificently painted and decorated dress in the Minoan style, with long skirt ruffles and an entirely open chest, so that her bare breasts are on display, nipples outlined in gold. Despite her reputation for being hired by the most noble men in Rome, her mouth is a latrine, not sweetened in any way by the fragrant mastic resin she constantly chews.

"It's all about moving your arse," she says matter-of-factly when our resident choreographer tries to alter her dance routine.

Our choreographer prides himself on his classical knowledge, even if he does spend most of his year creating routines that will be shown in the amphitheatre as light-hearted breaks from the more bloody elements of the Games. "Ariadne was said to have a dancing floor made for her by Daedalus himself, designed to mimic the shape of the labyrinth he created to imprison her ill-fated monstrous brother," he points out loftily. "It's described in the *Iliad*. The steps you take are supposed to be reminiscent of a maze. You see?" he adds, demonstrating a few twisting turning steps of the dance he's attempting to teach the troupe of dancing girls. "It's said to have been depicted on Achilles' shield."

Luna rolls her eyes. "If you say so," she says, still chewing. "But if you don't move your arse and jiggle your tits a bit, the men get bored. And a bored man is a limp man. And you don't want them. They don't pay well. You got to get them a bit *interested*, that way, when you've finished all this dancing nonsense for the day, there'll be a nice evening invitation to one of the villas up on the hill waiting for you, won't there?" She winks, lasciviously. "I'm sure the girls know what I mean."

The other dancers nod. Dancing for the Games is only a side-line. The real money comes from wealthy men, who might spot you and be persuaded to give generous gifts as well as the money they owe for services rendered.

The exasperated choreographer turns to me for support.

"Don't look at me," I say, hiding my laughter at their exchange. "I'm sure both of you know what you're doing, in your own ways. I'll leave you to come up with a compromise."

A voice calls out. "I'm looking for Marcus Aquillius Scaurus?"

I turn and immediately bow my head at the sight of a senator standing behind me, surrounded by not only assistants and scribes, but also bodyguards. "Aedile. We weren't told to expect you."

The Aedile looks flustered, as usual. Despite officially being the senator in charge of all the imperial Games, and therefore the Flavian Amphitheatre itself, he is not a naturally commanding man. He gestures vaguely in the air and an assistant presses a scroll into his hand. "Yes, yes, didn't know myself… ah, well it appears the Emperor likes all administrative matters to be carried out *very* correctly, so it has come, ah, let us say, ah, *forcefully*, to my attention that in fact Scaurus' contract as manager of this amphitheatre ought to be renewed, it is too vaguely stated in the first one he signed, you see, ah, er, where is it? Ah yes, here." He indicates a section of the scroll. "You see, it states that Scaurus is appointed as manager 'up to the inauguration of the amphitheatre and for one hundred days of Games afterwards,' during which time he may neither resign nor leave Rome. But of course that was… some time ago and ah, the Emperor is, ah, displeased that our contracts are not up to date. He wishes Scaurus to agree to another season, after this one is complete." He hesitates. "In actual fact, he, ah, would prefer to agree on several years of service, being, ah, not *fond* of changes in personnel related to important administration. But in the meantime, we must definitely ascertain that Scaurus will be continuing as the manager here for the remainder of this season, and all of next season as well. Where is he?"

I hesitate, but there's no stalling the Aedile, no way of escaping this meeting. "I'll send Karbo to fetch him, Aedile." I gesture to Karbo, who bounds away.

I try to make polite conversation, although my head is whirling. I had completely forgotten Marcus' original contract and that it only bound him for the first hundred days. He is free! He could leave at any time and no-one could force him to stay. For one wild moment I imagine him leaving right away, but try to calm myself. The season will have to be completed. "You must be looking forward to the season?" I ask, growing aware that I should fill the awkward silence.

"Oh, er, yes, yes of course," agrees the Aedile vaguely, leaving me with the distinct impression that he has absolutely no interest in the Games and barely frequents them. Certainly I never saw him much after the opening day last year, until the closing event. He always strikes me as more of a scholarly man, someone who would be happier in some dusty study somewhere, reading the ancient poets and making notes to himself. How he ever got chosen as Aedile for the Games is beyond me.

Marcus is striding towards us. I want to intercept him. I should have gone to fetch him myself, how stupid. If I had found him alone, I could have explained what the Aedile was here for and suggested that he at least ask for time to consider what he wants to do. I might even, given the circumstances, have had the courage to remind him of his desire to return to the family farm, encouraged him to make this his last season. Of course, there is a risk that he would simply leave and go to his farm without me, but if nothing else he is my legal protector, and Karbo's too, I would have more time to persuade him...

"Aedile."

"Ah, Scaurus, good to see you again, you are, ah, well? Confident with the season's plans?"

"Yes," says Marcus. "It's going to be spectacular. Bigger and better than ever. It's taking up every moment of our working day. Was there something you needed to discuss?"

I watch, anxious, as the Aedile re-explains the matter of the out-of-date contract to Marcus. I hope to see a flicker of reluctance, even think he might outright refuse. He might state that this is his final season, that he wishes to return to the family farm and that as such he cannot agree to further service. But his face stays serene.

"Of course," he says.

A weight sinks in my stomach. How many more years does Marcus intend to run the Games? He said, when I first met him, that one season was enough, that he would inaugurate the empire's greatest amphitheatre and run its first one hundred days of Games, as contracted, then he would retire, buy back the family farm and live there, content as a farmer. He delayed only because he lost Livia and Amantius, and even in the depths of grief, he suggested it would be only for one more year. Is this what will happen? He will go on and on, one season of Games rolling into another, the farm slowly rotting away? Will I be stuck in this world too, unable to leave because I want to be close to him, but unable to live the kind of life I would really like because he will not leave the Games? Will he remain oblivious to what else he could be doing with his life, oblivious to me? Perhaps he thinks I will always be here too, but I am growing tired of the Games, beginning to hope for something else in my life. I watch, my face carefully blank, as he presses his seal onto the soft wax of the new contract, signs his name. He is bound, not just to this season, but to the next as well; that small piece of papyrus is a year and a half of commitment, of choice taken away. I bow my head as the Aedile departs, but cannot bring myself to say goodbye, my throat feels constricted. If Marcus is bound here, am I bound too? Or must I break the bond between us in order to be free of this place? If I were to leave this job, would I lose Marcus too? The thought makes my stomach turn over. Clearly Marcus does not feel the need to leave this role, nor has it occurred to him how I might be feeling, he has barely glanced at me during all of the conversation, has not even silently raised his eyebrows to ask,

Will you be here too, are you committing to this too? My shoulders slump as a wave of weariness washes over me.

"At least that's out of the way," says Marcus, as the Aedile and his entourage wander out of view. "Can get back to what I was doing. Why do these people never ask for an appointment?" He turns away, about to leap down the final tier of seating and make his way down the steps back to the hypogeum.

"Are you happy doing another year after this one?" I ask, the words coming slowly, sullenly, out of my mouth.

He turns back, surprised. "We need that contract to keep the team safely employed with us," he says. "There's over a thousand of us reliant on this amphitheatre. Those who are paid need to know they'll keep being paid, and the slaves we've been loaned from the imperial household probably get better treatment from us than they could expect elsewhere, thanks to your work on their barracks and food," he adds with a smile. "So I doubt they want any changes to personnel."

I nod.

"Did you need something?"

"No," I say.

"Right, back to it," he says cheerfully. "At least we can sleep easy knowing we all have jobs for the foreseeable future. You never know when you get a new emperor. I was worried he might not renew the contract, but apparently he likes what we're doing enough to keep us for now. So you can spread the good word to the team."

And he's gone, leaping three seats at a time and disappearing down into the gloom of the hypogeum.

I do what I have to do, one task after another, but a weight is pressing down on me. He didn't ask me if I was happy staying. He didn't even *think* to ask. He assumed that I would want to carry on here. He never mentioned his own retirement, not even as a far-off possibility.

"Idiot," says Cassia that evening after hearing my mournful account. "Want one of us to have a word with him?"

I gulp more wine than I'd usually take, draining the cup. "What's the point?" I ask. "It didn't even occur to him."

Fabia tickles Emilia under the chin and the baby giggles, trying to keep her balance and failing, rolling over onto her blanket on the floor with a surprised air, unsure how she got there. "Perhaps he was thinking of keeping everyone around him safe, rather than his own desires," she says.

"Yes, exactly," I say. "That's what he said, more or less."

"Well, that's what a good man would do, isn't it?"

I sigh. "I *know* he's a good man. I don't need another season of the Games to prove that to me. I want to leave."

"Leave," says Fabia.

"With him."

"Then speak to him."

"Can't find the words," I say, a miserable groan escaping my lips. "Why is it all so hard?" I demand.

"Because you're making it harder by not telling him how you feel."

"He didn't hesitate! Nothing! He just said, oh yes, no problem, here's my seal, good to have seen you, Aedile!"

"Perhaps he doesn't want to leave till he's sure *you* want *him*," says Cassia, wiping the countertop.

"Very funny. He's shown no interest in me that way at all."

The last piece of work the builders do, at my request, is to set small plaques into the walls, which create a complex numbering system identifying every pen, trapdoor, passageway and lift. Larger areas, such as Fabius' medical area and the spoliatorium where the armour is stripped off, are named rather than numbered. I add the numbering to our diagrams and encourage the team to familiarise themselves with it. We need to be able to refer to lift twenty-two and have people use the correct lift, or say that pen six contains lions that need to be sent into the caged lift numbered three and know they will not end up in the wrong place, perhaps loaded in with gladiators who are not expecting them. Not being able to see each lift at a glance means we are more reliant on planning every show's exact sequence in advance and sticking to those plans, to avoid any errors. I spend time each evening studying the plans, trying to commit the layout of each floor to memory. When I close my eyes all I can see are endless corridors, animal pens, lifts and labelled drawings.

"The work's done," announces the head builder to Marcus a week later. "I'll need you to sign it all off, agree that we've completed the works as requested, to the proper standard and that you are satisfied, on behalf of the amphitheatre, as its manager."

Marcus never wanted the works, but he has nothing much to say about how they've been completed. The building has been done at speed, to a good standard, and has even weathered an earthquake along the way, proof of its quality. He makes a show of walking through the whole of each floor, checking that the work matches the diagrams sent by Rabirius at the start of the works, checks that every one of our twenty-eight lifts rises and falls smoothly, that the thirty-six trapdoors of the arena floor can open and close, unimpeded by any of the new brickwork. It takes most of the morning. Finally, he affixes his seal to the scroll proffered by the head builder, stating that the works have been approved.

There are handshakes and farewells as the head builder and his apprentice leave. Marcus and I are left standing alone in an empty corridor, next to one of the lift shafts. We are silent for a few moments.

"I don't like the feel of it," I say. It feels like a stupid thing to say, given there's nothing here that wasn't here before: the morgue, the lifts, the physician's area, the gladiators' entrance and the undertakers' exit, but before it was one wide empty space with a high ceiling, which even when full you could see across it, through the jumbled but organised chaos of equipment, performers and our own staff. Now the ceilings feel very close and you can't see anything except the area you're in, can only hear noises from other parts. I find it hard to breathe here.

Marcus chews his lip. "Enough to make you want to leave, isn't it?"

I can't believe what I'm hearing. "What?"

He clears his throat. "Sometimes I think it might be time to pack it all in."

"Leave the amphitheatre? Go back to your family farm?"

He shrugs. "Maybe."

Is this it? Is this the conversation I have been dreaming of? Is it my moment to speak, to encourage Marcus towards making some kind of declaration?

"When?" Too blunt, too awkward, too much to ask.

He looks away. "Oh, who knows? I've signed that contract…" He clears his throat again. "Anyway, I can still hear the noise that lift's making upstairs, it's irritating. Someone needs to oil it. I'll go and sort it out."

He's striding away before I've opened my mouth again and

131

so I stand watching him walk down the tight corridor, before he takes a sudden right and disappears from view.

It's dawn and Marcus sets off to visit Patronus, to spend a morning finalising which gladiators will be used on which days to ensure an even spread of skills and experience, styles of combat and levels of fame.

I head to the amphitheatre. I need to familiarise myself with its final form. I know every part of it above ground, the high-ceilinged corridors of the larger floors and the endless entrances of the ground floor, the darker narrow top tier corridor, seen only by slaves and women. I know the seating tiers, have sat in all of them, including the Emperor's own imperial box, to understand what can be seen from each space. And until last year the hypogeum was only an empty area under the arena floor, barely worthy of the name but fully my domain. But now it is a wholly different place. Two storeys where there was only one, intricate passages where before there was only one wide-open space. I must make it my own even though I dislike it. I must grow to know it intimately, because once it is put into full use it will only grow more complex. There will be noise, there will be doors and cages that must be kept securely locked or lead to certain danger, even death. There will be our numbering system, which I believe I have learnt but still worry about in anxious dreams where I call out a number and a lion leaps out from what should have been a safely closed cage, or I hear a number followed by laughter and ridicule from the crowds when they should be gasping in awe, because dancing girls have appeared rather than wild beasts. So today, in the quiet before we begin the season, I have decided that I will walk the hypogeum alone and make my peace with it.

I make my way through the Forum, which is slowly coming to life, and enter the amphitheatre with confidence, lighting a large lamp with brisk fingers before I descend into the hypogeum's lower floor.

But down here, all alone, the darkness unsettles me. The lamp has five wicks, it is plenty bright enough, yet I hesitate before I set off down the central passageway of the lower floor. I look left and right at each junction, noting the numbers are indeed as I recall them.

"Sixteen." A whisper, echoing in the dark passageway.

I freeze at the junction labelled twelve. Sixteen is another four plaques away, it is in full darkness, I would have to take more than twelve paces to be closer to it.

"Fifteen."

I can't move. The lamp shakes in my hand. I could raise it above my waist level, could hold it up and beyond me, at arm's length and I would see further, might see who is ahead of me, who is down here in the dark with me, but I don't dare. I take a step back, try to steady my breath. I daren't even ask who is there. There's a light ahead, but it's tiny, like a glimpse of sunlight from a crack in the floorboards of the arena, but that is a whole floor above us. It has to be a lamp, but if it is the person should be so much further away from me... I am growing even more frightened in my confusion

"Fourteen."

I don't recognise the voice that whispers the question, other than it sounds like a man. They are moving towards me but I cannot yet make them out, although shadows are shifting now, I can see the shape of a person, but only when they move. Fourteen? My mind is whirring. If that is what they can see they are... walking backwards? Towards me?

I am bone-cold with fear from trying to work out too many things at once. I want to turn and run back up the passageway, back towards the stairs which will take me out of here, but I am afraid that if I do the unseen person, the man, will follow, that I will hear footsteps running behind mine and they will come closer and closer and –

I take one step back and another, trying not to make a sound, open my mouth so that I will breathe more quietly and bring my lamp down lower towards me so I can try and see their light better.

"The morgue?"

I let out a gasp of fear and the person turns, their lamp held up high.

"Who's there? Answer now!" There is no trace of the soft sibilant whisper, it is a loud command. The raised lamp illuminates a tall man with a longish face, bright eyes fixed on me. Domitian? It cannot be. Domitian?

"Speak your name!"

"I – Althea."

"Althea who?" He comes closer. I am face to face with the emperor of Rome. Domitian. His eyes are wide, perhaps he is even frightened himself. "The scribe. What are you doing here?"

I'm amazed he's remembered who I am, he never gave any previous trace of interest in me or my role here.

"Inspecting the hypogeum, Imperator."

I try to step back and bow my head and in my confusion, I stumble, clutch at the bare brick wall to try and stop myself, mindful of the lamp in the other hand, and find myself falling on my backside, a sudden and humiliating bump to the cold floor. I scrabble back to my feet, where Domitian is standing, watching me like an odd performance, something gone confusingly wrong. He makes no move to help me as most people would when someone falls in front of them, only raises his own lamp to inspect me more closely.

"Your hand is bleeding," he remarks, as though commenting on the weather.

I look down. He's right. I have scraped my hand and it is bleeding, though not badly. It stings, though. "It's nothing, Imperator."

He doesn't reply, but looks expectant. "You may continue," he says after a long pause, irritated.

"Continue?"

"With whatever you were doing," he says. "You were inspecting the area?"

"Yes," I say.

"Proceed. I will go on with my own work. You will not be in my way," he adds as a sort of gracious afterthought.

"Your work, Imperator?"

"My own inspection of the building works." He looks at the nearest plaque. "I like the numbering system, it is very orderly. Did you invent it?"

"Yes, Imperator."

He nods, satisfied.

I don't know what to say. "Should I... attend you?" I stammer at last.

"No," he says. "Continue your work."

There is an awkward moment when I have to pass by him in the tight corridor, twisting myself to avoid any contact, but he simply pushes past me and continues down the passageway, whispering again to himself as he moves away from me, his voice echoing through the darkness. "Ten. Nine. Eight."

I stumble down the corridor and take the first turning to

my right, finding myself inside the room where the animals will be butchered after the games. I lean against the cold rough wall, my whole body shaking with shock at the encounter. After a few moments, I quiet my ragged breathing, then make my way through the side passages towards the Gate of Death. I do not wish to be in the hypogeum alone with Domitian wandering around. His behaviour leaves me unsettled every time I am near him, wondering whether he is about to praise me or grow impatient. And after last year being alone in the dark with a man I do not know well is frightening in and of itself.

The key for the Gate of Death is in a tiny antechamber at the far end of the hypogeum. I make my way there as much by touch and memory as my lamp, which I hold very low. I change the lamp into my left hand, reach tentatively up the wall, rubbing my hand across its rough texture till I touch the cold metal of the hanging key, and lift it down. Strabo likes to joke darkly that he doesn't need Charon's hammer, this key alone could finish off a fallen gladiator. He's probably right, it is twice as long as my hand and very heavy, with Cerberus, the three-headed dog that guards the underworld moulded into the bronze of one end while its three prongs at the other end are as thick as my fingers.

I follow the last part of the corridor, make my way up one flight of stairs, still listening for Domitian, but I can't hear him, which makes me more nervous. The crack of light ahead of me at the end of the second flight of stairs is a welcome relief, and I push hard on the door leading to the arena, make my way through it. I've never been so glad to see the cold light of dawn in my life, it feels like the full midday sun compared to the darkness below. I step further out, shove the heavy door behind me, make my way to the Gate and use the heavy key to unlock it for the day before hanging it back up on its hook. I heave on the low-set handle to open the Gate and slip out into the welcome hustle of the day. It may be cold but there's life and noise around me, street sweepers, carts making their way out of the city having made their deliveries, and guards... the Praetorian Guards who should have been with the Emperor, a small cluster of them. They are not in their formal uniform, rather in togas, clothing designed to let them slip unnoticed through crowds, looking out for troublemakers and protecting the Emperor from them. Domitian must have told them to wait here and make themselves unnoticeable. Despite being half-hidden by the Colossus Sol statue, they still look highly conspicuous, even from here I can see their gladius sword hilts poking out of their togas and their short military haircuts, but knowing that the Emperor is all alone inside the amphitheatre is making them nervous; they don't want to be blamed should any harm come to him.

"You!" bellows one of them, not doing a very good job of being discreet. "Come here!"

I indicate myself, eyebrows raised.

"Yes, you, you stupid girl! Come here."

I make my way over. There's twelve of them, trying to maintain their usual intimidating presence while hiding at the base of the statue. The absurdity doesn't make me want to laugh though, it only makes me more anxious. I wish Marcus were here.

"Were you inside the amphitheatre?"

It's not something I'm able to deny, seeing as they've watched me emerge from there. "Yes."

"Doing what?"

"Inspecting the new hypogeum," I say.

The Praetorian Guard looks uncomfortable asking this next

question, it makes him look like he isn't doing his job very well. "Have you... did you see the Emperor?"

"Yes," I say.

"What was he doing?"

"Inspecting the hypogeum."

The Guard looks me up and down, evidently beginning to suspect that something else was going on... an assignation? But surely not. I'm clearly a nobody, not showy enough to be a she-wolf, only slightly too well-dressed to be a slave girl. But a nobody, nonetheless. If the Emperor wanted me in his bed, he would have sent for me and I'd have had no choice in the matter, would have presented myself at his villa to be done with as he pleased. He wouldn't have come creeping round the Flavian Amphitheatre at dawn to meet with me in secret. The Guard's trying to formulate a question that will clear all of this up, but he can't think of one.

"Has – has he finished?" he says at last.

"I don't know," I say truthfully and my own confusion must shine through because the Guard blinks once or twice, shrugs and finally makes a vague gesture of dismissal which has me all but running back to the insula.

Marcus stares at me when I relate what happened later that day. "All on his own? Not with Rabirius or the chief builder?"

"All alone."

Marcus shakes his head. "I don't understand him. He's too strange for my liking. I worry we'll see a darker side to him one day."

"He frightened me," I confess. "I didn't know who was down there with me and I –"

Marcus puts an arm around my shoulder at once. "I'm sorry," he says. "You shouldn't be there alone in future. I would never forgive myself if something happened to you."

Held against his chest, I breathe in his words and the scent of him, the warmth of this embrace. I lift my other arm to hold him closer, but he has let go of me, is already moving away.

"The opening Games are one week away and we're behind. Three of the lifts aren't operating smoothly, we'll have to make adjustments to their mechanisms and half the scenery and props are still down at the warehouses. I don't fancy getting any of it down those stupid corridors, but we don't have a choice. Draw up a plan for the shifts the slaves will be working, Althea, we may have to do later hours than usual, maybe even work into the nights. The gods only know how much lamp oil we're going to burn through in the hypogeum just to keep it well-lit enough to see what we're doing."

And he's gone, striding out of the courtyard. I raise one arm and smell it, his scent on my skin, drop it with a sigh. I never think fast enough, move fast enough, to hold him to me, to speak the words that would make him understand my feelings. Because you're too afraid, I berate myself silently. Because you think he will not feel the same way. "Coward," I mutter.

A voice comes from above. "I thought that's how it was with you."

I startle. Maria is in her usual watching place above me, but I'm so used to her I hadn't even noticed her presence. "I'm a coward," I say, face tilted up to her, helplessly honest in the face of her certainty. "I don't think I'll ever find a way to tell him."

"You didn't used to mind telling him things to his face, as I recall," she says.

She's thinking of the day, years ago, when I turned on Marcus, screamed truths into his face that were honest but also too cruel, borne of fear, my own and the team's need to survive. "I was desperate."

She lets out a chuckle. "Perhaps you'll get desperate enough again."

I shake my head. "I imagine it when I'm alone and it's always easy. When he's in front of me, it isn't."

"One day you'll find the words. Venus will guide you."

I let out a deep sigh. It feels about the right weight for what I'm holding inside me, day after day. "If you say so."

"Are you questioning what a goddess can achieve?"

"I'm sure Venus could find the words," I say. "But I don't think I can."

"Venus cannot resist a lovestruck mortal," says Maria, making herself more comfortable on her balcony cushion. "She will seek you out one day when you least expect it and lend you her voice."

"I hope so," I say. "I can't do it by myself, that I do know."

"Do what?" asks Karbo, appearing through the gateway after a morning at the stables.

"Lunch," I say. "Are you coming with me?"

We leave the courtyard and make our way to Cassia's popina. We usually eat breakfast and dinner there, managing with bread and cheese for lunch, but I want to stay in the light, to see Cassia's friendly face and keep Karbo close to me.

"What you doing here?" she says by way of greeting. "Didn't I see you leave as I was pulling up the shutters?"

"Yes," I say. "But it was only a quick trip. I had to unlock the Gate of Death so deliveries can be made, that's all."

"Lunch?"

"Yes," Karbo and I say together.

By the time I've eaten, the trembling in me has died down. Domitian's behaviour is unusual, we've all realised that already, but so far he hasn't done anything worrying, other than appear when we're not expecting him. And he seems pleased with our work, or at any rate not displeased, which is all one can hope for with emperors. I spend some time playing with Emilia, and her chortles and embraces calm me further.

Emilia may not have been formally adopted, but it's clear by now that she's here to stay. I make my way to Balbus' toyshop and spend some time looking at his beautiful collection of toys. Most are not priced for the likes of insula-dwellers, they are instead put into carefully arranged wooden trays and leather carrying-cases and taken, on command, to the fine villas of Rome, where wealthy matrons and fond senators will have them laid out for their young children to choose, price no object. Some pieces, such as large-scale wooden toy horses or wooden swords, exquisitely carved and jointed dolls dressed with care by Balbus' wife, are made on commission. Other smaller pieces are there to catch a child's eye, to make them beg their parents for a set of marbles or a painted board game, a little wooden cat or tiny pottery jug and plate for a beloved doll.

"They're lovely," I say. "I was looking for a rattle for Emilia. Something pretty."

He shows me carved wooden pieces, or painted gourds to be held with both hands, dried seeds shaking inside when moved.

"That one," I say, taking a fancy to a tiny bright orange gourd with little black figures painted on it, like a vase. The figures are cats, stretching, curled up, pouncing after mice. Karbo will like it too, he can shake it for Emilia as she is too small to hold it properly yet.

"A good choice," says Balbus. He charges me less than he should, waving aside my protests. "I shall have to retire soon," he confides. "My eyes aren't what they used to be, the smaller pieces are getting harder to make. One slip of a carving knife…"

"What will your clients do?"

"Ah, who knows? I am sure there are other toymakers who will take my place. I have no sons to pass the business onto. The shop will have to close."

I nod, pay for the little gourd, bid him farewell, then turn back at threshold as a thought strikes me. "Balbus, did you never take on an apprentice?"

"There was a lad many years back who showed an interest, but his father wouldn't have it. I had an apprentice before that, but he moved out of Rome to set up his own business in his wife's town."

I come back to the counter. "Would you take on an apprentice now?"

"I'm too old to teach a child," he says. "I wouldn't have the patience. Or the years left to me," he adds with a resigned shrug.

"I'm not thinking of a child," I say.

I catch Quintus the next morning at Cassia's popina.

"Put Emilia down," I say. "I need to take you to Balbus."

"Excuse me?" says Cassia, pouring wine with one hand, turning my pancake on the spitting griddle with the other. "Who's looking after this baby while I serve the customers?"

"You'll thank me for this one day," I tell her. Emilia starts to cry, but I ignore her and pull the bemused Quintus with me, making my way round the side of the building to where Balbus is pulling up the shutters of his shop. "Balbus, this is Quintus."

"The man who found the baby," says Balbus.

"He's more than that," I say. "He's the boy who wanted to be your apprentice. Quintus, show him that little horse you've been carving."

Quintus hesitates. His neck flushes, but he pulls out the tiny carved horse from a fold of his tunic and holds it out to Balbus with a hand that trembles slightly, betraying his feelings.

The two men talk, Quintus growing in confidence as he speaks, Balbus' gnarly fingers stroking the little horse, feeling without looking how Quintus has worked with the grain of the wood, not against it, turning little knots into the dappled hide of the animal. After a while I turn away, to let them talk more seriously and when eventually Quintus and I return to Cassia's popina, we are both beaming and not even Emilia's loud wails and Cassia's thunderous expression are enough to sober us.

"Are you even going to tell me where you've been?" she demands.

"I'll leave that to Quintus," I tell her.

When I next see Cassia, she stops serving customers and puts her hands on her hips.

"So you've set up Quintus as an apprentice for Balbus?"

I grin. "Yes. He'll have a room in their insula apartment, be apprenticed to Balbus for one year, then take over the shop. He can spend some of each day looking after Emilia while he does his carvings, like before. And in a year's time, he'll have his own business, right next door to yours. You can thank me later."

Cassia splutters. "What do I care what job he does? I only care whether someone is going to help out with the baby."

"And he will."

"Well…" She struggles to think of something to reprimand me for and instead gestures at her customers, who are watching, amused. "I'm very busy, Althea. I don't have time to chatter with you right now."

"You're most welcome," I say, making her a mock bow.

BLOOD ON SAND

W E CRAWL HOME THE NIGHT before the opening Games, three burly slaves accompanying us to the insula with burning torches to ensure our safety. The hypogeum still smells damp from the fresh brickwork. But everything is laid out correctly, or at least I keep telling myself so, running through lists in my head even as we trudge home in the dark. Animals grunt and roar in their cages, the arena's sand has been scattered, the lifts have been tested and oiled, the dancers' costumes hang in multicoloured rows, the armour and elaborate helmets have been sent to each gladiatorial school. Tomorrow Domitian will arrive to an amphitheatre filled to bursting capacity.

Cassia has left a covered pot filled with vegetable porridge and a loaf of bread on the doorstep of my hut, the porridge is lukewarm but we are grateful for it. Marcus, Karbo and I sit around the pot with spoons, eating in exhausted silence by the light of a small lamp. Letitia mews and licks up the scraps she is offered, but mostly she wants stroking, although even Karbo is not willing to play. Instead he curls up on his bed with her and they fall asleep together almost at once, I can hear little snores from him.

"Sleep well," says Marcus when the pot is empty and we have

sat in weary silence for a few moments, too tired to get up and go to our beds.

"I'm not sure I'll sleep at all," I say.

"Everything is ready," he says. He stands, rubs his lower back, offers a hand to lift me to my feet. I take it, feel the warmth of him, the firm strong pull he offers, but even though I would willingly stumble into his arms if he offered, right now I am so tired I don't even feel the rush of desire at his touch that has welled up in these past months.

"It will all go well," Marcus says.

I nod, because there's no point admitting I'm nervous, we both are. I make my way into my hut and lie down on the bed, try to match my breathing to Karbo's, reach out a hand to stroke Letitia's warm fur in the hopes her calm will soothe me.

My dreams are a confused whirling, where naked dancers stumble out of malfunctioning lifts and dangerous animals escape, rushing past me into the imperial box, to the horror of Domitian and his guests.

I wake in darkness, but when I come out of my hut a tiny glimpse of pale sky on the edge of the horizon at the other end of Rome tells me it will soon be dawn and I couldn't sleep if I tried. I wash, shivering at the cold water, then dress. When I finally wake Karbo and we stumble downstairs, Marcus is ahead of us, irritably massaging his neck and carrying his toga.

"I've got a crick in my neck," he complains, "and I'll have to put this stupid thing on in case Domitian wants to see me. Karbo, you'll have to help me. Not now, when we get there."

"Let's have breakfast," I say. "There's really no point being even earlier than we have to be. Everything is arranged."

"Is it?"

"Yes," I say, as confidently as I dare. When he is anxious, Marcus barely eats, while Karbo and I get some comfort and confidence from having a meal inside us. "You need food. So do I. We're not going to get any lunch today, are we?"

"No," agrees Marcus. "Come on."

Cassia is opening the shutters, but she knows what day it is today and already has the fire going. "I made you something heartier than pancakes and bread," she says. "Eat this."

She's made a thick barley porridge and filled it with dried dates, figs and nuts. Marcus wrinkles his nose at a sweet breakfast, but eats it nonetheless. The heat and sweetness is filling and warming and Cassia gives each of us a hot spiced wine to go with it. It's more of a winter drink, but in this cold dawn and with a long day ahead, we're grateful. Marcus twists his neck from one side to the other, trying to loosen up the muscles.

"Someone should massage your neck for you," says Cassia, looking meaningfully at me.

"Can't get to the baths today," says Marcus. "Though that's where I'll be spending most of tomorrow, I'll tell you that right now."

"Massage his neck, Althea," says Cassia more firmly, seeing that her hint has not been sufficient to get the result she was hoping for. "You can't spend a day in agony, Marcus."

My cheeks grow hot, but I move over to stand behind Marcus, place my hands gently on his neck and shoulders. "Where – where does it hurt?" I ask, afraid to move my hands now that they are in contact with his skin, warm beneath my cold fingertips.

He reaches up and takes my right hand, moves it higher up his neck. "There," he says.

I use my left hand to support his head while I massage his neck. His muscles are hard, knotted up.

"Aaargh."

"I'm sorry," I say at once, stopping.

"No, no, it was a good pain," he says, grimacing. "Carry on. It was helping."

More confident now, I continue, enjoying the chance to touch him without him seeing my face, stroking and pressing his neck and shoulders. I make sure not to catch Cassia's eye, who is smirking mischievously at me.

"Right. No more putting it off," says Marcus, tipping back the last swallow of his wine. "Thank you, Althea. At least I won't be hunchbacked today."

He's already walking away, Karbo trotting after him.

Cassia winks. "It's easy to find an excuse to touch a man if you're looking for one," she says. "If you're going to try and arrange my love life," she adds, "I shall arrange yours."

"Shush," I hiss back, but I can't help a grin as I walk after Marcus and Karbo.

The amphitheatre looms above us in the pale light. Slaves are already positioned around the entrances, some busy setting up the rope walkways that will control and guide the crowds as they approach us, others standing in each entranceway to deter any would-be spectators who have not been issued with a token to the first Games of the season, a prestigious day when only the best people in Rome get seats for our opening spectacle. Even we, the team, must show the small, red-painted tokens that Marcus devised to indicate staff. Stallholders are getting ready, the opening day of the Games is a busy day for merchandise.

We make a tour of the hypogeum, ticking things off

interminable lists, Karbo carrying a whole bucket of scrolls as he trails behind me and I tell him what I need to check next. Scrolls detailing animals, timings, gladiators and their bouts with matching referees, dancers, singers, extra sand for the arena floor and when it needs to be laid. On and on. Marcus has disappeared somewhere, muttering about insufficient lighting, demanding more lamps, more torches. I can only hope we don't set fire to the place. A burning arena floor would certainly look spectacular, but not in the way that Domitian and his guests will be expecting. Most of the senate is here today so the seating will take longer than usual: the more important the attendees, the more fuss they cause.

By the time I eventually make my way upstairs again the sun has fully risen and I stand blinking in the bright light.

"Thanks be to Apollo it's not raining," says Marcus as he strides past me.

It's rained off and on these past two weeks and we really don't need rain on Games days. It spoils scenery and people don't like sitting in it, so we end up with half-empty seating, which dilutes the atmosphere. Today's fresh spring air and bright sun bodes well for our opening day; it will put everyone in a good mood.

We carry on with preparations as our performers arrive, the singers and musicians settled into their places around the amphitheatre, mostly close to the imperial box so that the Emperor can hear everything perfectly, but also at strategic locations around the seating, so that everyone will hear the stories and songs which will add to the excitement of the fights they will be witnessing.

Now the crowds, who have been building up for over two hours, are allowed in. I make my way up to the first floor and look out, feel the familiar thrill at the sight of so many people, all of them about to enter the amphitheatre, expecting to be entertained. They will only see the performers, but it is we who entertain them really, it is our team that has spent months preparing these spectacles, conjuring these stories for their amusement. I catch sight of Secundus, bustling along the queues, making his pitch. I can't hear him from here but can imagine his patter all too well, *Lucky pecker, Dominus? Domina? Untold wealth... sons... women...crops...the blessings of the gods.* His jovial demeanour is already making him a sale as the crowds stream inwards, entering the vast arches. Time to go to the very top of the amphitheatre, to the women's section, to take up a position where I can intervene, should a noble lady of Rome wish to make a fuss about how many slaves she can have with her, or the lack of an awning to protect her from the gentle warmth of the spring sun. The lack of an awning annoys Marcus, too; he had hoped to have one installed this past winter but the idea of that being done at the same time as the hypogeum was too much to bear.

The seating is full and trumpets sound as Domitian and his party arrive. Marcus and I meet in the corridor leading to the imperial box, standing by as they pass to ensure all is well. The Aedile, anxious and flustered as ever, is supposed to be in charge of these Games and is therefore standing in front of us, but only wringing his hands, rather than making a gracious gesture of welcome as Domitian comes striding down the corridors at a fast pace, the rest of his group hurrying to keep up. His wife Domitia is a floating cloud of colours, a whisper of silks and perfume as she keeps pace with him, head high, one disinterested flicker of her eyes in our direction as we bow our heads. Ahead and behind them the endless tramp of feet as the accompanying Praetorian

Guards sweep by. The silk drapes of the imperial box swish open, Domitian and Domitia enter, along with family members and hangers-on who have been given the honour of sitting with them today. Already in the box are their personal attendants, who arrived more than an hour ago to add the final touches necessary for imperial comfort; cushions, gilded glassware, trays of exquisite morsels of food, fans, even boardgames should the Games not be of sufficient interest.

"The gods help us if we're boring enough for those to be necessary," Marcus muttered when he saw these being carried in.

"Maybe Domitia isn't a fan of gladiatorial combat?"

"She better learn to be. He's obsessed with the Games. He's going to be here for practically every show. As if we don't work under enough pressure as it is."

The drapes of the imperial box close, the signal that the imperial party are seated and ready to be entertained. "I need to go below and get ready," I say.

He nods. "Good luck. Be careful."

My nerves are growing. I want to touch his hand, to be embraced, even if only for a moment, but he is already striding away, making his way to the nearest entrance to the seating areas. He must take up his place, give the signal for the Games to begin. I watch him disappear, then turn and make my way down into the hypogeum, glimpsing the empty arena floor, ready to be filled with spectacle.

The two levels of flickering torch-dark rooms beneath the arena are pulsing with life. Lift doors open, men and animals are taking their places, willingly or otherwise. I make my way from one dark archway to another. On the lower level, Funis is standing by the team of bull-leapers, the gigantic bull in a cage behind them. He nods, serious as I pass, all his attention on the next few moments. Strabo is watching over a pure white bull, its horns painted gold. A cage is being closed up, containing three men, shaking, clutching at the bars. Criminals, our executions for the day.

The upper level. Gorgeously clad dancers and singers, the court of Crete. Amidst them stand two figures even more ornately dressed, destined to receive crowns and become King Minos and his ill-fated Queen Pasiphae. And finally a man, dressed in odd swirling robes, stands by a wooden cow containing one of the two star performers of this season's Games.

This year we are trialling a new approach. Marcus is somewhere above me, as ever, sitting near the imperial box. I used to sit in the opposite part of the amphitheatre, close to the box for the Vestal Virgins, each of us able to see half the amphitheatre perfectly as well as each other. But I am bowing my head to a dresser, who fits me with an elaborate ruffled dress in bold colours and laced sandals. This time I will be standing in the arena itself during the opening crowd scene, able to see everything at close hand, to direct events with a gesture, a low voice which the crowd cannot hear. In theory, it will give us better control in large crowd scenes requiring complex instructions. In practice, it will put me rather closer to the arena action than seems desirable. I will be barely five paces away from those about to be executed.

The doors into the arena are each held by a slave, ready to pull them open on Marcus' command, which will be communicated with a long low whistle.

Bursts of light fill our dark space as door after door opens. On cue, loud music fills the amphitheatre and over three hundred of us emerge into the empty arena: dancers, slaves, singers, bull-leapers. As we do so, a palace frontage appears from the floor and narrow seating arises on both sides of it. We are in Crete of long ago, the court and its performers. I walk with the other courtiers, slaves who usually sweep and clean the amphitheatre's seating, now brightly arrayed in costumes that our tailors have spent all winter making. We take our places, seated safely above the arena's still-clean sand. Our first king takes his place amongst us, golden crown glittering.

The bull is released, the crowd gasping at the size of him, the leapers already spread out across the arena so that all parts of the audience will be able to see the show about to unfold.

The bull snorts, confused by the bright light after darkness, the loud music. But when he spots movement he does not hesitate. He gallops towards the first bull leaper and the crowd gasps as his sharp horns come within a fingernail of the leaper's bare skin.

Again and again the bull attacks and each time the leapers, men and women, arch out of the way with their perfect, life-or-death timing and begin to show off their more elaborate skills, the first leap bringing a resounding cheer from the audience, unable to believe the acrobatic strength and speed on display. All around the arena floor they perform, certain to die, before, unbelievably, surviving. The court of Crete applauds, the king grants a laurel wreath to one bull-leaper. But as he completes the gesture his crown falls, golden light rolling over the arena floor and he sinks to his knees as the bull is led away, the leapers taking their place among the rest of us, chests heaving from the exertion.

"When the old King of Crete died," recites the chorus, "many men claimed the throne, but Minos made a vow. That if Poseidon should send a bull to show his favour for Minos being King, he would sacrifice that bull to show his gratitude."

There is an expectant silence.

"And Poseidon sent a bull from the sea."

Rippling blue cloth spreads across the arena floor, pulled by invisible hands and in the midst of it, in front of the Cretan court, a hole opens up and the white bull with golden horns steps out. Well trained, as I lower my hand amidst the crowd, it sinks to its knees, acknowledging Minos' claim to the throne. I sigh with relief. Our hours of rehearsals with a docile ox standing in for the mighty bull of the tale have paid off.

The man playing Minos picks up the golden crown and fits it to his own head, before crowning the woman beside him, creating Queen Pasiphae. Together, they accept applause from our own court and the crowd around us, taking their places on the top tier of seating in front of the painted palace.

"But when the time came, Minos would not give up the bull for sacrifice. Instead, he sacrificed a lesser beast."

A laughably small and mangy-looking bullock is led out and its blood spilt. The crowd murmurs. They know this moment signals the downfall of Minos and all his court. The gods cannot be treated like this, cannot be lied to or made fools of. There will be a retribution, and it will be terrible.

"And Poseidon was angered."

The blue cloth whispers, rises to almost cover the painted palace like a vast wave, but subsides, as though the god had shown mercy at the last minute. As it lowers, it ripples across the lap of the Queen. The cursed touch of Poseidon, seeking vengeance for the offences of her husband.

"He made Queen Pasiphae desire the bull, filling her mind with crazed lust."

Our crowned queen makes her way down the seating. King Minos tries to hold her back as she kneels before the white beast,

153

kissing its muzzle, stroking its flanks. Then she summons the man in the long robes.

"She demanded that the King's chief inventor and architect, Daedalus, build her a cow of wood, that she might mate with the creature."

Daedalus gestures and the model cow is wheeled out, to many ribald shouts from the crowd as Pasiphae climbs inside it. I gesture and the docile ox is led towards it, where it obligingly simulates mating with the unresponsive model. In past seasons Carpophorus has been known to suggest that a bull should really mate with a woman. I grimace at the thought, raise my hand and the man holding the wooden cow unfastens a latch and from the belly of the cow emerges, not the still-concealed Pasiphae, but a man, who drops to the ground in a crouch, as the cow moves away and our crowd of courtiers step back with gasps of horror.

"Now Minos knew the true horror of what he had done, for Pasiphae, his queen, having given way to a bestial lust for the sacred animal, was delivered of a son. But not a human son. A beast. A monster."

Painted black all over, naked muscles rippling, Felix stands. He is a good height, made taller still by the magnificent helmet he is wearing. Glowing silver, surmounted with two vast horns in black, the front covers his face entirely, moulded into the shape of a bull's face, its muzzle protruding. Two large eye holes have been covered over in a dark fabric, so that the man inside can see out, but his opponents cannot see his eyes.

The crowd oohs and leans forwards, but falls silent at the sight of his hands, which he has raised up into a fighting stance. Black leather gloves cover his hands up to the elbows. But where his fingers end, there are glinting silver knives, sharp and awaiting their first victim as a lift ascends and the door opens. A screaming man is pushed out and into the merciless arms of the horrifying figure. The blades are quick, the man has no weapons, can only writhe in agony as they slash at his arms, chest, finishing with his throat, blood cascading onto the sand of the arena. The spray of it hits one of my feet, the warm blood landing on my bare toe. I swallow down a wave of nausea. The deaths, seen this close, are different. From the seats in the amphitheatre, they are a play, a story, even if grisly. Here, they are very real, the warm blood of a dead man touching our living skin.

"The Minotaur."

The black figure moves, paces first to one side to meet the man emerging from the second lift, then to the other to meet the third and final lift. Three men lie on the now red sand, their blood spilt and spilling, their lives lost, their last sight a monster from a dark myth brought to life for the pleasure of their Emperor.

"King Minos, horrified at what had come from his actions, called on Daedalus to make a maze, a palace of so many rooms that no man could find his way through it, that the monster might never emerge."

Every lift we have operates in unison, the arena floor trembling with their movement, delivering up black walls from the ground, taller than a man, which create the fabled maze across the entirety of the arena, trapping the silver-knifed killer in the centre as the palace sinks away and we, the court of Minos, shrink back, trembling, into a small huddle. There is a huge round of applause from the audience at the impressive structure.

"The Labyrinth."

At the centre of the labyrinth, our Minotaur stands on a raised platform, making him taller than the maze itself, taller than a normal man. He lifts his arms to show once more his glinting knife-claws, still dripping with blood. The chorus open up their throats in a bellowing roar, giving the monster a terrifying, echoing, inhuman voice.

There's a deathly silent pause, all of us frozen in place, before the chorus speaks again.

"But across the seas another queen gave birth to a child with an equally fearsome destiny. A man. A prince. A hero."

The maze sinks, disappears into the floor, taking with it the entrapped Minotaur. The court of Crete disperses through the arena doors. I follow everyone, kneel by a grate in the arena wall to watch the next part.

"Theseus."

The crowd erupts into cheers and applause as, in the centre of the arena, a trapdoor opens and Carpophorus emerges. Naked to the waist, his well-scarred skin gleaming with oil, sword in hand, in every respect the famous bestiarius that he is. I can hear higher-pitched cries of admiration from the upper levels of seating, Carpophorus has always been one for the ladies and they in turn have never held back from showering him with gifts, as well as granting him admission to their bedchambers whenever they can get away with it.

Carpophorus turns this way and that, sword held aloft, enjoying the absolute focus on him by the crowd, the empty arena his stage.

"He was trained for glory and destined to be a hero."

I can rest for a while. What follows is first a brief interlude of dancing girls and actors, then a series of gladiatorial bouts, using high-class gladiators, designed to show off Carpophorus' fighting skills and those of others. There will be no deaths here, the sequence is supposed to show his training period as a young prince and impress the crowd with a showcase of superb gladiatorial combats. These will last at least two hours, made up of multiple bouts of different pairings, many conducted simultaneously. Everything is proceeding smoothly.

The final part of the afternoon's combats includes a demonstration of archery and a return to our theme of Crete and bulls. While pairs of gladiators continue to whirl about the arena floor with their weapons glinting and clashing, Funis and his team of handlers release bulls, who, confused and irritated by the movement going on around them, try to attack the gladiators, only to be shot down by archers. A dangerous sequence for the gladiators who need to keep out of the way of both bulls and arrows, but the crowd loves the mayhem and threat of it all. We finish the day on cheers and applause as well as a delighted smile from Domitian, who leaves at a fast stride again, leaving us to manage the exit of the other sixty thousand people, which goes smoothly, always something of a surprise. Marcus is beaming over a job well done; he raises his arm in a salute to me from a distance and I grin back, relieved and happy that all has gone well. It's a good omen for our new season. I hurry down the steps into the hypogeum, nodding at everyone, praising the performers and our own team, but as I reach the lower floor and the medical area, I see Fabius outside it, looking worried. He hurries over and takes my arm.

"Come with me."

"What's wrong?"

"A gladiator has died."

None of the gladiators died. "You mean a criminal?"

"No. A gladiator."

I'm following him down the central passageway to the medical station. "Who?"

"Primus."

It's a show name, *First*, belonging, I dimly recall, to a young gladiator who made a name for himself last season, tipped for great things. From Patronus' school. "I never saw him killed?"

"He took an arrow to the arm."

"He can't have died from that."

"He was spitting blood."

"From an arm wound?"

We've reached the medical station. Draped over Fabius' table is the body of Primus, his helmet fallen to the floor. Clearly dead, and yet his body is untouched, except for a small wound, no longer bleeding, on his upper arm. Fabia is holding the arrow that caused it gingerly in her hand,

"Poison," she says, grim-faced. "It has to be."

We stand over the body, looking down at Primus' face. He can't have been more than twenty years old, with a long career still ahead of him as a top gladiator, if he fulfilled his potential.

"Does Patronus know?"

"We've sent a messenger."

I'm trying to recall the sequence of events. "There were four archers."

"Five," says Fabia.

"I hired four," I say.

"There were five in the arena."

It takes a while and we have to consult several witnesses in our team. But eventually it is confirmed that yes, there were five, not four, archers in the arena today, and we can only account for four. The other has disappeared, slipped away somewhere in the darkness of the hypogeum and no-one can give a good enough description to make me think we have any chance of finding them.

"Why would they want to kill Primus?"

No-one can think of a reason. Gladiators don't kill their rivals, they train alongside them, see each other as comrades in arms. They kill only if they are ordered to, and only in the arena. Primus was well-liked, a good fighter.

"A mistake?"

"Who was the fifth archer aiming at?" challenges Patronus. He has arrived and he is angry. We will pay for Primus, of course, but still, he has unexpectedly lost a good gladiator and he is not best pleased. It takes years for a gladiator to be trained well enough to perform at a venue as prestigious as the Flavian Amphitheatre and had we wanted a man to die as part of today's performance, he would never have offered up Primus. If not a criminal, some poor-quality fighter would have been chosen instead, one with no promise, or one who had caused trouble by being rebellious.

Marcus is grave. "We don't know," he says. "We've been looking at where the arrow was fired. There were six people in the vicinity. Primus and three other gladiators were the closest together. Funis was there to direct the bulls, although he was partly obscured by a piece of scenery. Another animal handler was just visible, we think, because they were by the trapdoor where the bulls were emerging. And Strabo was in the nearest doorway, but it would have taken a master archer to even try and hit him."

"It was right below the imperial box," says Strabo.

Marcus turns to him, horrified. "Are you suggesting it was an assassination attempt on the Emperor?"

Patronus is shaking his head. "If so it was a very poor shot. No archer with even a small amount of training could miss so badly."

"But they didn't hit Primus very well either," I reason. "The arrow almost missed him, it just caught the edge of his arm."

"It didn't need to do anything more than that," says Fabius. "Not if the tip was poisoned."

Marcus heaves a sigh. "We'll probably never know what really happened," he says. "The archer slipped out, and no-one can think of any identifying marks or even anything particularly noticeable about him. No-one was looking at him." He touches Patronus on the shoulder. "I'm sorry, Patronus. You will be compensated for Primus, of course. I will attend his funeral myself. And our team will be told to be on the alert for anything like this happening again."

He speaks with confidence and Patronus reluctantly departs, his assistants carrying Primus' dead body and the other gladiators from his school silently trailing behind their fallen comrade. But I'm wary of Marcus' certainty. In the busy arena we didn't notice the extra archer today and with a team of over one thousand of our own, as well as a few hundred extra performers appearing at each show, how can we possibly be sure that no one else will be able to infiltrate our events in the future? I can only hope that the death of Primus was intended. Some quarrel or trouble he'd managed to get into without anyone knowing of it, now brutally settled.

"It's a bad business," says Marcus. "Send the celebratory drinks and cakes down to the warehouses. I don't have the stomach for them and we don't even have a big enough space to gather everyone together here anymore, except for the arena floor and that's covered in blood. But that shouldn't stop the team celebrating. Aside from Primus, it was a successful opening day. Domitian was pleased."

I make the arrangements. The rest of the day and evening is

subdued. Usually we would have celebrated with the team and gone back to the insula to share stories of the day, eaten a good meal, perhaps arranged for some of the butchered bulls to be made ready by Cassia for a shared feast, signalling the start of a plentiful supply of fresh meat for the season, which everyone looks forward to after a long winter of less exalted fare. But instead we morosely eat a vegetable porridge at Cassia's counter and retire quietly to our own huts. Even Karbo, who usually chatters on incessantly after exciting events, is downcast.

"Do you think someone wanted to harm one of our team?" he asks in the darkness, his voice cracking. "Would they come after us, to where we live?"

"I doubt it," I says reassuringly. "They wouldn't have to wait for a Games day to target one of us, would they? Perhaps Primus was involved with something dubious."

"Like what?"

"Gambling. Throwing a fight. Maybe a love affair... who knows, Karbo, go to sleep. Don't worry yourself about it."

Eventually Karbo's breathing slows and tiny snores emerge. But I lie awake for many hours, tired but unable to sleep, reliving the day over and over again, trying to recall any small detail that will help us understand what happened to Primus. And why.

CHARON

NOW THAT THE FUSS OF the opening day is over, we settle into the season and the rhythm of the days – most days are a show day, with the odd respite, and Domitian attends far more regularly than his brother Titus used to. We get used to welcoming the imperial entourage rather than it being a novelty. We've done about fifteen shows when Luna performs for the first time.

The morning hunt and executions over, it's time for something lighter, but still linked to our theme and relevant to this afternoon's gladiatorial bouts.

Twenty slaves freshen the pale sand that covers the arena floor, then fetch buckets with special holes in the bottom, each bucket filled with sand of four different colours, specially tinted for us. Orange, green, blue and black. They walk in a pre-agreed pattern, creating an outline on the sand of Ariadne's famous dancing floor, a maze across our arena. No sooner are they done then the musicians strike up a lilting tune and the arena doors swing open, our dancers take their places, Luna amongst them, in her much-anticipated starring role as Princess Ariadne of Crete.

"Spit that out," hisses the choreographer, who can see her chewing away at mastic gum as usual.

Luna rolls her eyes at him and spits out her mastic with

fearsome accuracy, landing the little white ball at his feet, before winking at me and stepping through the door, to be greeted with cheers from the crowd.

She's no slouch, she has in fact learnt all the steps the choreographer requested of her, a twisting turning dance with many quick steps, so that the women appear to dance their way through a labyrinth of their own, the music growing faster all the time, and yet none of them scuff the sand or disturb its intricate pattern. Luna's role requires her to reach the centre and then dance her way back out of it, which she does, although I note that she has made sure to include her own elements. Her breasts tremble with every step, her hips sway seductively from side to side and the mostly male audience sits rapt with attention, leaning forward, clapping and cheering her name when she's finished. She bows and waves, then leaves the arena floor, bringing her past me in the darkness as a messenger reaches her, holding out a tiny scroll. She pauses briefly to unroll it, frowning at the writing in the poor light, then winks at me and waves the scroll in the air.

"Straight from the imperial box. Told you... arse and tits." She gives a wiggle and laughs. "See you, Althea."

"Goodbye Luna," I say, wondering whether the summons has come from Domitian or one of his guests. "Enjoy your evening."

"Not as much as he will," she calls over her shoulder.

The lighter part of the entertainment over, we settle into the gladiators' rounds. These require less in the way of management, as the referees make sure everything proceeds smoothly.

I make my way down into the hypogeum. I'm still not used to how many rooms there are, the maze-like feeling hasn't gone away with familiarity. Closed doors, glimpses through open walls, little alcoves, the built-in cages and their occupants meet you round every corner. It keeps me jumpy, which I dislike. There is something unsettling about never knowing what is behind some of the doors, of not knowing who or what you might come across. More than once I jump when I come round a corner and find myself facing a gladiator made half-human by an elaborate helmet, many shaped like animals.

A towering black-cloaked and hooded figure steps out of the darkness, blocking my way. A masked face shows only the glitter of eyes behind it.

"Strabo!" I yelp.

The figure pushes back the hood and lifts away the mask, revealing our stolid team manager Strabo's kindly face and squint.

"Sorry, Althea, didn't see you there."

The role of Charon regularly falls to Strabo, a good-hearted quiet man. He's an unlikely person to take on such a dark part. Charon, ferryman to the underworld, will emerge onto the arena after a bout where gladiators have died or been half-killed and take them out of their misery and into the darkness by slamming a hammer down onto their heads, then dragging their body out of the Gate of Death.

"You gave me a fright," I say, trying to smile, my heart beating faster than it should do.

"Ready to go on, if I'm needed," says Strabo. He nods down at the long-handled, heavy hammer he's carrying.

I grimace. "Sure you're alright doing that?"

"I don't mind," he says. "It's better to finish them off if they can't be saved. Unkind to let them linger when there's no hope."

He has always taken this view, unflinching and dutiful, seeing the task as a kindness, which in a dark way I suppose it is.

He lifts the mask back onto his face, pulls the hood over it.

It's still only Strabo underneath, but I step back. To stand face to face with Charon, alone in the darkness, is disconcerting. "I'll see you afterwards," I say and he walks away, the long cloak making it seem he is floating, adding to his otherworldliness.

There are two bouts today where it's possible that a gladiator will die, hence Strabo standing ready. Usually the battles are intended to demonstrate the fighting skills and excitement of a well-matched pair of gladiators. The crowd has its favourites, bets are made, the odd wound here or there will be seen to by Fabius and no-one will perish. But extra excitement from time to time does not go amiss and so some bouts allow for something more dangerous, for the chance to actually kill an opponent, perhaps when a gladiator has displeased their trainer or is weakening and no longer a star performer, or not loved enough by the crowd to be protected from a bloody end.

I'm still down in the hypogeum when there's a triple whistle followed by a long single note.

Our carefully established protocol begins. Our physician Fabius hurries past me, a slave opening the door allowing him into the arena. I stand in the doorway, out of sight but able to see the fallen gladiator, who is lying jerking in the sand, his feet and hands scuffing up little gusts of sand while the victor soaks up the applause of the crowd. Fabius bends over him for a moment, then looks up into the seating area and locks eyes with Marcus, shakes his head while gesturing, a strong quick hand movement from one side to the other, a clear agreement of what is to come, then retreats.

The chorus has been watching Marcus. Now he gives a low whistle and they spread their arms wide, then speak, deep-voiced and solemn, summoning a being from the other world.

"Charon."

Another doorway opens and the hooded masked figure advances, sunlight glinting on the hammer it carries.

Fabius has returned to the shadows of my doorway and we stand together in silence as the crowd grows quiet, watching each slow step. Charon stands over the fallen gladiator, whose body is still jerking in a way that is making my stomach churn. He pauses for dramatic tension but does not hesitate, the hammer rises and falls, a sickening crunch and the gladiator lies still, while the crowd lets out its breath in a collective sigh, which turns to applause.

"I never get used to it," I confess, as the door to the arena closes, leaving us in the flickering torchlight. "It's worse than the other deaths."

Fabius nods. "There was no hope for him," he reassures me.

"I know," I say quietly. The protocol we have is strict. Fabius must inspect the gladiator. He must clearly indicate to Marcus that there is no hope whatsoever of anything being done for him medically. Then and only then will Marcus summon Charon. Usually there is no need, a gladiator will be killed outright. If he is badly wounded but still conscious, the crowd or the Emperor may be asked to decide whether he should be dispatched by the victor, an honourable death. But to kill an unconscious gladiator, there is no honour in that, it would make a poor spectacle, and yet they must be dispatched. Hence Charon. The dark ferryman who takes souls across the River Styx from our world to the underworld. This is the role Strabo must sometimes play.

"Well done," says Marcus, as he passes Strabo later. He pats him on the back.

Strabo bows his head. He is not distressed at these moments, seeing it as a duty and a quicker release of a suffering man than allowing him to twitch alone on the sand. There is an orderliness and righteousness to what he does.

Domitian is in attendance for the much-publicised show in which Hercules and Theseus will face the Amazons.

Our first glimpse of Billica is certainly impressive. With or without her consent, her mousey-brown hair has been dyed and interwoven with additional hair pieces to make it both spectacular and wildly excessive, a scarlet that would rival any soldier's shield, stacked and cascading from her head to well past her waist, surmounted with a magnificent golden headdress to indicate her place as Hippolyta, Queen of the Amazons, though I'm not sure the stories say anything about the Amazons having red hair. She is wearing a skimpy loincloth, attached to decorative leather straps which cross over her chest, the same as all her women are wearing, which have no purpose other than to draw attention to their bare breasts, now helpfully outlined for the audience's benefit.

They carry multiple weapons, from bows and arrows to swords, clubs, battle-axes and more. Billica-Hippolyta wears knee-high boots in scarlet leather, her women lighter shoes along with trousers in bright colours, under which, Labeo has helpfully informed me, is protective armour. I don't bother pointing out that it's hardly very protective if it's only protecting their legs, rather than their heads and chests, surely more vulnerable to weapons. Five of our scene-painters have spent the past two hours painting black tattoos on their arms, backs and thighs, an element that makes them look particularly exotic and savage, though I am unsure how authentic any of them are. I suspect the scene-painters have let their imaginations run wild about what a tribe of wild women would have decorated their skin with. At any rate from a distance it looks very dramatic.

A quarter of the women are on horseback or in chariots, the rest are on foot, although many arrive in the arena sitting behind the main riders, so that they seem more of a horse-bound tribe than is the case for real Amazons.

Labeo's women do not hold back; the male gladiators from Patronus' school are highly trained but are not getting an easy afternoon of it. Both sides sweat and rage, swearing and mocking one another as the fights go on. The better-known gladiators are given their moments to shine, sometimes within a ring of shouting minor gladiators, the better to draw attention to their bout while giving the illusion of one vast battle.

At last it is the turn of Theseus and Hercules to fight Queen Hippolyta. Billica's chariot whips round the arena, circling the two men, who are elevated onto a piece of scenery resembling a large rock. Her sword glints as she slashes at them with it, her women returning to their chariots and horses. The two men are in danger of being overcome. When she eventually leaves her chariot and battles with the two men face to face, I think Carpophorus really might not complete the season, which would be awkward, given that it revolves around him. Billica is fearsome and as Patronus said, does not care about being wounded, receiving cuts, one to her arm, one to her leg. She fights on, bleeding, but she is slowly overcome, despite the shouts of encouragement from her warriors below the rock. At last Theseus grabs at her hair and holds her down, while Hercules disarms her with a passionate kiss and claims her golden belt, given to her by her father, the god of war Ares, and endowing her with superhuman strength. Billica is not willing to play along with the mythology. She has to be forcibly obliged to accept the kiss but legends are legends and the crowd cheers the finale. Three gladiators drag Billica out of the arena so that Carpophorus can take a bow and the Amazons join Patronus' gladiators in a victory lap of the arena.

"Domitian says it was delightful and wants to know if we'll be having the Amazons again," reports back Marcus.

"Not so different from other men as everyone keeps implying, then?"

The new hypogeum has a special butchering room on the ground floor, close to an exit for easy access. With close to one hundred animals killed every day, the after-show butchering is always a long job. Skins are removed and sent over the other side of the Tiber to the leather-workers' district for fur and leather; we get wafts of the tanning work from time to time near the insula; it's an unpleasant smell. If there's something unusual or of good quality, like a fine leopard skin, it'll eventually make its way to the imperial palace, freshly tanned and ready to be included as part of Domitian or Domitia's winter wardrobes or made into an elegant rug. Meanwhile the carcasses are butchered for food. Marcus brings home something every day for Cassia to feed the insula. Good quality specialities are sent to the palace, the rest is given away outside the amphitheatre at the end of the day, an eager queue growing as soon as the show finishes, waiting for the handout. Some people skip the Games entirely, keen to be at the front of the line and receive the best or largest pieces available to feed their families. Meat is a keenly anticipated rarity for plebians and the Games season brings the best chance of having it at the table.

I poke my head in at the door of the butchering room. There's a pile of dead animals, perhaps twenty still left. The butcher and his three assistants are sweating; it's a hot day and even away from the sun the rooms within the hypogeum are getting warm now that we have poorer air flow.

"Nearly done?"

"Yes. All smaller animals now, easier."

I nod. "Send one of your lads for the cleaning crew when you're done, won't you? They'll need to wash the room down."

"Yes, yes."

The butcher is a grumpy old thing, but fast with a knife. He doesn't care about the stink that surrounds his work, but I do and so we have the room washed down with several buckets of water whenever we get the chance, sluicing it into the drains. One of his assistants heaves up two large buckets of pieces of meat and hurries past me to the exit where the queue will be waiting, each person holding a container to carry home whatever they are given, a leg of a sheep or deer if they are exceptionally lucky, more usually ribs and offal, sometimes meat from strange animals like lions or hyena, which have an odd taste about them. Still, once they're in a stew with plenty of seasoning they'll be a welcome change from the usual vegetable and grain porridges.

"Billica looked amazing," I tell Patronus, finding him about to lead his gladiators back to the barracks.

"She was furious," he says. "Raging and crying when they pulled her off the arena floor. The Briton slave we have who understands her says she was screaming about being dishonoured by making it look like she lost to the men and she didn't like being kissed by them, either."

"The crowd loved her," I say. "If she could calm down enough to receive more training she'd have a great future as a gladiatrix. She's already a good fighter and the audience likes something a bit different."

"I've tried telling her that," says Patronus. "She spits and hisses when I try to talk to her. The slave says he can hear her muttering about killing us all at night, pacing up and down in her room, barely sleeps till she's exhausted."

I wave him off, sad for Billica, hoping that her successes in the arena may begin to assuage her rage.

Being new and different, the bull-leaping becomes one of the season's must-see element of the Games, something people have heard of but not often seen. We make room in our schedule for more events featuring the performance. The female leapers, in particular, are favoured, whether because of their partial nudity or simply their skill and daring, I'm unsure. But certainly the days when we advertise their appearances are very well attended and I see fashionable women about Rome copying elements of the clothing they wear, adding a flounce to the bottom of their tunics to imitate our court of Crete, or having hand-painted elements added to their ordinary tunics, this last very popular as the simple pigments they use are not water-fast and so can be washed away, then added anew in different combinations. Instead of the usual hair wraps we all wear, young girls are plaiting their hair into tight rows or tying wraps tighter around their faces and in brighter colours, so as to emulate the bull-leapers' style, which was born out of practicality but has become something of a fad.

The days grow warmer and the ladies of Rome insist on bringing parasols to the Games, complaining about our lack of an awning, fearing that the sun's rays will darken their carefully cultivated fair skin. The parasols block the view for anyone behind them and Marcus and I are regularly called on to settle disputes.

There's a burst of trumpets.

"That'll be Domitian," I say. "Places, everyone." We never

171

keep the Emperor waiting once he arrives. Inside the Emperor's entrance I stand unobtrusively out of the way and watch Domitian and the procession that moves about with him. I take up my place as members of the Praetorian Guard and bodyguards sweep ahead, then Domitian and his wife Domitia, followed by a couple of dozen servants and slaves.

Domitia is magnificent in flowing jewel-toned silks, her hair towers, if possible, even higher than the last time I saw her at the opening Games, back in March. There's more than three heads' worth of hair in there, so gossips whisper, held on a wire frame to create the pyramid of curls rising above her face. Her ornatrix must be kept even busier than the one preparing Billica for the arena. This is certainly a woman who is enjoying the trappings that come with being an empress. Her face has been powdered very pale with chalk. Cassia keeps some in her apartment but she can't wear it except in the very depths of winter; her skin goes too dark in the summer, chalk over the top of summer-brown skin looks odd. Domitia is careful to stay out of the sun, like all rich women. Behind her, in her retinue, is a slave carrying a parasol.

The procession makes its way to the imperial box and there's a lot of coming and going as everyone gets settled into their proper places, whether in the box, left outside as bodyguards or waiting for further tasks, should they be required. I give a small impatient sigh.

"It always takes a while to settle everyone," says a voice behind me.

I jump. In the shadows of one of the archways is Stephanus, his long frame clad in a toga blending into the white stone all around him.

I'm silent, unsure what to say.

"Attention to detail," he comments with an approving air, looking at my wax tablet, which I had been consulting while waiting for further trumpets to indicate that we could start the show. "I'll not keep you," he adds. "We all have places we are supposed to be."

He turns and walks away, towards the imperial box. I watch him go, frowning. He never says hello or goodbye. Appears from the shadows and then leaves again. It's unsettling. Not for the first time, I wonder how much influence he has over Domitian, what exactly his shadowlike role consists of.

Today I won't be in the arena. I make my way to an area which will give me a view of the imperial box and the Emperor. It always takes longer to seat important people. Aside from getting all their accompanying bodyguards, slaves and other hangers-on organised and in their places, it's the fussing over whether the cushions are to their liking and the re-draping of their togas and pallas once they've sat down, making sure they've been served a drink and a snack if they'd like one that adds time. Domitian has a glass of wine in one hand and picks up a small cake with the other. Domitia also has a glass of wine but is shaking her head at any food, instead summoning a slave girl with a fan. That will be a boring afternoon for the girl, fanning the Empress hour after hour. Though as a result, the girl does have a front row seat in the imperial box at the Games, so I suppose that's something.

Marcus gives me a nod and we make our way in different directions, he to watch from his place near the imperial box, I to oversee the workings down in the hypogeum for most of the morning.

Come the afternoon, the black-sailed Athenian ships are setting sail across a rippling cloth sea. To liven up the voyage, today's sailing is the setting for many gladiatorial bouts, including the classic secutor gladiators whose helmets appropriately recall a fish. Additional gladiators are dressed as sea monsters and even a few in crocodile-leather armour. All of these are being valiantly fought off by the Athenian 'sailors', or rather some of Rome's finest retiarius gladiators, who traditionally have a sea-like aspect to their weaponry, fighting with a weighted net, a three-pointed trident, and a dagger. There's no mention of sea monsters in the original myth, or indeed any difficulties at all on the voyage to Crete, but we are always happy to add some embellishments.

I should be able to watch this part, the gladiatorial sessions require little from me, but instead I am in the very highest seating area, trying to convince a lady to be reasonable about her parasol.

"How dare you?" she hisses. "My slave will hold my parasol where I tell him to. And no-one will tell me otherwise. Hold it higher," she adds and her slave obeys.

"But it is blocking the view of the two ladies behind you," I say. "Perhaps if it could be lowered, at least?"

"Certainly not," she retorts. "And those are not ladies. They are plebians and should know their place."

The two women behind look furious.

"Perhaps you'd like to move to a different part of the arena," I suggest. "There is more shade on that side?"

"Absolutely not," she says. "And you're blocking *my* view. Move. I want to see Charon finish off that man."

"Charon?" I frown. I've not heard the whistle signal, nor the chorus summon Charon. I turn, looking down into the arena.

Through the rippling waves, now growing still as our slaves slow their actions, comes the dark figure of Charon, striding across the arena to where a fallen gladiator is holding up his hands to ward him off, yet appears unable to stand.

174

"*Move*," says the woman, pushing me to one side.

I lose my balance, teetering on the stone terrace seats, watching in horror as Charon's hammer falls and the gladiator is dispatched to the underworld.

"Do you *mind*," says the outraged lady as I shove past her.

"No," I throw over my shoulder, taking the stone steps at a run, making for the nearest exit, tearing down through the narrow corridors and steep steps followed by more steep steps, rushing back into the darkness of the hypogeum, half-falling down the last steps in my rush to reach our team and find out what has gone wrong.

"Where is Strabo?" Marcus is yelling. "What in Hades happened out there? That gladiator wasn't supposed to die! He only had a minor cut to his leg, he would have been fine."

"I don't know," I say, still shocked. "Karbo, find Strabo, immediately." I wonder what has happened. Has Strabo lost his mind? Is he killing people with no warning, wielding his hammer against anyone in his way?

Marcus has already gone striding down the corridor and Karbo rushes away but from behind me comes a familiar voice.

"Althea?"

I turn in sudden fear but Strabo is wearing his usual clothes; a scruffy tunic belted over his substantial middle. His face is anxious.

"Why is everyone yelling for me?"

"Where have you been?" I ask, my voice shaking.

He looks bewildered. "Helping Fabius in the physician's bay. There was a gladiator in the first bout needed stitching up. We've only just finished."

I stare up at him. "The first bout?"

"Yes."

175

"And you just finished now?"

"Yes. What's happened?"

I swallow. "The third bout had a young gladiator in and he got cut on the leg, couldn't get up. Charon came out and finished him off."

Strabo stares back at me. "Charon?"

"Yes."

"But I was with Fabius."

He is confused, anxious. I can't see any dishonesty in his face. "I have to ask Fabius to confirm you have been with him," I say, my voice shaking. "I don't want to disbelieve you, Strabo, but no-one else plays Charon except you."

"But I wasn't called on to be Charon," he says.

"No-one gave the order. We need to go to Fabius."

We make our way to the physician's bay and Fabius confirms, confused that I am even asking, that Strabo was with him, from midway in the first bout until now, helping with the young gladiator they have been patching up and who is about to be taken back to his barracks. A few extra people nod, confirming what I'm being told.

"Strabo!" Marcus' roar has people cringing. It's rare to see Marcus this angry and I step in front of him, hands up. He only stops because I am in the way, my palms pressing against his chest.

"It wasn't Strabo," I say. "It wasn't him, Marcus."

"How can it not be? No-one else plays Charon." He glares at Strabo and Strabo, shaken, stares back, his own hands rising to protest his innocence.

I push harder against Marcus' chest, afraid that in his appalled anger he will go for Strabo, despite our protestations. "It wasn't him. He was with Fabius all the time."

"He was," confirms Fabius again.

"Then what's going on?" demands Marcus.

"I don't know," I say, lowering my hands as I see him gain control of his initial rage. "We need to find out. Strabo, where's the outfit?"

"And the hammer," adds Marcus.

Strabo blinks, then recovers. "In the chest by the fourth door into the arena," he says. "Where we always keep it."

We make our way there, Marcus striding ahead, while I half-run behind him and Strabo, Fabius and a group of slaves follow us.

The fourth door into the arena, always used by Charon, is closed, as it should be. Beside it is the chest, its lid thrown open. It's empty.

"Search the hypogeum," Marcus orders. "Everyone. Now. Every part of it."

With over one hundred people scouring both levels, the search doesn't take long. Close to the end of the arena by the Gate of Death, someone lets out a call that brings us all running. In a dark niche, sometimes used for smaller animals, but today unoccupied, its metal gate unlocked and swinging half open, is a bundle of black cloth, Charon's cloak. Marcus pulls at it, revealing not only the discarded mask but also, with a heavy scraping across the brick floor, Charon's hammer, covered in blood.

There are whispers down the crowded corridor, gestures against bad luck as the news is passed along. Marcus holds up his hand and everyone falls silent.

"Someone took the opportunity of hiding their evil intentions in plain sight," he says. "They used this costume to murder a man who should have lived and thought they could pin the blame on Strabo, who fortunately was with Fabius all the time and can be vouched for. You are all to be careful until we find out who did this."

It takes a while to dismiss the team, to send everyone about their business and I note that they leave in little groups, no-one wanting to walk alone through our dark underworld, now grown darker. I have to give orders to make everyone do the work they should be doing, sending the cleaning team about their business of washing down the seating areas, sweeping the arena clean of the sand bloodied by a man who should not have died today. Strange that we see death every day and yet still are shocked by it when it is unexpected, when it comes unbidden and unplanned for. When I've made the rounds and can see everyone doing their work, I go back to Fabius, who is comforting Strabo.

"Who would do that?" asks Strabo. "And they thought you'd think that I –"

"Do you have enemies I don't know about?" I ask him.

He looks shaken by the very idea. "No! What have I ever done to anyone?"

The men he has dispatched to the underworld over the years, standing over gladiators taking their last dying breaths, before swinging down the hammer... but they were beyond saving, he was doing them a kindness. Still, perhaps they had family members who did not see it that way or... but why not accost Strabo somewhere, a quick knife between his ribs on a dark street? This smacks more of shifting the blame onto someone else, of concealing the true murderer, than of a punishment specifically for Strabo. "Go and have a drink," I say. "We will find out what is going on here," I add with far more confidence than I currently feel, but I have to do something to cheer him.

Fabius frowns. He knows I am putting on a false front of certainty, but he pulls Strabo by the elbow.

"A drink is what we both need," he says jovially. "Come along, now, if a physician tells you that you need a drink, you don't argue."

Strabo follows behind him, shoulders heavy.

"I don't know what is going on," says Marcus, his voice strained. "Two gladiators killed by someone and we can't find them, can't stop them? Last time there were six people it could have been aimed at. This time there were dozens of gladiators and two of them were down, then Charon comes out of nowhere, unsummoned, no checks made and kills one of them."

"What did they have in common?"

"I keep asking myself that. I've no idea."

I think of the gladiator being stripped of his crocodile-leather armour, the helmet in the shape of a vast-jawed beast crumpled like the skull within it and shudder. "Who was he?"

Marcus shakes his head. "A slave. Name of Eros. Even more minor than the last one. A nobody, he'd barely finished his training, they put him in this scene because all he had to do was make up numbers and not disgrace himself. Patronus is furious, he's threatening to stop supplying us."

A horrible thought sweeps over me. "Siro."

"What about him?"

"What if he was part of this as well?"

"Why would he be? He wasn't a gladiator. Primus and Eros were gladiators."

"All of them were slaves linked to the amphitheatre."

"Someone has a grudge against the amphitheatre?"

We're both silent for a moment. "The manure daubed on the front…" I mutter.

"It's a long way from a bit of manure to three murders," says Marcus.

"The Urban Cohorts need to be informed."

179

"They're all slaves. The Urban Cohorts wouldn't care unless their owners made a fuss. Domitian was hardly likely to care about a slave he didn't even know the name of. Patronus will be compensated for Eros, just like he was for Primus."

"So we do nothing?"

"We'll have to draw up plans to keep everyone safe. For starters, no one goes anywhere alone."

"The whole team? Over a thousand of us?"

"Everyone," says Marcus firmly. "You and Karbo especially. Go everywhere with someone else or not at all. Same rule for everyone. I need witnesses if this happens again."

"Again?" I feel cold at the idea.

"We don't know who did it, so we haven't stopped them," says Marcus, his face grim.

"The rule goes for you, too," I remind him. "Don't go anywhere alone."

It's been a long day and Marcus and I are standing side by side in exhausted and worried silence, elbows on Cassia's counter, eating a richly seasoned stew of antelope. Quintus is rocking Emilia and the popina is busy with customers, eating alongside us or dropping by to collect their dinners to eat in their own homes. Karbo has been picking the first broad beans and now he comes running down with an armful of the fresh green pods, which he proudly shares out to all the customers. Cassia finds a sheep's cheese to slice up to go with them and everyone compliments Karbo and me on our successful gardening as they pod the beans and eat them with the salty cheese. Karbo strokes the inside of the pods, admiring the soft white lining.

"It's furry like Letitia," he says.

Even Marcus smiles. "They're delicious, Karbo," he says. "A

real taste of summer to come. Well done, the pair of you. You're practically farmers."

My fantasy moment: the beans were to lead to a conversation about his farm... but it seems inappropriate after what has happened today.

Quintus stands, holding Emilia.

"I have an announcement to make," he says and the popina falls quiet. "Now that I am working towards owning my own business and live here in the insula, I feel I should take care of two things that are important to me. I am going to adopt Emilia."

Everyone applauds and Cassia puts a hand to her chest, tears welling up.

"Also, I would like to marry Cassia," says Quintus. "If you'll have me?"

Cassia's cheeks turn a hot pink and she looks towards her father Cassius, who nods his approval. He doesn't look surprised, Quintus must already have asked for his permission.

"I – I suppose," she says, shrugging, her tone suggesting she's agreeing to an extra loaf of bread being delivered rather than a marriage proposal. But her eyes are very bright and when a cheer goes up from the customers and Quintus approaches her, she holds up her face to be kissed and then, flustered, takes Emilia from him and busies herself with the baby while the men slap Quintus on the back and the women embrace her. I hug Cassia amidst the hubbub, my arms entwined with several other people's. Emilia stares at everyone, astonished at the sudden noise and finding herself in the midst of a crowd, but pleased at all the smiles and pats she is receiving as part of the celebratory fuss.

"He's a good man," says Cassius, when I finally reach him to congratulate him.

"He is," I agree, turning to Quintus. "You look after her, now," I say, in a teasing tone.

"You know I will," he says, his face earnest.

I hug him. "I know," I say.

When the hubbub has died down, I make my way to Cassia for an extra embrace, just the two of us instead of a cluster of people.

"Did you know he was going to ask?"

"No! Father did. He'd already given his blessing."

"Are you happy?" I ask.

She tries to shrug again. "He'll do," she says. "He's a good man, he's been kind to Emilia and he didn't have to be."

"Your cheeks are too pink and your eyes are too bright for 'he'll do', you know," I say, laughing.

"I've been burnt once," says Cassia fearfully, her voice low.

"He's not like Rullus," I say, embracing her more tightly. "He's kind and he loves you, we can all see it."

"Thank you," she says in a whisper, her smile returning.

"For what?"

"His apprenticeship," she says.

"It didn't take much doing," I say. "Balbus is delighted with him and Quintus... he was made for that job. When's the wedding?"

Cassia is beaming again. "He said he asked me now so that we can get married in June."

It's a lucky month for weddings, a good choice. "Only a few weeks to get ready then, we'll have to rush all the preparations along. You ready to be a wife?"

Her cheeks get, if possible, even pinker. "Not much choice, have I?" she says, her voice a little hoarse.

Now that Quintus has made his feelings and intentions clear,

Cassia unbends. He showers her with tokens of his affection, from flowers to carvings he has made, and she glows with his attention, offers first her cheek and then her lips for kisses as he passes, nestles into his arms, beams on him when he plays with Emilia. She looks after him in her own way, cooking little treats, weaving him a colourful belt, tutting over the state of his shoes and ordering new ones from the cobblers. She spends time preparing her white wedding tunic, adding embroidery, also in white, to the hem and neckline.

Fabia is delighted with the news. "Now my little one will have a proper mother and father," she coos. She sits on the floor of the courtyard and allows Emilia to crawl over her lap, tickles her and then strokes her hair as the child grows weary and falls asleep. "Someone lift her off me, she's getting so heavy."

Cassius comes to take her, carrying her drowsy over one shoulder back to their apartment.

"You should have your own baby," I tell Fabia.

Fabia laughs. "One day," she says, getting stiffly up from the position she's been stuck in for the past hour. "I have enough to be doing with the new school. We've got twice the number of gladiators we had before."

"How is Sadiki working out?

"Good," she says, nodding. "He works hard and he's respectful. I could do with two of him."

"You'll manage," I say. "You always do."

Billica's turn as Queen Hippolyta of the Amazons has been a raging success and we ask Patronus and Labeo for more bookings to re-run the battle regularly over the season. Labeo is delighted. Patronus agrees, reluctantly mollified over the unexpected gladiator deaths by the higher price Billica now commands as a popular, billed gladiatrix. Painted images of her, red hair flying as she wields a sword from her chariot, adorn advertisements for the Games and I see plenty of obscene graffiti around the amphitheatre mentioning her name and what men would like to do with her in the bedroom. Labeo was right, she is beginning to make a name for herself, whether she wishes to or not.

Meanwhile the deaths of Primus and Eros have been reported, but there's been little interest from the authorities. They were both slaves, they were both gladiators. Their owner Patronus has been compensated by the imperial purse, they clearly feel that this sort of thing is to be expected amongst the low-life of the Games performers. Marcus gives instructions that there should be a guard at each door leading to the arena floor during shows, so that the Charon episode cannot be repeated. Strabo must show his face if he is called upon and Fabius must escort him to the arena door to show that his service really has been requested. All of us try not to walk about the place alone, although with the endless corridors and side rooms this is sometimes difficult. I can feel the nerves amongst the team and am glad when the programme shows a space of three days without shows, one of which will be Cassia's wedding. It would be nice to stop looking over our shoulders for a few days.

THE THRESHOLD

C ASSIA'S WEDDING DAY IN LATE June dawns with a bright blue sky and the promise of heat to come later. For now, there is a light breeze and the courtyard is full of women with flowers in their hands, following Julia's orders while over-excited children dart in and out, part help, part hinderance.

"Morning, Althea."

"Secundus! What are you doing here?"

"Brought a gift for the bride, of course." He holds out a bronze phallus on a chain. "Lucky pecker, can't have a bride getting married without one, now can I?"

"Thank you," I say, taking it. "Will you be with us for the festivities?"

"Got to get home," he says cheerfully. "But wanted to make sure I wished her luck."

"You're a kind man," I say, giving him a quick hug. "I'll give her your blessings."

"Enjoy the day," he calls out. "May Juno bless the bride."

"Juno's blessings on the bride," echo the women, still placing pots of water filled with flowers on every available surface.

Marcus clatters down the stairs to go with Fabius and Cassius to the auger, who will say whether the day is auspicious for the wedding. This time there is none of the dread in my belly as there was when Cassia almost married her horrible cousin. I run up the stairs to Cassia's apartment and find Fabia already dressed in a pink tunic trimmed with beads and flowers tucked in her hair, worn loose for once. It makes her look younger, less like her usual scholarly self. She is rocking Emilia in her cradle.

"I'm washing," calls Cassia from the other room.

"I'm so happy for her," says Fabia. "She deserves Quintus, after…"

"Yes. I woke up joyful today, not like that awful day last year."

Cassia appears, skin still pink from being rubbed dry, her eyes bright with excitement. I embrace her, getting wet from her still-dripping hair.

"I'm so happy for you," I say.

"I'm happy I didn't marry Rullus," she says with feeling. "Juno saved me for a better man."

I take the towel from her and rub her hair dry, pull a comb through it as it dries, then help her dress in the white tunic of a bride, adding the elaborate knot of Hercules to her belt and her mother's flame-gold veil to her hair. I can already hear noise from the courtyard, the inhabitants of our insula gathering to celebrate. A cheer goes up.

"That'll be your groom arriving," I say giggling. "Better not keep him waiting."

I lift out Emilia and give her to Fabia, who staggers slightly under her growing weight. "Ready?"

"Ready."

"Cassia?"

She beams at me as I take her by the hand. "Ready."

I open the door and let Fabia out, then lead out Cassia to

whoops and cheers. I cannot help laughing with pleasure. To see our whole community gathered here, the courtyard filled with flowers and happy people, is a lovely sight. Opposite stands Quintus. His face lights up at the sight of Cassia. He holds out his hands towards her and I lead her to him. He does not stand on ceremony, clasping her in his arms and whispering something to her, which makes her smile even wider. Then he lets her go.

"Sorry, Althea," he says, still beaming. "I could not resist."

"I'll forgive you for loving her," I say, taking her hand back. "You need only wait a few more moments."

The priest declares that all the signs are good, the bridal pair have the blessing of the gods on their wedding day and for their marriage. He pours a libation of wine to the gods. Then he turns to face the crowd. "Who gives this woman to be wed?"

"I, Althea Aquillius, give this woman, Cassia Umbrius to be wed," I say. I squeeze Cassia's shaking hands in mine and place them gently in Quintus' outstretched palms. His hands are steady, warm as I close his fingers over her hands, his face alight with love, his eyes only on Cassia's face.

"Now you must swear your oaths," says the priest. "First you, Cassia."

Cassia's eyes are brimming as she repeats the traditional vows, invoking all the marriages of the past as she creates her own. "When and where you are Gaius, everyman, I then and there am Gaia, everywoman," she says.

"When and where you are Gaia, everywoman, I then and there am Gaius, everyman," echoes Quintus. He puts an iron ring onto the third finger of Cassia's left hand, then takes a loaf of unleavened bread from the priest and breaks it above her head, before passing it to the priest who takes a chunk of it and places it on the altar.

"I am part of your family," says Cassia, completing the words of the ceremony.

Applause and cheers break out. Cassia and Quintus are seated on little stools before the altar and feed each other pieces of the bread. But we are impatient, we call for kisses and, giggling, they acquiesce, at which more cheers break out and the feasting can begin.

A pig has been slaughtered for the occasion, stuffed with fennel seeds and herbs and slowly roasted in the baker's oven overnight. Within moments a long table has been laid out, made up of every table in the insula. Julia hands flowers to the children, who lay them down the middle under Adah's direction as the women carry in great platters of food. For once, Cassia is not the caterer, but there are many delicacies to be eaten. Wine sweetened with honey and fresh green salads filled with parsley, onion, mint and coriander accompany the fragrant roasted pork eaten with bread rolls studded with olives and nuts. A traditional wedding cake made with grape juice is ready to be shared out. We also have a peach cream, which is Cassia's favourite, blackcurrant tart with a thick custard and figs in a richly spiced syrup. There are many toasts made, offering good wishes, which inevitably lead on to bawdy songs as the afternoon wears on, and later on there is dancing round the courtyard, hands clasped as circles weave in and out of one another.

Before dusk comes we take care of another important matter. Fabia places Emilia on the floor at Quintus' feet and he adopts her, lifting her up from the ground as he did from the street and naming her, to much applause and blessings from the crowd. He gives her a tiny crescent moon-shaped protective necklace, and Fabia fastens it about her neck. Emilia stretches up inquiring fingers but cannot grasp it and is distracted by Quintus handing her to Cassia, who covers her little face with kisses.

"Making Cassia a wife and a mother all on one day? You are quick, Quintus!" calls out a wit and everyone laughs.

It is time for the bride to leave for her husband's home. Quintus is planning to come and live in the insula with Cassia and Cassius, as they have a large apartment, but the rituals must be observed. Two of Quintus' brothers make for Cassia and grasp her arms.

"We're kidnapping you, Cassia!" they shout jovially. "You're part of our family, everyone heard you say it, and so now you must come with us!"

Cassia is laughing but trying hard to hide it, instead pretending, as she should, to be afraid of leaving home. "Oh, oh," she cries out rather weakly. "Father! Althea! Fabia! Julia! Maria! Save me! I am being taken against my will!"

Trying to keep a straight face, the other members of Quintus' family lay hands on her and begin to drag her towards the gate, Quintus leading the way, Cassia's hand held tightly in his. We all follow them out into the street, where a larger crowd has gathered. It is good luck for as many people as possible to see the bride, so our neighbours lean out of windows and come out of their homes as we turn down Virgin's Street, clapping and cheering as we pass.

"I am being kidnapped!" cries Cassia in a louder voice, getting into the spirit of the occasion, widening her eyes and reaching out to Marcus. "Someone save me! Marcus!"

Marcus laughs at her poorly disguised giggles and throws handfuls of nuts into the crowd, followed by everyone from our insula. Children scatter to catch them and the crowd responds with shouted obscenities which will convince any evil spirits not to harm the happy couple.

Quintus' family home is only two streets away, so our procession there is quick. The door is opened to receive Cassia and now she gives up her feigned fear and outrage and turns to face us all to repeat her consent.

"When and where you are everyman, Gaius, I then and there am everywoman, Gaia," she says, beaming up at Quintus. "I am part of your family."

We cheer as Quintus sweeps her into his arms and carries her across the threshold. A few of us follow inside, where Quintus' mother and father greet Cassia with a bowl of water and a burning brazier, indicating that she will be mistress of the home and hearth, before leading the couple towards Quintus' bedroom, where the bed has been draped with brightly coloured blankets and strewn with rose petals.

Shyly Cassia sits on the bed and is joined by Quintus, who pulls her into his arms and kisses her, to a final round of applause and bawdy shouts. I wink at Cassia as I close the door and she smiles back, cheeks pink.

"All right, back to the insula, there's a lot more wine to be drunk!" calls out Marcus and everyone follows him back to our courtyard. "Music!" he cries when we get there and grabs my hand and Fabia's, leading us all into a wild dance round the courtyard.

After several rounds I break away and collapse, laughing and panting, onto a bench where Marcus joins me.

"That was well managed," I say, filling up our cups with wine.

"Oh, you have to control these things or everyone gets silly and starts insisting on staying outside the door while the marriage is consummated," he says. "It's not really what you want is it, everyone giggling outside the room on your wedding night? I had an uncle who took care of such nonsense for me and I was grateful."

Heat creeps up my neck that has nothing to do with the dancing. "Yes," I say, "I mean no, not what you want." The idea of a wedding night, of what Cassia and Quintus will be doing now, flusters me, the thought of Marcus and his bride… The first night I went to Marcus' house as his newly acquired slave, I heard him in the bedchamber with Livia, he kissed her lips as we left, never to see her again. I am torn, as always, between desire for Marcus and the sad memories of Livia and his tiny son Amantius, feeling a guilt I have not even earnt, and wondering if this is how Marcus feels when he thinks of being with another woman, if it is part of what holds him back…

"What are you thinking of, all serious like that? Sad to have lost a friend? She'll be back tomorrow morning you know, looking after customers like always. You won't even have time to miss her."

I force a smile. "Oh, I know. We're lucky not to be losing her. And she is so happy with Quintus, he is a good man. Not like…"

I don't even say his name, I don't want it to pollute this happy day, but Marcus reaches out a hand and places it over mine. "I thank the gods he is gone," he says. "I never wanted to hurt someone so much in my life as when I heard he laid hands on you. But he wasn't even man enough to deserve that, he was better off being humiliated by Cassia."

I sit rigidly still. The warmth of Marcus' hand on mine, his words of protection and care, are leaving me breathless. I want more. I want him to say something else, something about me deserving better, deserving a man who loves me, a man like…

"Quintus is a good man," says Marcus, removing his hand from mine and sitting back, taking a sip of wine. "He'll make

Cassia a fine husband. And a baby already," he adds chuckling, "no doubt with another one in a year or so."

His fingertips are so close to mine. I could reach out myself, could take his hand and say…

"Dance with me?" Funis is standing over me, hand outstretched.

I hesitate, hoping for a brief moment that Marcus will intervene, will offer himself as my dance partner, but he has been distracted by a toast called out by Fabius, who has joined our table.

"The happy couple!"

"The happy couple!" says Marcus, raising his cup.

"Come," says Funis and I rise, take his hand and follow him to the other side of the courtyard, where we join the dancers. We clasp hands and enter the circle, taking steps first one way and then the other.

"It must be a happy day to see your friend wed to a man she loves," says Funis.

I smile up at him. "It is," I say. "She deserves every happiness. They both do."

"Knowing who the right person is to bring you happiness is a gift of Venus," says Funis. "When we see that person, we should take them by the hand and make them our own, without hesitation."

We turn in the dance, our steps taking us one way and then another. Funis is a graceful dancer, he guides my direction with ease as the circle of revellers attempts a more complex sequence. I realise, stumbling with shame, that I am not gazing at him as he is at me, but instead twisting my neck in an effort to spot Marcus. I look at Funis and he meets my gaze with a serious look in his eyes.

"Does it make you think you would like to be married yourself, one day soon?"

He's hinting. If I were to clasp his hand more firmly, smile more widely, he would guide my steps away from the crowd and to a quieter part of the courtyard, into the shadows of Julia's tumbling vines and flowers, where I would be embraced. He would be kind, I would be treated lovingly, not just now but in the future. I look across the courtyard, to where Marcus is laughing with Fabia, and although Funis can sense my longing he knows it is not for him. He is no fool and I do not want to lie to him or give false hope. Gently I pull my hand away, touch his arm but with a sad smile rather than the flirtatious one he is hoping for. "It does."

THE GATE OF DEATH

W E ARE USED TO PLENTY of strange sights at the Games. But even the audience is whispering at the drunken ex-senator in the front row of the amphitheatre and his chosen companion.

"Have you seen her?" asks Strabo, eyes wide.

I nod. "Unbelievable."

The she-wolf chosen by the ex-senator as his companion for the day is wearing an outfit that has everyone gaping. She is clothed only in a breast-band and briefs of tightly fitted pale leather, decorated with a leopard pattern, which then extends over the rest of her bare skin, so that every part of her is painted with dark brown spots. Her hair hangs loose, but a hairband is wrapped round her head, from which poke sewn-on ears of leather, the whole headpiece also decorated as a leopard. Her face has been painted, her eyes in the Egyptian style, her nose in black, her cheeks with sweeping strokes to illustrate whiskers. Her feet are shod in delicate sandals and from the back of her leather briefs swings a real leopard tail.

The prostitute has imbued herself with the spirit of the large cat she is embodying. Sinuous, she drapes herself against her client, bends backwards over his knees, slinks along the walkway in front of his seat, crawls up his body, her arms draped about his neck, licking his face with an enthusiastic tongue. He, delighted, holds onto her via a bejewelled leash and collar. He rubs her leather ears, tickles her under her chin, rubs her belly. The audience looks on, part amused or bemused, part outraged that a senator, even one no longer in office, should stoop so low in public.

"We have to get them out of here before Domitian arrives," I whisper to Strabo.

"Can Marcus get rid of them?"

"I suppose," I say. I'd like to deal with the matter myself but I doubt that any senator will listen to a woman, let alone one as drunk as this one appears to be. But Domitian has made it pretty clear already that he does not care for sexual misconduct even in people's private lives, let alone a public display like this. "Where is he?"

"I'll go and find him."

Marcus is not impressed when he spots the couple. "What is that?"

"They've been like that since they got here. And the show has to start shortly."

Marcus looks appalled. "I'll deal with it. If Domitian sees that we'll get in trouble for allowing lewd behaviour at the Games."

Marcus' intervention has the ex-senator leave fairly promptly, but only after the leopard-woman has rubbed herself against Marcus' knees, winking up at him as he argues with her client.

"Thanks the gods Domitian didn't see that," is all he says when he gets back to us. "Come on, let's get the show started and hope nothing else like that happens," he adds, rolling his eyes at our helpless giggles.

Today Billica is back as Queen Hippolyta. The crowd cheers

when her name is announced, the plebians stamping their feet as the first chariots come hurtling out of the arena doors. I kneel by a grate to watch as Billica makes her entrance, tumbling red tresses surmounted by her golden crown, face contorted in a violent grimace.

She's unstoppable. Labeo's gladiatrices are well trained and are putting on impressive battle scenes, they're not there just to be pretty, but even they look nervous when she's close to them, jerking away from her or looking over one shoulder when they should be concentrating on their own bouts. But Billica ignores the women. It is the men she goes after, sword in hand, teeth bared, lunging and swiping at them. They fight back, but she almost stabs one to death, he escapes with a severe cut to his side and has to be taken at speed to Fabius below. She fights every minor gladiator she can get close to and kills two criminals, one by cutting his throat and one who she runs through with her sword, but her eyes return again and again to Carpophorus and the gladiator playing Hercules. It's them she wants, the heroes of the arena. She gets closer to them and even though Carpophorus is very experienced and so is his fellow gladiator, still my hands clench as she finally enters into combat with them. Patronus is right. Carpophorus is mindful of the referee, aware he is there to put on a good show. Billica just wants to kill. She snarls at the referee when he tries to intervene and her sword comes too close to comfort to his leg. He steps back, alarmed, but the crowd is loving this, the savage woman turned loose, wild and untrainable. They shout her name, they shout encouragement and cheer her on. Marcus, seeing that things are about to get out of hand, makes a gesture and the chorus announce that Hercules and Theseus overcame Queen Hippolyta, claiming a kiss from her as well as her sacred belt. Carpophorus and his co-gladiator take the hint and nod to two other gladiators and the referee.

It takes five men to hold her down and wrest the sword from her hand, during which the referee gets a cut on his arm, before today's Hercules is brave enough to lean over her for a kiss and even so he is careful to put one hand on her forehead, pushing her down so she cannot suddenly lunge forwards to bite him. He kisses her lightly and the crowd cheer, but Billica, heavily restrained, still manages to spit in his face as he holds up her belt. Her chariot arrives and she is forced back into it, now weaponless, and swiftly driven to the exit door. A more docile performer would have been granted a victory lap of the arena with their sword still in their hand, I think, a chance to soak up the applause, but no-one trusts this woman.

The exit door is right by my grate. I stand up as the chariot is driven in. Four men are waiting in the shadows and before the wheels have stopped turning they have laid hands on Billica, gripping her tightly and pulling her out of the chariot, then forcing her to an open lift, into which they throw her. she falls, landing hard on her knees as they slam the door shut, but she's immediately back on her feet, reaching through the bars to the man who is locking the lift door, running her nails down his arm so hard she draws blood.

"Stupid bitch," he swears, raising his hand as though to strike her back, but then thinking better of it when her face shows nothing but eagerness for his hand to come inside the cage where she can grab it and bite him. Instead he shouts for the lift to be lowered and receives an answering shout. He makes an obscene gesture at her and then walks away with the other men.

There's a tiny pause before the ropes tighten, indicating that the lift is about to move. I step out of the shadows and Billica's head jerks with fear at the unexpected movement. When she sees me she swallows and stands still.

"You're a good fighter," I say softly. There is something so animal-like about her that it's like admiring the strength of a tiger, while fearing it.

Billica does not say anything. The lift begins to move down to the lower level, where she will be chained and taken back to Patronus' barracks. As she fades out of sight I see that her eyes are full of tears.

It's late in the afternoon of the same day and I should already be gone, but after the cleaning shift was done and the arena made ready for tomorrow's hunt, Funis has arranged for a large herd of zebra to be brought through the Gate of Death and across the arena floor, to a pen we have erected where they can sleep the night and eat the cut grass provided. I wait for everything to be done and once the animals have been locked up in the pen Funis and I settle down in the seating area to ensure they grow calm and don't try to escape, though I'm fairly sure the enclosure is solid enough to contain them. I don't want the conversation to stray into marriage territory again, so I bring up something I have been curious about.

"You never told me who your father was," I say.

He's very quiet for a moment. "I don't talk about him much," he says at last. "He is a senator."

I stare at him. "A senator?"

He gives a short laugh. "Didn't think I was that well connected, did you?"

"Um... gladiators aren't... usually..."

"I know. Slaves, prisoners-of-war and misfits. Not the sons of senators, as a rule."

"Then... how?"

He gives a sigh, the story is a heavy burden he carries. "My mother was enslaved as a child, just as you were. She came from the Kingdom of Kush."

"Dodekaschoinos."

"That's right. She was brought to Rome very young and sold to the kitchen of a fancy patrician villa. She peeled vegetables and washed dishes, she cried for her mother at night and ate whatever was put in front of her. That was her whole life until she was nineteen. By then she was the assistant to the cook, she'd learnt to cook and make herself useful and some other child peeled the vegetables and cried at night. The old master died and his son took one look at the slaves in his household and decided he'd have his sport with them. There wasn't a slave he didn't bed in that household, male or female. But he took a particular liking to my mother and she was called for pretty regularly. When she told him she was with child, he stopped calling for her. I grew up in that villa, slaves are expensive to buy so if you can breed them yourself, why not? I had my mother with me, but it was a cowed household. Whippings came easy and any slave could be called on to warm the master's bed."

There isn't very much I can say.

Funis sighs again. "He became a senator. His family background made him believe he was superior to everyone, better than even most of the senators in Rome, he was obsessed with how high class he was, his public image was everything to him, never mind what went on behind closed doors. He married a wife from one of the best families, then mistreated her while obliging her to go about in public as though she were the happiest woman in the world. And while most masters would not care if there were a few slave boys about the place with a passing resemblance to themselves, I saw the look in his eyes when I stood in front of him, the recognition and then the hate, how repulsed he was to see his own features in a slave boy."

"But you're free?"

"I waited. Learnt to fight. Found a gladiator trainer and asked him to buy me. My mother begged me not to do it but it was the only way out. The trainer made the offer to the household steward, who was fond of my mother. He agreed a price for me and sold me, the senator was only too willing to get me out of his house. But when he found out who had bought me he was furious: rather than disappear quietly into Rome I was going to be a gladiator? The lowest of the low? He felt it would be degrading for him if it were known I was connected to him, though I doubt anyone but him would have cared. He said he would make it hard on my mother out of spite, so I said I was an Egyptian, used the fighting name Sobek. I trained harder and longer than any other gladiator at the school, started to make a name for myself."

"Sobek the crocodile god?"

"Yes. I wore a suit of crocodile armour and a helmet with crocodile-shaped jaws."

A cold shiver runs down me. "You wore crocodile-leather armour? Like Eros, the gladiator that was killed by Charon?" My mind is whirring. "You were close by when the first gladiator was wounded with a poisoned arrow. Have these attacks been meant for you? Is your father aware of you being here? Wants to harm you?"

"Who knows?" he says, apparently unconcerned. "If that was the plan, they didn't carry it out very well. I'm still breathing."

"Be careful," I say, shaken by his revelation. "It's a dangerous life to be a gladiator, let alone one who is an enemy of people in power."

He nods but his mind is still on the past. "I never got what I wanted. I asked over and over to buy my mother. I offered a ridiculous sum for her. But he stuck to his word and wouldn't allow her to be sold. She got ill and still he wouldn't allow it. She died a slave." His voice is very bitter.

"Did you keep fighting?"

"For a while, but then I started training other gladiators, and the animals. I had a knack for working with them, so I did well and after a while I was worth more out of the arena than in it. I was glad to have made it to the end of my fighting career without suffering a bad injury or losing my life. One of the beast hunters needed an assistant and when he died I moved to Ostia and took over. I've been one of the top animal providers to all the arenas in the Empire for years. I'm proud of what I've accomplished."

"You weren't sure about coming to us, though."

"That was for other reasons."

I wait, but he does not speak again. I say it for him. "Your father?"

"He's still a senator here in Rome."

"Does he know you are here?"

"He'll find out, I expect. He's had spies keeping an eye on me for years. I've been warned more than once not to come back to Rome, not to be too visible. He preferred me in Ostia."

"Warned?"

"At knifepoint. In dark alleyways."

"Why?"

"He does not want his bastard son by a slave woman being famous for being involved in the Games. He worries someone would find out, ruin what he likes to think of as a spotless reputation, though his whole household knows better. If Martial got his hands on it he'd have it written up and circulated round Rome before you could blink, a tasty bit of gossip."

"Plenty of senators have illegitimate children scattered about. And most of them slaves."

"Not ones who were gladiators and now supply the Games as beast hunters. Disreputable trade."

He's right, the work we do places us in an underclass side by side with gladiators and whores; something of the glamorous and desirable about us, yes, but still disreputable. Desired and disdained, all in one.

"But you came back to Rome anyway?"

He looks at me, dark eyes serious. "I came because you asked me."

"You said that once before."

He smiles. "Ah, so you did hear me."

"I did."

"But you didn't ask what I meant by it."

I look down; his gaze is too direct. "I knew what you meant."

"And?"

I look up again. "I don't know."

I have told him much more than I have said out loud. "Is there someone else?"

My head moves, but it is neither a nod nor a shake.

"You're not sure?"

I sigh. "Neither is he."

"Ah."

We stand in silence for a moment.

"I should go," I say.

"Wait," he says.

I wait.

"I *am* sure," he says. "I am sorry he is not and that evidently it is painful to you, so painful that you cannot see who else you might turn to, who else you might have feelings for. But I am sure. I want you, Althea. I saw something in you on that day in Ostia and it drew me back to Rome, a place I am rightly wary of, because I told myself I would be a fool not to see you again, to see if I was right. And I was. I have grown to love you. You are a rare woman. You have a good and kind nature, you work hard and you are quick-witted. And I see you yearning for something greater, for someone to love you."

I look at him. I am not trembling, not swept away with desire as I am when I daydream of Marcus making a similar declaration. Instead it feels like a friend speaking to me, like speaking with Fabia or Cassia, someone I can trust to tell me the truth, someone with whom I can speak truthfully. "I don't love you," I say. "I do not mean that as an unkindness, but as a truth. I could not make you happy."

"I thought you might say that," he says, not distressed by my refusal. "But perhaps if you were not yearning for something that cannot be, you might open your heart to something that could be, to something that is already waiting for you."

"But what if I never love you and you love me?"

He smiles. "You see? Already you are imagining what could be. You are imagining what it would be like if we were to walk through life together, if you would become my wife. If you wish to work with me in my business, we could do that. If you are tired of the Games, as I think you are, then I will sell the business to Carpophorus and you and I can live quietly somewhere on a farm, or in any business you choose."

"Is that what you would want?"

"Yes," he says, with absolute certainty. "I want you to be my wife. I do not care what work I do, I have proven myself already, now I want something new. A different life. A happy life, away from the harshness that is Rome and the Games. Family. Friends. The small joys."

"And if I never loved you?"

"I would still love you," he says. "And there are plenty of marriages where love is never thought of, never planned for at all. So we would already have more love than those."

"Perhaps."

"But?"

I shake my head. "I cannot marry you, Funis. I love –" I stop myself. "I love someone else, as you have already realised, and I cannot marry someone else while... while there might be a chance."

"And is there a chance? That Marcus will stop being an idiot and see what is right in front of him?"

I'm hot. "I –"

He chuckles. "You cannot think I don't see how you look at him. I don't know how he doesn't see it, but I am not blind."

I swallow. "He doesn't see me because I'm always there," I say at last. "He doesn't think of me that way."

"Then he's a fool."

"Cassia and Fabia would agree with you," I find myself saying.

He laughs out loud, a big laugh, startling a passing dove, which takes off with a flutter of wings. "Oh, so everyone sees it except him?"

"Apparently."

"Not blessed by Venus to see what's right in front of him?"

"No."

He sighs. "I cannot believe I'm even going to offer to do this. Do you want me to tell him?"

"No!" I say hastily, horrified.

"No? You'd rather wait until he comes to his senses, one day? After not doing so for – how many years have you known him now?"

"More than two years."

"And you'd rather wait? Or keep waiting, I should say?"

"Yes."

His eyes are sad, but he forces a smile. "Then know that I will keep waiting too. For you. We will see who can be the more stubborn. Marcus, for not seeing you, or me, who sees you every day in my dreams."

"You should find someone else," I say.

"So should you."

We laugh together. I touch his arm quickly, wanting both to comfort and to show gratitude for his declaration and acceptance of my refusal combined, but not wanting him to take it for anything more. "Thank you."

"I have done nothing."

"It is not nothing to offer your heart," I say. "I have not been brave enough to do it."

"Then perhaps you should."

"I don't know how."

"When you are desperate enough you will," he says. "The words will come out of your mouth because you can no longer bear to hold them in."

A voice comes from behind us. "Funis, my friend! You still owe me a drink!"

It's Secundus, who has finished selling for the day.

"So I do," agrees Funis, grinning. "You told me your life

205

story and I promised you mine in return. We're going to need several drinks this evening." He looks at me and lowers his voice to a quiet tone. "I will keep waiting."

"I'm sorry," I say.

"I may win yet," he says, getting to his feet and holding out his hand to pull me up. "I can be stubborn too."

I watch them go, unsure of my feelings. Why is it that Funis can offer everything I want from Marcus, when Marcus is unable to offer the same? Perhaps he just doesn't feel the way I hope he does, and never will. Perhaps he sees me as someone with whom he works, at best a friend and nothing more, neither now nor in the future. And if that is the case… would marriage to Funis be the right choice? Should I accept that plenty of marriages are based on practicalities and a respect that might grow into friendliness and care, yet still without thoughts or hope of romantic love ever flowering?

My steps back to the insula are slow. I walk through busy streets without hearing the noise of daily life around me, my mind uncertain. Have the dice of fate already fallen this way or that, showing what path will be followed? Funis' words, *when you are desperate enough*, make me wonder whether I will know that moment when it comes, whether I will find it in myself to speak to Marcus, to tell him that I love him and find out, at last, what his own thoughts and feelings about me are.

I make my way to the popina, dandle Emilia, eat a platter of olives and salad, scoop up soft fresh cheese mixed with herbs using fresh bread, pass the time of day with some of Cassia's regular customers. Karbo arrives and wolfs down his evening meal before dashing off to play with his friends. I am too tired for much conversation. I pass Emilia back to Cassius, who has been entertaining her by playing peekaboo behind an old dishcloth, wave goodnight and make my way upstairs.

I lie awake for a while, thoughts still turning over, but it is all too confusing and eventually I drift to sleep.

When Karbo and I arrive at the popina the next morning, Emilia is wailing and Cassia is rushed off her feet.

"She's teething," she says.

Karbo and I pull faces to distract her but Emilia is grumpy, with flushed cheeks and a sullen tiredness about her we don't often see. She chews voraciously on a piece of stale bread, evidently the only thing giving her gums any satisfaction.

"We have to go," I say to Cassia. "I'll try and leave a bit earlier and come back to help you, once the gladiators start."

"Thank you," she says. "I'd be grateful for that. I don't know what to do with her when she's like this."

"It's hot," I say. "I'll take her to the courtyard fountain later and she can play in the water, she'll like that."

The walk through the Forum, though familiar, is always interesting. There's such a mix of people; from the lawyers and senators to street sweepers and shit carriers, she-wolves making their way home, soothsayers and priests…

"Can we go swimming in the river this evening?" asks Karbo.

"After I've helped Cassia with the baby," I say.

"Can I go with just my friends?"

"Only in the shallows," I say. "The current's too strong, I don't want you getting swept away."

At the amphitheatre, the zebra are calm; none have escaped, one is even lying down, most are chewing grass. There's no sign of Funis.

"Shall I check if he's in the hypogeum?" asks Karbo.

"Yes," I say. "You won't need a lamp if you leave the arena door open, you can call down and he'll hear you if he's there." I'm always a bit anxious that Karbo, or indeed any of our team, might leave a lamp burning and start a fire. Hidden in our maze of rooms and corridors, no-one would know until a blaze had built up.

Karbo makes his way to the arena door closest to the Gate of Death, pausing to try and stroke the zebras, who are having none of it, retreating to the edge of their pen, as far away from him as they can. Disappointed, he pulls open the arena door and disappears inside. He appears again immediately.

"Althea!" His voice is a desperate whisper.

"What?" I ask, already hurrying towards him.

"Come quick!"

I break into a run, join him in the doorway. His face is grey as he points down into the darkness, trying to edge away from whatever he has seen.

"I can't see –" I start and then stop.

On the brick floor, in the dim light, lies Secundus, one arm stretched out so that his cloak is pulled back to reveal the tiny phalluses with which he made his living. He is very still. His head is covered in blood which have come from three holes, neatly spaced out in a small area of his temple. I don't understand what kind of weapon would make such a wound.

Karbo, who has seen all sorts in the arena, is whimpering. I kneel down, touch Secundus' neck, but he is already too cool to be living. I snatch my hand away, stare down in disbelief.

"What if someone wants to kill us? What if they're here?" whispers Karbo.

"They're gone already," I say. "Whoever did this, they're gone. Go and get Marcus. Now."

I wait with the door propped open so that I can see Secundus from the arena. Despite my certain words to Karbo, I'm too scared to be alone in the darkness with a corpse. I stare out at the vast amphitheatre all around me, wonder at how calm the zebras are. My world is growing darker and I am afraid.

Marcus arrives at a run, followed by a panting Karbo. He does not even speak to me, just looks down at Secundus in disbelief and silence.

His presence gives me courage. I squat down next to the body, trying to see the wound better. Secundus' eyes stare up at me, empty of the laughter that always accompanied his presence.

"I know what it is!" says Karbo.

"What are you talking about?" Marcus snaps.

"What made those three holes in his head."

"How could you possibly know that?"

"The key!"

"Key?"

"To the Gate of Death, it has that shape. And you could kill someone with it if you hit them hard enough."

I look down at Secundus, his face pale in death. The holes. "Bring it here," I say.

Karbo is up and running before I've finished talking, disappearing down the long corridor, his footsteps echoing.

"I'm sorry," I whisper down to Secundus, patting his shoulder, hoping he might still feel my touch and find it comforting. His jovial smile and the constant patter that tripped easily off his tongue, the jokes and puns, the endless innuendos his merchandise allowed him to make… tears well up, trickling down my cheeks.

"It's gone!" I hear Karbo yell before he's even got back to us.

I knew this already, I expected the key to be gone as soon as I realised it had been used for this purpose. Something very dark is happening and I cannot bring it into the light, cannot work out what is going on. I am afraid, because someone is killing people and I have no idea how to stop them, nor who else might be in danger. I had feared for Funis, because of the crocodile armour and his past, but I must have been wrong, I cannot see how Funis is involved here. Unless… he was going drinking with Secundus last night. They were going to share life stories. Funis would have told him everything he told me. Is he dead because of that knowledge? I can feel the back of my neck grow cold. I know the story too. Am I next? But why kill Secundus and not Funis, if they were both out late, surely it would have been just as easy to kill Funis or indeed both of them. I am growing more and more confused, but no less afraid.

"I'm sorry," I whisper again, and close Secundus' eyes. I stand and stare directly at Marcus.

"What is going on?" I ask.

In the shadows his face is more lined than usual. "I don't know," he says.

"I am going home," I say. "With Karbo. You will have to complete today's Games by yourself. Send a messenger for the Urban Cohorts. They will have to investigate what happened. They will take what's been going on seriously now it is a Roman citizen and not some slave they don't care about. And you can go and tell Secundus' family."

He doesn't argue, only steps aside so that we can leave. I take Karbo's hand in mine and we walk, in silence, back through the

Forum, up the stairs to our roof hut, where I lie on my bed and listen to Karbo whispering to Letitia as they play in the sunshine.

I sleep, eventually, when my thoughts have gone round so many times that I am dizzy and sick. When I wake the heat tells me it's already afternoon and I sit on the edge of my bed, head in hands, more weary than if I had not slept at all. At last I drag myself to my feet and push the door open. Karbo is in the doorway.

"We need to eat," I say, my voice croaky from sleep.

"Already have. Marcus brought some food." He points in a vague direction behind our roof hut then leaves. I can hear him clattering down the stairs.

My feet drag. For the first time since I realised my feelings for him, I don't want to see Marcus. I don't want to discuss what is going on. I hope he has left some food and gone away.

He is there. Looking out over Rome, his back to me, hands on the wall. I wonder if I can pick up the plate of food at my feet and return to the hut without him noticing me. My stomach rumbles at the fresh salad, flatbread and a crushed chickpea dip thick with olive oil on the plate, as well as the ripe peach sat by its side. I crouch down as quietly as I can and place the peach on the plate, then grimace. My throat is dry with thirst but in order to pour water from the temptingly-full jug into the empty cup sat by the plate, I will most certainly draw Marcus' attention.

I start pouring and Marcus turns at once.

"Althea –"

"I don't want to talk," I say.

"What?"

"I don't want to spend hours going over and over it, how it could have happened, what's going on. I don't want to hear what

Secundus' family said when you told them or how they'll get by without him."

"They –"

"Something bad is happening, Marcus, and I'm afraid. For me, for you, for Karbo, for all of us. This life – it's too dark. It's too much. And you have –"

"I have what?"

"Willingly signed up for another year. Without asking me if I wanted that! And will there be another year after that? And another? Will you just keep saying yes, while the roof tiles fall and your family farm becomes nothing but a memory, something in your imagination?"

"The farm?" He looks bewildered and it makes me angrier.

"Your family farm! The one you told me about when I'd barely met you, when I was still your slave. You told me it was all you wanted, it was your dream for the future and you'd go there as soon as you could. The amphitheatre, the Games – that was just to have enough money. You couldn't wait to be rid of this job and now you can't get enough of it, no matter how dark it becomes, no matter who dies or who is in danger!"

"Livia – Amantius –"

"I know! I know they died and took away everything you cared for. But I hoped you might care about – about Karbo," I fumble, putting his name before mine, like a coward, "– about me, that you would take us away from here, that we…"

I stop. Marcus is staring at me while I rant, his face showing confusion at my sudden rage. "Never mind."

Marcus takes a step forward. "I do mind. I do care. I did not know you were so unhappy."

"You think I can be happy with all this going on?"

"No, of course not, but aside from this matter…"

I wave him away. "You don't understand anything. I shall make my own arrangements. I will find a different job, a safe place for Karbo and me to live. You won't have to worry about us."

"But I thought… one day… that we…"

"You thought what?"

His words stumble out. "That I… we… that one day I would return to my family's farm and that you and Karbo…"

"Yes?"

"Would be there too."

"Would we?"

"You are always there," he says.

I almost gasp. "And I would be *what* to you? On the farm? A farmhand?"

He blinks. "Of course not."

"Then what?"

He half-shrugs, searches for words. "My wife, I suppose."

"You *suppose*?" I'm half-laughing, half horrified, tears welling up, the anger burning my neck and cheeks.

He knows he has made an error. A bad one. "I didn't – I meant…"

"You assumed I'd tag along, wherever you went, whenever you felt like going," I spit out. "You assumed that because I always do tag along. Because I'm 'always there', as you have just so perfectly phrased it."

"I –"

"You don't even know how I feel for you! You don't see me as someone to fall in love with because I'm always by your side. You suppose I'll have to be your wife because you can't think of what else I would be. You take me for granted and more fool me for letting you do that, for hoping for a life by your side even

213

without any hope of love. This is my last season of the Games, with or without you. I'm not living like this anymore. And I'm taking Karbo out of this world. It's not safe." I've been speaking so fast I'm gasping for breath, my voice wavers.

Marcus is staring at me. "You feel…?" His voice trails away, he cannot believe what I have just said.

"Yes!" I say, my voice bursting out too loud after being held in for too long. "Yes, I *feel* for you. I love you! I desire you. I can't stop thinking of you. I can barely breathe when your arm brushes mine. And everyone knows it! Everyone but you. How can you not see it? How can you not feel it? Funis wants to marry me, but I turned him down because of wanting you and you don't even know or care or look at me, I'm just there, just always *there* and you don't see me except as your right hand, sorting out messes and doing what I'm told. I've had enough. I want more. I deserve more. I'm done with moping about for you. I want happiness and fun like Cassia, I want a husband who loves me and children who are safe and happy like Emilia."

"But I —"

"But nothing. I am not wasting my time and love on a man who doesn't even see me when I'm standing right next to him!"

I hear him calling my name over and over as I run across the rooftop and down the stairs. I make my way, eyes blurred with tears, through the courtyard and out into Sand Street, run down the street and spend the rest of the afternoon until dusk, sitting by the edge of the slow-running Tiber river, crying until I can cry no more.

The next day we stand side by side at Cassia's and eat in silence. Cassia looks at my red eyes and Marcus' stony face and her cheerful morning chatter fades into uncertain silence. Emilia cries and neither of us coos at her. Marcus does not swing her in the air before work, as he usually does, I do not sit on the floor to tickle her tummy.

We barely talk in the following days. We speak only to carry out our work and our voices are flat. I make sure other people are always around us, including insisting that a slave accompanies me everywhere while I am at work and when Marcus asks for me to go somewhere where we can speak alone, I refuse, until he stops asking. I carry out my tasks and leave as soon as I can each day. I forbid Karbo from being at the amphitheatre and hire another messenger boy to take his place. He grumbles, but spends his days at the stables and playing with his friends.

I hurt every day. I cry every night, silently, so that Karbo will not hear me. But there is nothing more to be said. I have spoken my heart and Marcus does not feel the same way. So I go about my business and he goes about his and I harden my heart. I will finish this season of the Games and then I will leave this job and Rome itself and take Karbo with me.

THE BURIAL CHAMBER

THE HEAT OF ROME IN August is unbearable. Stray dogs pant on street corners, desperate for shade. Only the lizards bask in the sun, their bright green bodies whisking away if you get too close. Broad-brimmed hats of straw or felt protect anyone who must work in the middle of the day and by the time the gladiatorial bouts are on, the crowd in the amphitheatre is thinning, women and children and anyone who isn't an ardent fan losing their will to stay any longer without an awning. But our Games are no longer the focus of daily life.

Rome is whispering a name.

Cornelia.

The Virgo Maxima, chief amongst the Vestal Virgins.

Found with? Seen with? Named by?

A man.

No one is certain of the details, she proclaims her innocence. But her name has been spoken by Domitian and now it is muttered across Rome. Her fate is already chosen, no grace given this time, no quick and simple execution of her choice, rather a fate worse than death. Domitian may have been kind the first time this happened but his patience has been tested and he has decided that only the punishment enshrined by law will do. The Virgo Maxima is going to be entombed alive.

I go up the stairs and see Maria settling herself on her balcony for the day, large breasts resting on a cushion. She looks sombre when she sees me, indicates the porridge I have brought with me from Cassia, guessing it is for Julia.

"I'm not sure she'll eat. She was crying last night."

"How did she hear? I thought it was only announced this morning."

"The Vestals know anything that happens to their sisters. They watch out for each other."

Julia's apartment is dark, there is only a faint light coming from the still-shuttered window. I cannot make her out in the gloom.

"Julia?"

"Althea."

Her voice guides me to her location. I pull the door open wider to let in more light and she is there, on the floor in front of her lararium, not so much in a position of prayer as of crumpled despair.

I put the porridge on the table and crouch down next to her. I have never seen Julia like this. She is always composed, even when events around her call for fear or anger. She is always upright in her bearing. If I'd been told she was at prayer I would expect to find her standing in front of the lararium, arms outstretched, palms upwards, her voice clear, carrying her prayers to the gods as she did for the first two Vestals condemned to die. Instead here she is, shoulders heaving, slumped sideways on the cold floor.

"Julia," I whisper, frightened by her loss of control. "Julia."

She sobs, a snotty, gulping sound, lacking all her usual grace. I open the window shutters, then light two lamps, my fingers clumsy. The room filled with light, I look back at her, hoping she will have pulled herself upright, but she is where I left her. I crouch down again and pull at her arm, like a child aghast at its mother weeping.

"Please come and sit, Julia."

She pushes me away, but gently, then puts one hand on the floor and heaves herself upright, her body slow and heavy. She follows me to a chair and sits in it. I bring her a glass of well-watered wine.

"Have you eaten?" I gesture towards the porridge but Julia only shakes her head. Her face is streaked with tears, there is snot beneath her nose. She does nothing to wipe them away. Thoroughly unsettled, I fetch a towel, dip it in water and wipe her face with it. She does not stop me, only sits still, staring at nothing.

"You heard," I say at last, unable to think what else to say.

She blinks so slowly that her eyes stay closed for a moment and fresh tears seep from under her lashes. When she reopens her eyes her gaze moves to meet mine.

"To be a Vestal is a hard life," she says. She swallows, her shoulders tight. "So hard. You are chosen when nothing but a child. What does a child of six know of thirty years' service? How would a little girl know she is giving up the chance of love and family? She knows only the fear of being taken from her mother and given to a household of women who serve some higher purpose which means nothing to her. A household fire that must be tended. A job fit for a slave and yet of such great importance that Rome will fall to dust if you fail? What nonsense is that to a child?"

She stares away again, back into her own past and that of every Vestal chosen, since the first times.

"A house full of women who grow more bitter with every

day that passes and they understand more fully what has been taken from them. Or instead grow so proud of their sacred duty that they become insufferable, that they preen and go about in public as much as they can, relishing the only thing that has been given to them in exchange for their snatched lives: the reverence of plebians. They attend the Games, are taken to the box reserved only for them, see the Emperor himself bow his head, feel the crowd's veneration and tell themselves that it is worth it, that their crippled lives are worth it after all, for are they not respected? Are they not given freedoms any woman in Rome would beg for? Do they not live in luxury, with slaves to wait on them and a sacrosanct destiny?"

"Cassia said…" I begin.

"One or two look beyond pride and bitterness. They yearn for something denied to them and when they see its form, they bring such danger upon themselves, unable to resist what is forbidden."

"Were you…?" I don't dare ask the question.

"Oh, I was one of the proud ones," says Julia. "I found my pride early and it sustained me when I wanted to cry for my mother. I held my head high, I spoke to my slaves with all the rudeness a child has in them and grew only ruder as a grown woman, whipped them for the slightest error, the slightest sign of disrespect. If there was a chance to be seen in public, I would go. My hair must be braided just so, my robes had to be whiter than white. I *felt* how sacred my very person was and I revelled in it. Thank the gods I did not see what I could have yearned for until I was freed from my service."

"Your husband?"

"I was thirty-six and I returned to my family's villa, a retired Vestal. Those first days, that first month, oh, I missed my former life. From one day to the next I was nothing, a shadow of my former glory, my place taken by a mere child, six Vestals just as there had always been, as there will always be. My family were proud, of course, such an honour to have given a daughter to Vesta's service… but it is a greater honour when she is a distant, white-robed figure in a temple. When she is nothing but a spinster in your household who used to be a Vestal, it is not the same, is it? When you see that she must eat and wash and use the toilet like everyone else, her sacredness dims."

I try to imagine Julia in her family's villa, the inviolability of her former life drifting away from her, day after day, as she became a woman for the first time, no longer a priestess.

"Is that when you met your husband?"

Julia gives a half-laugh. "Can you imagine my family's horror? A carpenter? It was their own fault, I suppose. They barely spoke to me, weren't sure whether I was to be treated like a Vestal or just a spinster, neither of whom you'd spend time in idle chitchat with, would you? So they mostly left me alone while they decided what to do with me. They didn't even consider marriage."

"Vesta does not share her handmaidens," I murmur. It's a common phrase; it's considered ill luck to marry a retired Vestal Virgin, so if they leave Vesta's hearth when their time is up, these women of thirty-six who have lived such a strange life, accustomed to freedoms and riches, then find it hard to settle back into normal life. And of those few who have married, rather too many lost their husbands early, adding to the superstition, not taking into account that if you marry after thirty-six, your husband is likely to be fairly advanced in years himself.

"Indeed," says Julia. She has gathered herself; the thought of her husband has revived her; she sits upright again, sips some wine, but still refuses the porridge.

"How did you meet him?" I ask. I've never heard the full story of Julia's marriage.

A faint smile emerges at last, the memory of him still making her happy. "Woke up late to a half-empty house, everyone had gone about their business for the day, mostly keeping out of the way because they knew there would be noisy building works. No-one bothered to tell me. The whole house echoed with hammering. I followed the noise out to the garden and there was a man up a ladder, taking an ancient vine down from its pergola, which was half-rotten and about to fall on someone's head. I demanded to know what all the noise was about. He didn't know who I was, had no idea about my past. He looked down at me from up there and said, 'I am here to rescue this lovely vine, Domina, and make a new home for it, so that it can flourish once again.' I stood there and watched him. He didn't speak to me again, only gently, gently took the vine away from its support. It lay over half the garden while he took apart the collapsing pergola and rebuilt a fresh one. Then he took the vine and twined it back onto its new home so that it would be safe and have space to grow. It took him two days and I sat in that garden and watched him all the time. He didn't speak to me. He whistled, he patted our family dog and he talked to the vine when he'd finished, said a few words of blessing over it and wished it many more years of happiness and fertility, of growing grapes for our household. And that was all it took. When he was leaving I asked his name and he told me his nickname. I said no, he must tell me all of his name. He paused then and looked at me and he told me all of his name and asked for mine. I told him. The next day he returned. He asked one of the slaves who answered the door if he could speak with me and when I arrived he looked at me and said, 'You were one of Vesta's handmaidens,' and I felt my heart sink because I thought, he will never marry me and already that was what I wanted. I said nothing, only nodded, and he smiled and said, 'I knew it when I saw you move. But I would like to marry you anyway.'"

We laugh out loud and both of us have tears that have risen up at the same time, the thought of this man, this carpenter-nobody, daring to say such a thing to a woman from a well-off family, a retired Vestal Virgin no less and yet the romance of it, the simplicity of what had been felt between them, the power of it. If Marcus said such things to me... I push the thought away.

"How did he know you wouldn't slap him round the face for insolence?" I ask.

"My mother did," says Julia. "But it was too late by then. I insisted on marrying him and my family cut me off with no money. I had money from my time as a Vestal, some people leave money to Vestals in their wills. So I bought the insula and we moved here. My family were appalled. No-one of their class lives in the Ninth Region. They never spoke to me again, not to this day."

"I'm sorry," I say.

She shrugs. "I hadn't lived with them since I was six. They hardly felt like family. And I was tired of taking care of a make-believe hearth to look after the people of Rome. I thought there must be better ways to do that. The insula was already crumbling then, but I rented out rooms and kept the rents as low as I could so that soon enough the place was full of waifs and strays. Cassia's mother was one of them and even when she found a good husband she refused to leave, opened up the popina downstairs instead and started making her weekly soup for beggars alongside the food trade. She understood what I was trying to do, it felt like we really were providing a home and a hearth for the people of Rome, not just pretending, even though that sounds blasphemous from a Vestal Virgin's mouth. Marcus was one of the strays, an injured soldier from a penniless shamed family, wondering what to do next in his life. I could see what a good man he was and he became a good friend. He came to visit me when my husband died, sat with me while I cried and cried, went home and wrote letters to me, each one with a pressed flower from Livia."

She has skimmed over her husband's death and I don't know whether to ask about it or whether it is something she would rather not tell me, even when she is telling me more than I've ever heard about her life. We sit in silence for a moment.

"It was quick," she says at last. "The marriage and his death. He died on a sunny day, his hand to his chest and gone. I know everyone whispered afterwards that Vesta does not share her handmaidens, that he died because he loved me. But we had such happiness together. Three years we had, one year for every decade I served Vesta. And it was so much, after so little, it filled my heart after all those lonely proud years."

My eyes well with tears again. I have never heard Julia sound like a woman. She always sounds like a Vestal; certain, complete, inviolable. I have never thought of the loneliness a child would feel on being thrust into that life and all the things they would have been forced to leave behind, from their family to the chance of ever making a family of their own...

"Did you know her?"

Her shoulders slump, heavy. "Cornelia was in my care. Came to the Vestals after me and you were supposed to care for the one that came after you, to be her guide. When I left she said she would leave too, when her time came, but when it finally came she was on her way to being the Virgo Maxima, greatest among equals and she couldn't resist the honour, the importance of it. So she stayed past her time, stayed for the glory." She gives a half-sob again. "She could have left and been free, she could have lain in the arms of a man and no harm would have come to her and instead she stayed for the supposed glory – there *is* no glory, she should have known that by then – and because she looked, because she looked out beyond Vesta's hearth and saw a glimpse of what she might have been, what she could have claimed in life and was tempted, reached out for what was forbidden…"

"They say Domitian has decided there will be no mercy this time."

"The burial chamber."

"Perhaps he could be persuaded? With the other two he –"

She shakes her head. "He's making an example of her. She is a warning to the senators of what he can do, of the power he wields. That he will not always be gentle, not always find a kinder way to proceed."

"Why is it a warning to the senate?"

"Most of the Vestals are daughters of senators."

"You don't think he'll change his mind?"

"No."

"What can we do?"

"Nothing."

"What will you do?"

"Be there when it is done. It is all I can do."

"We will be there too," I promise and she touches my hand, her eyes full of suffering only she fully understands.

Cassia, Fabia and I make our way early to the Temple of Vesta. There is a crowd waiting outside, despite the heat already rising. Marcus has gone with Fabius to another part of the route. I am glad we do not have to stand together in silence, witnessing yet another dark moment.

I spend my life looking after crowds in the amphitheatre, I know what they are like. They are raucous: talking, singing, shouting, jeering. Even when they think they are quiet and attentive, they are not. They whisper to each other, adjust their clothing or give a cough, all sixty thousand of them. They cannot help but make noise.

This crowd is silent. No-one speaks, no-one coughs or adjusts their clothing. They are cowed in a way our crowds never are, not even when we dispatch criminals. This is no common criminal, this is a Vestal Virgin being put to death in a way that even a hardened soldier would blench at, for they expect to die by a quick blade in the glory of battle, not by the slow, slow lack of food, water and air. And a Vestal is a sacred being, they cannot bring themselves to think of her as impure after bowing their heads all their lives any time they saw one of the six white-robed figures. They are afraid; they know that this is right and proper, what they are doing, she must be punished, but also they know that you must not harm nor kill a Vestal and in their stomachs they know that this death she will be put to is a lie, that leaving her alive in that tiny room, sealed underground with a lamp and a couch, a few days' worth of bread and water, milk and oil so that all can claim they never hurt her is nothing but deceitfulness... and who is the deceit for? Not the crowd, they know it is a falsehood, not the Vestal who is going to her certain death. It surely cannot be for the gods, for the gods see all and know all, they would not be taken in by this pretence. And so if everyone knows it is a lie and yet we are still going ahead with it, then we are indeed harming a Vestal Virgin and perhaps the gods will be angered with anyone who was there, who took part in this sham? The crowd's deepening sense of dread weighs down their feet and tongues, keeps them still and silent.

Today's procession will leave the House of the Vestals and make its way north-east, to the Colline Gate, one of the great gates of Rome. The burial chamber will be on the inside, in the area known as the Evil Field, Campus Sceleratus. Cornelia will be interred within Rome, but only just. A dead body should not be buried within the gates of Rome, but she will not be dead when she is buried, so all is well, another law will have been upheld by this performed pretence.

"Julia said she would be here," whispers Fabia. "Where is she?"

We look about us but we cannot see Julia anywhere. I wonder whether she has entered the Temple of Vesta to pray but I am not sure anyone is allowed in today.

The crowd finally makes a noise, there is a brief rustle and low murmur as she emerges. The chief Vestal Virgin, the Virgo Maxima, once the most revered woman in Rome, even above the Empress. The woman once named Cornelia, condemned by the college of pontifices, is now named the empire's most reviled, shamed, despised being.

She is tall, with the perfect bearing of a Vestal. Pale skin from the decades tending a fire indoors, long dark hair. She has served beyond her thirty years, but, chosen as a child of six, she is not yet old. She is wearing a plain, undyed tunic, like something a poor woman would be buried in, her hair is not bound with red ribbons into the elaborate braided hairstyle that Vestals wear, instead it falls loose down her back. But these deliberate debasements only serve to echo her robes of office, the yellowed-white of undyed linen recalls the white robes she would have worn, her fine loose hair is still crinkled from the braids she

226

has worn every day during her service. Her red hair ribbons and the red band that would have encircled her head are gone, but in their place we can see plainly on her arms and legs, glimpse from the neckline of her tunic, the thin red lines where she has been whipped by Domitian himself, as the law demands.

The crowd shuffles backwards and more than a few bow their heads without realising and then jerk them back up, remembering that she is no longer sacred. She was a bride of Rome, she committed adultery by lying with a man and so she is guilty of treason. They could jeer at her if they wished, could spit and curse and name her a whore, but they cannot bring themselves to do that.

We see her only briefly. The quick tramp of feet brings a litter close to her, into which she climbs, the plain drapes falling about her, hiding her shame from view. The bearers lift the litter with ease, she is a slim woman and there are four of them. There is a brief pause, a slow swirling of positions as the procession forms. At its head, Domitian, in his role as the pontifex maximus, Rome's leading male priest. His face is tight with what looks like anger, but from the way his hands are opening and closing by his sides, I wonder if in fact he is anxious. To have yet another Vestal fail in her sacred duty may be seen as a bad omen for Rome. He looks quickly behind him, to where the executioner, whose role it will be to seal up the burial chamber, and a whole group of additional priests stand. Behind and around all of them, the twenty-four bodyguards assigned to the Emperor in case there should be any trouble during this difficult ceremony. Beyond them, the closed litter. Behind it four sullen but well-dressed people, two men, two women. They must be Cornelia's family, once boastful of having given up a daughter to Vesta's service, who became the Virgo Maxima, now shamed by attending this false funeral, their daughter's body not an honoured corpse but very much alive, streaked with the whipping she has brought upon herself. Behind them, the gathered crowd becomes the main part of the procession, there is much shuffling and jostling, albeit quietly, for a good position, for no-one wants to be at the back of the crowd when we reach the burial chamber and miss seeing the ritual. Indeed some people have gone ahead to line the route and others even further on, are waiting in the Evil Field.

Fabia, Cassia and I find ourselves a little behind the family but there is a sudden murmur, a falling back.

Out of the crowd ahead emerge three women. Julia is the youngest, the other two are more wrinkled and shrunken than she, though they are still upright. Each one carries a burning lamp. I have never seen the other two women, but there is no doubting that these three are surviving Vestal Virgins, those who served out their time and were released, set free to live their lives as they saw fit. They have come today to escort their sister to her place of death, the only ones to give her honour when all honour has been taken from her.

Domitian turns to see what the commotion is and looks appalled at the sight of the three women, looks for a moment to his bodyguards, who tense, waiting for his instructions. But his hesitation means he has lost before he even opens his mouth. He closes it again and pretends he has seen nothing. There is no law to cover this moment, no ruling that says who may attend the entombment of a Vestal and who may not. Domitian jerks his head and steps forwards, the family step back, confused, and so it is Julia and the two women who walk just behind the closed litter, not speaking, holding their burning lamps, the little flames flickering at each pace the procession takes through the silent Forum, north-east to the Colline Gate, the route lined all the way with hushed crowds who gape at the sight, making signs against evil spirits and bad luck, for who knows what gods may be angered, what spirits may be woken by such a sight, such a deed?

The walk feels longer than it is, partly because of the sombre, funereal pace, partly because we cannot chatter amongst ourselves. Behind us, the procession is growing, the people we pass mostly falling in behind us, so that by the time we reach the Colline Gate there is a huge crowd. Ahead of us looms the vast arched stone gate, just before it are built-up ramparts, into which has been dug out the burial chamber. All we can see of it is a large square hole, as wide as a man's outstretched arms, descending into darkness, a wooden ladder joining the world above to the world below.

The procession stops and those of us who were close to the head of it find ourselves grouped in a half circle around the litter, placed on the ground, its bearers stepping away from it. The crowd behind us is vast, I am not even sure what anyone would see from the back. Perhaps people just want to feel the solemn nature of the occasion, and they are right in this, for even if it is soundless and even if nothing can be seen, there is something amongst us all that cannot be described, that can only be felt.

I watch Julia and the other two retired Vestals. They stand upright, they hold their lamps, they do not look about themselves, only wait to bear witness to what is about to come.

Domitian steps forward. He should pray out loud, as would be normal in a ritual or even at a funeral, but he does not, he holds up his hands, palms turned upwards to the sky and prays in silence, I can see his lips move but no sound escapes. I wonder what his prayers consist of, whether they are a prayer for Rome, defiled by this woman's actions, or a prayer for this woman, about to be executed in a manner which even I, who play a daily part in executing criminals, find horrifying.

He has finished praying, turns to the still and silent litter and draws back the drape. The litter shudders as Cornelia emerges to meet him. Her height means she stands almost eye to eye with him. She does not weep or fall at his feet to beg for mercy. She looks into his eyes with an expression of dignified curiosity, who is this man who dares to block the pathway of a Vestal? And after a moment it is he who lowers his eyes, who steps aside and brusquely indicates to her the ladder, forgetting to move with the ritualised care suitable to this moment.

She stands still for a moment, looking at the ladder and then she glances over her shoulder to where Julia and the other two women stand, one last sighting of her sisters. They raise their lamps in tribute to her. She holds their gaze, then turns her face away from them and steps forward to where the ladder descends into darkness. By the hole stands the executioner and his three assistants, who carry shovels.

She grasps the ends of the ladder, then takes her first careful steps down it, her feet disappearing from view, but then she pauses. Her loose tunic has caught on the ladder, she takes one hand off to free it. The executioner, seeing her difficulties, goes to help her but she pulls away, shrinking from his touch which would defile her sacred person. I see Julia's description of herself, the excessive pride she carried to make her strong, to rise above fear and loneliness, reflected in Cornelia's face as she continues to step downwards, the rigid proud bearing the only thing keeping her from crumpling, from weeping in terror. Perhaps she will weep when we are all gone, but she will not allow herself to do so in public, to be further dishonoured by weakness. She will take each step as though it were her choice; it is all that gives her strength.

She is gone.

The executioner looks downwards. He must see her disappearing into the chamber and closing its door behind her, for he gives a signal and two of his assistants draw up the ladder. His face is pale; he has been shaken by her disgust. He points, not speaking, and the three assistants pick up shovels and begin to fill in the pit that leads to the burial chamber.

We stand in silence, all of us, no-one daring to protest, no-one able to walk away until the thing is done. The only sound is the shovelfuls of earth hitting the ground below and it is deafening. Cassia and Fabia take my hands and they are both shaking. They will feel my own winces each time the heavy thud of earth drops a little less far.

The scraping, shaping sounds are almost worse, as the mound is smoothed. Can she hear them, I wonder? Can Cornelia, buried in a tiny room below us, hear these sounds? She cannot hear the crowd, even though there must be more than three thousand of us here, because we stand still and silent, afraid of what we are seeing, unable to look away.

The assistants look to the executioner and he, sweating without having done any of the work, gives an uncertain nod, turns to Domitian and stands waiting to be dismissed. Domitian, face pale, hands still clenching and unclenching, gives a small gesture to release him, his work discharged. Then he turns away and walks through the crowd with the bodyguards and the swaying, empty litter following him.

No-one dismisses us, the crowd. We stand a few moments longer, caught in the spell of what has been done here, then a few people recover and begin to move away, making gestures against evil spirits as they do so, hoping none will follow them home from this most ill-omened event.

I look for Julia, but she has melted back into the crowd

with her two sister Vestals. Cassia, Fabia and I walk slowly away, taking a longer route than is necessary to get home, so that we may avoid the crowds. We are walking through a tiny backstreet alley before Cassia opens her mouth. Her voice is hoarse, she has to clear her throat before she continues.

"How – How long do you think?"

Fabia's answer comes so fast it must be all she has thought of. "Maybe three days. At the most."

"She has food and water," protests Cassia.

"She doesn't have enough air," says Fabia.

"Could anyone have given her…"

"Doubt it," says Fabia. 'Where would she hide it?"

We don't talk about it in the insula, we don't gossip about how it all happened or speculate who will be chosen to replace Cornelia. The whole of Rome waits to see who the replacement will be, a child substituted for a Virgo Maxima, starting the cycle again, innocence taking back what was defiled. Only our insula does not take part. Each household leaves food outside Julia's door for many days, our offerings to Cornelia. Julia stays indoors, barely seen, nodding wearily to any of us if we happen to meet her in passing, going to the toilets or to collect water from our courtyard fountain, her face pale and her eyes rimmed red.

One day, a week after Cornelia was entombed alive, Julia finally emerges when it is dusk, takes up a little pot of red flowers and disappears for some time, returning when the streets are dark, carrying the now empty pot back to her apartment.

The next morning a messenger from Patronus arrives at dawn, panting, to tell me that this afternoon's Amazons scene will need a new Queen Hippolyta. Billica has committed suicide. I send

Karbo to Labeo to tell him to prepare one of his gladiatrices to take on the part and go myself to the Ludus Magnus, which is very quiet. A guard on the gate is particularly careful about checking who I am, sending word to Patronus, who comes to collect me himself, a far cry from the usual freedom I have to enter whenever I wish.

"Althea," says Patronus heavily when he sees me. His face is drawn. "What a season. Never had so much ill fortune." He makes a superstitious gesture to ward off further evil. "Two gladiators killed before their time and now this?"

"Where… how…?"

"She said she needed to relieve herself. It's the only thing we allowed her to do alone and without being chained. The rest of the time she was chained or in her own room in the barracks. Couldn't leave people in with her and she had a guard outside all the time. She was worth it, her price was rising all the time, but it was a lot of trouble to go to and she wasn't getting any easier to manage."

I hardly care about how she was to manage. "She was relieving herself and then?"

Patronus has to take a deep breath. "She took the toilet stick and shoved it down her throat, so that the sponge suffocated her."

I stare at him in horror. "She suffocated herself? Is that even possible?" I can't help thinking of the other murders. "She wasn't killed by someone?"

Patronus shakes his head. "She was all alone, she died by her own hand." He grimaces. "The undertakers had a struggle to get it out of her." He's quiet for a few moments. "Brave though," he admits at last. "Not many men would have the courage to do what she did."

I swallow. An ending shrouded in secrecy and fear, violent and obscene in its desperation. I think back to Billica's wild fury in the arena set against her eyes filling with tears as she was returned to her enslavement, humiliated time and again for the cheering crowds, forced to simulate submission to men she hated and could well have killed, had she not been held down and disarmed.

"Labeo can find someone to fill in, I suppose?" says Patronus. "I'll send him the crown we used and the hairpieces. She was always ripping them out anyway, we had to put them in fresh for each show."

There's not much I can say or do. I make my way to the Ludus Matutinus where Labeo is shaking his head.

"Told you, they don't know how to manage women. Wild thing like that, you have to tame her somehow, you can't have her chained up forever holding a grudge. But don't you worry. I've got one of my best girls on the job. Dyeing her hair right now, she'll do you proud this afternoon."

But the gladiatrix who performs as Queen Hippolyta is not the same as Billica. Her hair and golden crown are magnificent, she can fight, but the wild rage that used to emanate from Billica is not in her and she submits all too willingly to being kissed by one of Rome's celebrity gladiators.

On my way home I take a detour. On the still-fresh mound of earth by the Colline Gate, in an inconspicuous corner, is a little flowering plant, blooming red like Cornelia's hair ribbons, like the streaks of the whip on her skin. Like Billica's false hair, taken from some other nameless slave, crowning her as queen of the Games against her will.

THE MINOTAUR

S EPTEMBER HAS SOMEHOW ARRIVED, THE stiff politeness
between Marcus and me making every day a struggle. I
might have relented, might have given way to my feelings,
but first Cornelia's death and then Billica's were further steps
into the darkness and it only made me more resolute in my
decision to get away from the Games, to find another life. I have
attended each day of the Games, done everything required of
me, but I have kept myself aside. I have taken a slave everywhere
I go, I do not stay late to chatter or go to the baths with various
team members. I no longer stand in the arena for crowd scenes,
instead I take my place opposite Marcus in the amphitheatre or
watch scenes through a grille in the arena wall. I said I would
only complete this season and here it is, the morning dawns,
the finale of the last Games I intend to be part of. I expected
to feel excited, but instead I'm weary and sad. Part of it is the
lack of warmth between me and the man I love, but I also feel
sorry for Felix, whose last day it is today. He has played our
Minotaur all season and is a favourite in the arena, despite his
grisly battle style. Today his monstrous stage persona will be laid
to rest alongside him.

The team is gathered in the centre of the sand-strewn
arena, making the most of the light before plunging into the

hypogeum. Marcus is consulting a scroll of the day's events, his brow furrowed. At last he straightens his shoulders and looks up at everyone.

"Last day," he says and there's a cheer. "We have a lot to get through before there's any cheering," he reminds us. "Domitian will be attending and there's a very full programme. Everyone be careful today, stay with other people, look out for any trouble. Today we tell the whole story of Theseus and the Minotaur in the correct order. Ready?" He tries to catch my eye but I look down at my own notes, nodding without returning his gaze. "Right then. Carpophorus, enjoy your last day."

Carpophorus puts his fist to his chest in a salute. "I just want to say," he says, his deep voice wavering a little, "that I've been honoured to be the lead this season. I never thought when I was a slave boy that I'd be standing in the largest amphitheatre in the empire, playing one of the greatest heroes there's ever been. I'm grateful."

Marcus gives a warm smile and pats Carpophorus' vast shoulder. "We've been proud to have you," he says. "You're one of the best."

The amphitheatre is at full capacity, close to sixty thousand crushed together instead of the fifty thousand it can comfortably hold. I shake my head when the inevitable complaints are brought to me about ladies and their parasols. I don't care. Let them argue amongst themselves. I don't care about how fair their skin is, how many slaves they've brought with them, whose view of the bloodshed to come is obscured. I'm nervous something will go wrong today. It's the closing show, if the murders so far were somehow linked to the amphitheatre then this is the killer's last chance to strike.

Trumpets. Domitian's entrance.

The court of Crete emerges, a riot of colour and music. Minos makes his ill-fated decision, gaining the crown of Crete and losing the favour of the gods. The crowd gasps as the Minotaur rips apart today's unlucky criminals and applauds the appearance of their hero, Theseus-Carpophorus.

"You would not believe the number of women we've had begging for a night with those two," says Labeo, standing next to me as we watch the spectacle from the grille. "I don't think either of them have had a night without a companion this whole summer."

I roll my eyes. The labyrinth appears and disappears, taking with it the Minotaur. Felix will be downstairs, locked into a cell until the final scenes of today's spectacle.

"Sorry to lose him," says Labeo. "He's been an excellent performer. But can't change the rules. Gave him a good send-off last night. Big feast, some noblewoman in his barracks who paid handsomely for his time. Then I left him to drink with Carpophorus and Funis."

I see movement in the gloom. Funis, nodding as the bull-leapers stream out to give their final performance. The crowd roars at the sight of them and minor gladiators follow them out. While the bull-leapers perform at the centre of the arena, gladiators in bull-helmets are killing off criminals who are fighting blind, their heads and eyes fully covered by helmets. They've been given real swords, but they haven't got a chance. They are fighting in a terrifying darkness, symbolising the darkness of the labyrinth, taking the part of the Minotaur's victims.

Ships sail across the arena, our rippling sea of cloth appearing and disappearing twice, before the time comes for our hero to make his mark. In the darkness, Funis is speaking with

Carpophorus, who embraces Felix standing beside him, wipes his eyes, then steps out to a roar of applause. The chorus tells how Theseus convinces his father to let him take his place amongst the Athenians given in tribute, and sets out the agreement that if he is victorious, he will return home with white sails in place of the black ones billowing in the breeze. Below us, Felix is guided into a lift which will bring him into the centre of the labyrinth.

The bull-leapers retreat, the court of Crete takes their places, the labyrinth, containing its legendary monster, rises up from the hypogeum to greet Theseus on his arrival. The sea recedes. Luna, as Princess Ariadne, performs one more lascivious dance before handing a ball of thread to Carpophorus, who takes the opportunity to run his hands over her body, encouraged by the crowd, while the chorus creates the roars of the expectant Minotaur, pacing in his labyrinth.

Funis passes me on his way to the bull-leapers, heading downstairs to the lower levels.

I catch hold of his hand. "Funis."

He turns back to me at once, all his attention on me. "Yes?"

I take a deep breath, ready to make the speech I have been preparing, but all that comes out is, "No."

"No?"

I try again. "I thought – about what you said, what you – offered."

He takes a step closer, his hand tightens on mine. "Yes?"

"I – my answer is no, Funis. I'm sorry."

"Why?"

"Because…"

Below us, I hear the grinding of the lifts as the labyrinth reaches its final position. Only the truth will do, only the truth will finish this conversation.

"Because I love Marcus."

Funis smiles. "I know that," he says. "Everyone knows that except Marcus himself. What if he does not love you, Althea?"

I look down. "Then no-one else will do instead," I say.

"Are you sure?"

"Yes."

"For the rest of your life, even?"

"Yes," I say with more certainty, raising my gaze to his.

His eyes are sad. "Then speak to him," he says. "A life spent waiting is not a life. We must step forward to claim what we most desire."

I nod and he lets go of my hand, turns away into the darkness. "Funis?"

He pauses but does not turn his head to me. "Yes?"

"What will you do?"

"Take another step. When we misstep, we cannot stop. We choose another path, we walk on. We make our peace with the past, we do not allow it to claim our lives forever. Else we give it too much power over us."

He waits to see if I will reply, but I don't. He walks down the corridor without looking back, disappearing into the darkness.

Now comes the moment we have spent a whole season leading up to: the final battle between Theseus and the Minotaur. Reluctantly, I turn my attention back to the grille. Any members of our team who are not actively employed at this moment join me in watching. We stand silently in the dark, peering out at the sunlit arena, as Carpophorus, urged on by a screaming crowd, enters the labyrinth holding his ball of thread as required by the story. He abandons it when the Minotaur rounds a corner and the labyrinth sinks into the ground, leaving Carpophorus and Felix at the centre of the arena, clearly visible for their final battle.

They're well-matched. The crowd howls encouragements as the two fight, the Minotaur's swiping claws skimming Carpophorus more than once, so that he is bleeding, but these are light cuts and he fights on, sword glinting, body dripping in sweat in the bright heat of the sun and then – with perfect timing from years of performance – the blade slips between two ribs and the Minotaur sinks to its knees before our hero, blood gushing. Carpophorus twists his opponent's body and holds Felix up to face the imperial box, slices his blade across the black-painted throat.

My shoulders drop. It is over. All over. I will never have to stand here again like this. I am done. I can leave. I take a deep breath. Only a few last tasks to complete. Everyone is safe, the season is complete. Thank the gods. Carpophorus drops Felix's body neatly over a trapdoor, which opens to claim his body and lower it back down to the ground level in a lift. I make my way down the stairs, under the flickering light of torches.

As I arrive at the central room of the lower floor, I hear Fabia scream.

The lift has stopped, Fabius is at its door, staring down, aghast. In the lift is, as expected, the dead body of Felix, still wearing his Minotaur helmet.

But Funis is there also, eyes wide, hand to his throat, blood spilling over his fingers as he sinks to his knees.

"Open this door!" roars Fabius.

There's chaos. All lifts are locked to keep everyone safe, to stop criminals and animals escaping. The lock must be fumbled with while I stand in rigid horror and Fabia tries to reach inside, to grab at Funis' arm and pull him closer, but it's too late. He falls sideways just as the lock is undone, his eyes closing.

They try of course. Strabo drags Funis' body out of the lift cage, Fabius and Fabia bend over him, trying to stem the blood, but a cut throat is not a quick sword-swipe to a limb. Funis is dead.

We stand in the space, blood everywhere, thick red pools of it on the floor, soaking Fabia and Fabius' hands, Strabo's shoulder and face.

"Find Marcus," I say.

He will be in the seating area just by the imperial box, entirely unaware of what has happened here. From his vantage point, all he will have seen is a magnificent spectacle and Domitian's engrossed face, the cheering crowd.

We wait in silence. More and more of our staff hear what has happened and appear from one corridor and another, forming a crowd around Funis, whispering down the corridors. Above us we hear Carpophorus-Theseus claim his status as a legendary hero and Luna-Ariadne as his bride.

The crowd parts and Marcus is standing opposite me, his face grim.

"How did this happen?"

Fabius shakes his head. "We don't know. I saw Funis briefly after the bull-leaping. Someone must have attacked him and shoved him into the lift just as the trapdoor above opened to drop down Felix's body."

"The lift was unlocked?"

"It must have been, but then locked again once he'd been forced into it."

Marcus looks at me. "I have to return upstairs," he says, his voice low. "Today's Games must be concluded without Domitian knowing anything is amiss."

"Put him – put Funis in one of the side rooms," I say, gulping back tears, trying to keep my voice steady so I can be understood. "I'll stay with him."

Marcus hesitates for a moment, his mouth opens but then closes again and he strides away.

The spell is broken. Our team begin to disperse, Felix's forgotten body is carried away.

I follow two gladiators as they carry Funis down the tight corridor to the room that we use for the dancing girls' costumes. Hung on the walls are flowing tunics in reds, oranges, yellows, blues, violets, greens, all in vivid shades and made of the lightest linens, so that they will easily flutter about the whirling bodies of their owners.

I want to turn away, to say the room is too bright but that would be absurd. Instead I set down my lamp on a shelf well away from the costumes and sink to the floor, receive Funis' head into my lap.

"You can go," I say. "I will – look after him."

They look down at me, two fighting men lost for words, stricken at the fate Funis has met.

"On your own?" says one of them.

"Yes," I say. "Yes, I'll be – fine."

They back away into the dark corridor, still uncertain. I nod to them, try to appear certain in my intention so that they will not linger any more.

They turn and head back, slowly disappearing into the gloom.

Above us I can hear the low groan of the crowd as Theseus sails home but forgets to change his sails, his father believing his son to be dead, leaping to his death. And then the final roar of applause as Carpophorus is given a laurel wreath by Domitian and praised for his exemplary years as a bestiarius, honoured as one of Rome's great performers in the Games.

I sit, shoulders sagging, over Funis. Hot tears run endlessly down my face and on to his.

"I'm sorry," I say to him, the words coming out slowly and then faster. "I'm sorry you came here and we did not keep you safe. I should never have written to you, should never have asked for you to be our beast hunter. You should have stayed in Ostia where you were safe." I think back to the first time we met in Ostia, his sharing with me his real name, which no-one ever used. "Arikakahtani," I whisper. The name of a long-ago king, he said, a name bestowed by his enslaved mother, perhaps hoping for a brighter future for her slave-born child. "Arikakahtani. May the gods of your homeland find you and take you to your mother's shade, to walk with her in peace."

From far away the trumpets blast out. Domitian will be leaving, his brisk walk keeping his entourage hurrying as he exists the building. When he is gone the vast crowd will also be allowed to leave, the stairs and exits will be packed with people, eagerly discussing the spectacle they have just witnessed, comparing it to previous seasons, wondering what will be planned for next year.

A voice comes from the doorway. "Is he dead?"

I look up, startled. The older, portly man is dressed in a toga. I do not know him, but there is something familiar about him. Perhaps a senator that I have seen in the Forum? Behind him loom two bodyguards.

"Are you lost?" I ask.

He doesn't answer, just looks down at Funis's face in my lap. "Did you know him?" I ask.

243

"No."

His response comes so fast it sounds like a lie. I am very tired, my mind feels slow. I wipe away tears and snot. "Why would you come to see him if you didn't know him?"

He turns to go without replying and as he does so I see his face from a new angle and suddenly I know who he is. I move to stand up but Funis' body slides down from me. I bend to let his head down gently so that it will not bang down onto the brick floor. When I stand my hands are red with his blood and I look down at them in new horror.

"Wait!"

The senator turns back to me and as he does so I launch myself at him, press my two palms against his chest, then wipe them on his pristine white toga, two red handprints on his chest, blurring downwards in two scarlet streaks of accusation.

"Make your way out of here with his blood on you," I say, "so that everyone will know you are a murderer. Whoever held the knife, you held their hand. You're a monster. You disgust me. There is no beast in this arena so low as you. I'll spend the rest of my life telling people he was your son."

His bodyguards step forward, blocking me from any further contact while the senator stares down in revulsion at his soiled toga. "Be careful how you speak to me," he says from behind them. "Be careful what you threaten me with."

"You're a filthy coward," I spit at him.

One of the bodyguards hits out, his hand landing squarely on my chest, shoving me to the ground. I land hard on my backside, the second bodyguard stepping forward, one hand on the hilt of a concealed dagger in his tunic.

"Senator." A quiet voice, calm, a polite greeting amongst equals.

The bodyguard hesitates, steps back from the doorway, revealing the angular frame of Stephanus.

The senator turns away without speaking, his footsteps and those of his bodyguards quickly fading down the dark corridor.

I struggle to my feet, look down at the broken body in disbelief that it should still be there, that Funis has not risen from the dead or simply disappeared, that all of this was only some dark nightmare brought on by anxiety the night before the final Games of the season.

"I regret your loss." Stephanus' face is grave when I turn back to face him.

"This was murder," I say. "Not a mistake during the Games."

"I know."

I put my face close to his, my voice uneven with rage. He does not flinch, does not step back from my anger and proximity.

"So? Will something be done about it?"

"It was deliberately planned as a murder. It would be hard to prove."

"That's not good enough!"

"Leave it with me."

"Will you have him accused?"

"I will have him punished."

"For murder?"

"For whatever I can arrange."

I stare at him. "Whatever you can arrange? What does that mean?"

"You must leave it in my hands."

"How do I know I can trust you?"

"I believe in justice."

I look back down at Funis. "There was no justice here. He did not deserve this, he did not cause anyone harm. He –"

"He will be avenged."

I shake my head, tears falling again. "I wish I shared your confidence."

"It no longer concerns you," he says. "Bury your friend with honour and leave justice to me."

I wipe my face, sweat from the heat of the room and tears mingled, the taste of salt in my mouth. "I am done with this life," I say.

"The arena of the Games is a brutal place in which to dwell," he says. "Few can survive it for long. Most exit through the Gate of Death, eventually."

"For me it has been a place of loyalty and friendship," I say. "But it has grown too dark. I cannot bear it any longer."

"Perhaps it is time to leave."

I look down at Funis, at the patterned scars on his cheeks, one hand outstretched, the shining arm cuff hiding past scars beneath it. "He wanted me to. I intend to."

Heavy footsteps approach in the corridor. When I look back, Stephanus has disappeared; once again I have not seen him come or go, his footsteps always silent.

Carpophorus emerges from the gloom, the bulk of him filling the narrow doorway. "I heard," he gasps. "Is it true?"

I step back so that he can see Funis and he sinks to his knees beside him, a hoarse wail emerging from him. "Funis! My friend!" He shakes the body as though there is a chance that we have all been mistaken, that Funis can be woken from his bloodied sleep.

I grasp his arm, the vast muscles tensed in distress and growing rage. "Carpophorus –"

"Who did this?" he bellows. "Who did it? Tell me and I'll kill them with my own bare hands!"

"We don't know," I say, afraid that if he were told the truth he would kill the senator and then be executed for murder. "We don't know, Carpophorus, they got away –"

Carpophorus breaks into noisy sobs. "He was my friend," he howls. "He said we'd work together when I retired, he'd teach me what he knew and I'd be a beast hunter, like him. He didn't think I was an idiot like the rest of them do."

"Carpophorus –"

"Everyone thinks it. Dumb old Carpophorus, only good for a show in the arena and giving the ladies a good time, like a prize bull. That's what everyone's said about me, my whole life. But Funis didn't. He was my friend, he talked to me man to man."

"I'm sorry," I say. I have said nothing else these past months, one sorry after another.

"He knew how it is," sobs Carpophorus. "He knew what it is to kill your barrack-mate, your fellow gladiator. He came with us last night, me and Felix, we drank together and he said there was honour in a gladiator dying well. He made Felix proud to die and he told me he knew I would kill him properly, that I wouldn't hesitate, wouldn't cause any unnecessary pain or suffering. We faced today with our heads held high because of him."

One grief piling on top of another fills me. I will never hear anything good again, only wretched hopes and lives being dashed to the ground, shattering one after another like the tiny pottery models Domitian cast aside so carelessly when I first met him.

A year gone so fast and so much gone with it. Funis, Secundus, my dreams of a life together with Marcus, not one but three Vestal Virgins, Billica and the two gladiators who took blows intended for Funis, Siro, Carpophorus' hopes... nothing good is left. Only Cassia, Quintus and Emilia, the three of them shining amidst the rubble all around us. I do not even try to comfort Carpophorus. He is right to cry. I stand over him and my tears fall onto his heaving shoulders, trickling down to join his on Funis' empty face.

THE FARM

THERE IS ASH FLOATING IN the air, tiny fragments of grey thrown upwards in the hot air from the flames, then drifting outwards and away, slowly making its way towards the earth. Specks of it fall onto the men's funeral togas, the soft grey touching their black. The whole of our insula's community is gathered here on the road outside Rome where burials and funerary burnings take place, along with half the gladiators of Rome. They look strange without their armour and weapons, a motley crew of all shapes and sizes, scarred faces and bodies solid with muscle, expressions grave. They don't talk, only stand together like family, exchanging heavy embraces.

Carpophorus lumbers towards me, his face wet with tears. "I should have protected him. We knew there was still someone out there and —"

I shake my head and touch his arm. "There was nothing anyone could have done," I say. "We didn't know Funis was a target."

"But I could have —"

I put my arms around him, as much to make him stop talking as out of pity for his grief. Carpophorus is a good-natured man but I cannot go through it all again, what happened and why. I have enough of my own grief and guilt to live with. Funis was a marked man as soon as he left Ostia. And he left Ostia, despite his misgivings, in part because of me, because he thought there might be some future for us together.

Carpophorus sniffs, then pulls away. "Thank you, Althea," he says gruffly. "You don't know how it feels, when a fellow gladiator falls. We live and train together, but we have to kill one another too, or watch our friends fall to another's blade. It hurts."

"He admired you," I say. "He said he'd never seen such a fine bestiarius."

"He was the best beast hunter I've ever met," he says, tears falling again. "No-one like him. I'll sacrifice for him at the temple. Me and the lads, we all had a lot of respect for him. He was one of us."

I embrace him again, look over his shoulder to where Marcus is watching us. He looks exhausted, dark circles under his eyes and a slump to his shoulders I have rarely seen since our early days together. He catches my gaze and holds it a moment, then gestures to send Carpophorus his way.

"Marcus wants a word," I say, gently pushing the still-weeping hulk of a man away from me.

"You take care," mutters Carpophorus, patting my shoulder. I don't think he knows how strong he is, it's like being patted by a pile of falling bricks.

"How are you doing?" asks Cassia, appearing at my elbow. "When we get back to the insula I've got food ready for us all, made it last night. Everyone will be too tired to think about cooking." Emilia, on her hip, stares with interest at me, one dimpled little hand twined into Cassia's black curls.

"May Juno bless you," I say. "You are the mother of our whole insula."

Cassia looks down. "It's been a hard time. We need some good news. Got any for me?" she adds, making a tiny gesture towards Marcus.

"No."

"Then he's a fool."

I shake my head. "He's not ready. He doesn't know what he wants."

"Well, he better think about it, hadn't he? Or someone else will know a good thing when they see it."

I look at her and she shrugs. "Did you think I wouldn't notice the way Funis looked at you?" Her face is serious again. "I'm sorry."

"We didn't – I wasn't –"

"I know," says Cassia. "But you felt something for him?"

"He was a good man –" I stop. My shoulders slump a little further. "He wanted what I want. Love. A peaceful, safe life." I sigh. "I'm so tired I can hardly think any more."

"Come on," says Cassia. "We're done here. I've told Father to round everyone up and get them back to the insula. And you should get some sleep."

"It's the middle of the day," I protest.

"You're exhausted," says Cassia. "Don't argue."

We walk ahead of the others and when we reach the insula I hesitate but Cassia is right. I need sleep so badly. I make my way up the stairs and into my roof hut, where I lie down on the bed and sleep comes instantly; I sink gladly into it.

When I wake it's still light. I lie for a while, watching shadows on the wall. There is a lost bee in the room, buzzing helplessly round the walls. At last I sit up and rub my face. I don't know what will happen next, I only know that this life has grown sullied in my mind. There is too much death, too much sorrow, one way or another. I glimpsed something else when I spoke with Funis, the idea of another life away from all of this, and I liked it. Except… except it is Marcus I have longed for, all this time. The life Funis promised was the one I wanted to live with Marcus. But I cannot force Marcus to see me. If his eyes and heart are still full of his past life then I cannot wait and hope for a life together that is never going to happen.

I let the bee out and follow it to the hives and the vegetables. I have money. I can leave the amphitheatre and live somewhere quietly in the countryside, perhaps near a stables to make Karbo happy, for I would take him with me. Marcus can arrange the buying of a little house, nothing grand but enough for us to live in comfort, he would do that for Karbo and me.

I will leave. The amphitheatre. The insula. Marcus.

I swallow. How can I? How could I leave all the life I have built here? I don't know what to do. I want to leave but I can't imagine it. I can't imagine being without my friends. And without Marcus. But the very thought of him makes my feelings for him well up again. His face when he smiles and the warmth of his skin…

Jerkily, I kneel and start to weed the vegetable bed, angry with myself. What is all this whining? I have decided I am no longer happy yet I will not do anything about it because Marcus has not fallen at my feet and declared his love? What would Fausta say, if she were still with us? She would laugh at me for being a hopeless romantic, tell me to stop waiting on Venus, for she is a tricksy goddess and cannot be relied on. She would tell me to make my own way in life for men cannot be relied on either, they –

"Althea."

252

I twist to look up at him. "Marcus."

He has obviously not slept while I did; he still looks bone-weary. He is holding something wrapped in cloth, a small bundle, which he sets down as he lowers himself to the ground, sitting with his knees pulled up. I hesitate, but it feels silly to continue weeding, so I sit down a few paces away, my back against the hut. I want the sun on my face, am in need of its warmth and light. I tilt my face up to it, close my eyes.

He doesn't speak for so long that I open my eyes again to see what he is doing. He is staring down at the bundle with unseeing eyes, staring at something beyond it, that only he can see. I close my eyes again. I will not waste my days staring at him. I won't be some foolish girl who spends all her time fretting over whether the boy she likes looks her way or not. I am older than that, wiser than that, beyond that. I will turn my face to the warmth and the light and choose a happier life than this one has become.

"It's for you," he says.

"What is?" I ask, opening my eyes again.

He's looking directly at me, serious, about to share bad news or something that we will have to address. "The –" He jerks his chin towards the bundle, lying between us. "It's yours. Open it."

I lean forward, pull at the edge of the cloth so that the bundle shifts in my direction. Once it is close enough, I pick it up. It's a rough square shape, about as wide as my body and lighter than I expected for its size. I fumble with the cloth wrap and as I pull it away I see the maker's mark; Balbus the toymaker has made whatever it is.

It is a toy farm, made from wood. A house and stables set around a courtyard, complete with tiny wooden animals and even beehives. It is Balbus' very finest work, intricately carved, the sort of expensive toy for a child that the noble families of Rome buy for their offspring, who will certainly never be farmers. But…

"Oh, it's broken," I say. The tiny wooden pergola that should be holding up a woollen vine, delicately woven in brown and green with embroidered purple bunches of grapes, is broken, it lies flat and the vine tumbles over it.

"Yes," says Marcus. "I want you to help me fix it."

I frown. "Balbus would be better suited to that task than me. I mean it's his…" I trail off and look up. Marcus is watching me intently. I look back down at the farm, heat rising up my neck. It is not just the pergola that is broken. There are four tiny roof tile pieces lying in the courtyard when they should be on the roof. One of the beehives is lying on its side, the stable door is hanging off its hinges and the tiny wooden pigs have escaped from their sty. I look fixedly down at the little model, unsure whether I can meet Marcus' gaze again. The heat is in my cheeks. I make an effort and raise my eyes to Marcus.

"It's your family farm," I whisper.

He smiles properly, it lights up his tired face. "No," he says. "You're making the same mistake I made."

Flustered, I look back down at the tiny tumbledown vine. "But…"

"It is our farm. Yours and mine. If you say yes to marrying me."

I'm struggling to hold his gaze. In all my daydreams of this moment, I never struggled to look into Marcus' eyes. I was so confident, so self-composed. I said everything elegantly, I didn't whisper or trail off halfway through what I was saying. I couldn't feel my cheeks burning. "Yes?"

He reaches out and lifts the farm out of my lap, sets it aside. He's kneeling in front of me, his face only a hand's breadth from mine. "You were right, I said it all wrong before. I need to say it better."

"You –"

He puts one finger onto my top lip and brushes down to the bottom lip and the touch of it is so deliberately intimate, so unlike how he has ever touched me before, that I stop talking and stare up at him. Suddenly I can meet his gaze, I cannot look anywhere but into his eyes.

"I asked myself the question you asked me," he says, his voice very soft. "How did I not see you for all this time? How did I have such a woman standing by my side and not see her for what she truly is to me?"

His finger has gone from my lips, but his hand is in my hair, he strokes down the length of it, looking at the very tips of it in his fingers before returning his gaze to my eyes. "After Pompeii… I thought I had lost everything and everyone. But I was wrong. All the way through that horror, you followed me. You followed me to places no-one else would go to, through ashes and down dark streets. And when I thought I couldn't take another step you went ahead of me and pulled me by the hand. You stood up to emperors and you told me to my face when I was wrong… and still I did not see you, not really."

Very slowly, I lift my own hand and move it towards his face. He catches it in his own and presses my palm to his rough-stubbled cheek, his skin warming mine. I stare at him. My daydreams were nothing compared to this.

"I found my courage again because of you," he says. "That stupid naumachia we were forced into, I dived into those waters and I was afraid, but because you were watching me I felt safe, against all the odds. Then Domitian…" He takes a deep breath. "He's a strange one, he's had me worried at times, but I'd found myself again. I thought if all else fails, there is always the farm and when I thought of it, I thought of you there, without even thinking what that meant for how things were between us. You were just there, every time I thought of it. It was unthinkable for you not to be there."

His eyes drop to the tiny model farm. "I'm sorry I said it wrong, though. I knew by your face, before you said anything."

I try to pull my hand away, but he keeps it in place. "I –"

He shakes his head to stop me speaking. "It came out wrong because of Funis, the way he looked at you. It made me afraid and then I knew why. I tried to speak but it came out all wrong. I tried to say how much a part of me you felt, how it was unthinkable to be without you. But it sounded like I took you for granted, that I did not see you for what you are."

He takes his hand away from where it has been holding my palm to his cheek and my hand hovers in mid-air, uncertain. But he leans closer to me, puts both his palms on my cheeks, and his voice is soft and warm, full of tenderness. "I do see you, Althea. From the first day I met you I saw your courage and quick wits, your loyalty. Now I see the touch of Fausta on you, of Julia, Maria and Adah, Cassia and Fabia, how they have shaped what was already in you. I see the woman you have become in the years I have known you and how you shape those around you." He takes a deep breath. "How you have shaped me, from broken shards into a man again, who cannot imagine his life without you beside him because I *feel* you beside me, always, no matter where I am, you are there. I know your scent, I know what you will say before you even say it, I know the way you look when you are trying not to laugh or are about to cry. The only thing I do not know is how your lips feel when I touch them with my own, and I have imagined it so often since we last spoke like this that it has driven me mad."

Perhaps he moves, perhaps it was me, I do not know who breaches the tiny space left between us, but his lips touch mine and my arms slip about his neck, our bodies press together so that we end up kneeling, entwined among the flowers and vegetables, the sun's warmth shining down on us just as I imagined so many times and what I imagined is nothing compared to this.

I'm not sure that we speak much after that, little soft words perhaps, nothing that makes any sense except to the two of us. Marcus stands after a while and holds out his hand and I follow him to his hut without speaking. He undresses and there is one moment, one tiny moment where his back is turned and his face is obscured by his tunic, when I reach out to the tiny doll with hazel hair who sits above us on his household shrine. I touch her with one finger. I do not say anything, neither out loud nor in my head, it is not a proper prayer or even a speech. It is only an acknowledgement, from one woman to another across the years, of a shared love for one man. And then Marcus turns back to me and takes me in his arms.

He sleeps, afterwards, and I watch him, not touching him because I do not want to disturb his sleep, he is so tired. I stare at him. *He is mine.* It is such a wonderful thought that a smile grows on my face until I give a tiny giddy laugh, then pull my tunic back on and creep away, so that he can sleep on.

I make my way barefoot to the stairway, peer over the side to see what is happening in the courtyard below. The meal Cassia prepared has ended, the tables contain mostly scraps. There are still people sitting about, talking to one another, though their voices are low, the courtyard feels like a shelter where we have huddled to be safe from a storm.

I tiptoe down, nod to people here and there and go to find Cassia. She's in the popina, Emilia asleep in a corner, Quintus beside her, carving one of his little toys. They both look up at me, take in my lack of a belt, ruffled loose hair and bare feet.

"Say the word and my wedding veil is yours," says Cassia, in a falsely bored voice. "Been waiting long enough to pass it on to you."

I laugh out loud and she shrieks, runs and throws her arms about me.

"Yes! I knew it! Days I've been waiting for him to take that farm up to you! Quintus carved the pigs. I knew when I saw what Marcus commissioned that he'd bring it to you, I knew it! I saw him walk up the stairs carrying it, I've been holding my breath for *hours*, so don't think I don't know what you've been up to!"

Quintus joins in our laughter but Emilia stirs in her sleep and we all subside into whispers.

"What's all the noise?" asks Karbo at the doorway, munching on a bread roll left over from the meal.

"Marcus and Althea are going to be married," says Cassia.

"Oh, good," says Karbo.

"You say it like it doesn't matter!" says Cassia.

"They're always together. I thought it was already agreed," he says. "But will there be a feast, like there was for your wedding?"

"An even bigger one," says Cassia.

"With cream pudding?"

"With all your favourite dishes," I promise him. "Come to the roof and see something with me."

A curious lizard has been exploring the tiny farm. It lies in the miniature courtyard, basking in the last rays of the setting sun. When it hears me coming its tail swishes away two escaped pigs, almost but not quite returning them to their sty, while the lizard makes good its escape across the warm roof and hides somewhere in the wall.

"Is it for me?" asks Karbo, kneeling over the farm, carefully replacing the fallen roof tiles to the roof and the pigs to the sty.

"It is for you to come to with Marcus and me," I say. "It will be a new adventure."

"When?"

"I'm not sure yet. We will make plans."

"But the racing stables?"

"I don't know," I say. "But I know they are important to you."

He nods, setting the hives back in their proper places.

"I can see you will be a great help," I say. "A proper farm boy."

"Can I bring Letitia?"

"Of course. She will be a real farm cat and catch mice for us and have lots of kittens of her own."

Marcus appears, the weariness gone from his face, instead his hair is ruffled and his smile warm. "I woke and found you gone from me already."

I scramble to my feet and nestle into his arms. It feels easy and at the same time I am astonished by it happening at last, by the warmth of him and the certainty of my place in his arms.

"Ah, back where you belong," he says and kisses me. "When shall we hold the wedding, Karbo?"

"Right now?"

"I would agree with you," says Marcus laughing, "but it is my understanding that women like more notice for these occasions. Mostly so that they can enjoy the anticipation."

"And prepare the food?" I ask.

"That, too."

"And make ourselves more beautiful?"

"That's not possible in your case," he says, tightening his embrace. "But planning a feast, that *is* important. So I will allow a week or two. That should be enough. You have Cassia to help you, after all, and Cassia can make a feast appear out of nowhere. Now come down to Julia, I promised I'd bring you to her for her blessing as soon as I spoke to you."

"You told her you were going to speak to me?"

"I told her I had been a fool and said everything wrong. And she told me to do better next time and to bring you for her blessing when I did."

"She had faith in you doing better."

"More faith than I had in myself," he says. "Come."

Julia is standing in her doorway when we make our way along the walkway to her apartment.

"About time," she says, smiling when she sees us walking hand in hand.

We follow her into the flickering light of her rooms, softly burning candles placed about her household shrine. She stands before it, Marcus and I behind her. She takes a deep breath, then lifts her hands, palms upwards. She speaks in her priestess voice, the certain clear voice of a Vestal.

"To the spirits of this insula for whom I keep this shrine and to all the gods of Rome. I thank you for having kept Marcus safe all these years since he first came here, no matter how far away he has travelled. I thank you for having saved him and kept him from darkness when he lost all that was most precious. I thank them for sending a woman to stand by him when the realm of Hades called but he still had a long life left to lead. I thank you for giving him the courage to love again, for he is a man of great good heart and such a heart should not be wasted."

She bows her head and her voice grows quieter, softer. "I send word to the shades of Livia and Amantius, who walk hand in hand amidst fields of flowers, that the husband and father they left behind stands always true to them, but that they should rejoice, for he has been blessed once more by Venus and Juno, in finding a second wife worthy of his heart. May your shades walk always in peace and may Marcus be free to love again. May Marcus and Althea be joyful in their new love, built as it is on a rock of friendship and loyalty which has outlasted all darkness."

Tears fall down my cheeks. I am grateful to Julia for her wisdom in having spoken Livia's name out loud, for taking away the fear of not knowing how to say something of the kind myself to Marcus, for assuaging whatever guilt he may feel at loving another woman.

She turns to both of us, her face lit up. "I could not be happier for you both," she says. "When is the wedding?"

"Very soon," promises Marcus. "I will travel to secure the farm while Althea arranges the day and we shall be married as soon as I return. There is nothing to wait for. And once we are married, we will plan everything for the farm and leave next spring."

"Won't you have to give notice to the Aedile that you no longer wish to be the manager of the Games?"

Marcus shrugs. "They have plenty of time to find a new manager, everything works well, there's more than five months to choose someone before a new season starts. There's no more building to be done, the team is complete. Whoever takes over will have an easy life of it. When I return I'll give notice. It will all be settled."

He is so certain that he makes me feel confident. Yes, he signed an agreement to continue as manager for next year's season, but that can surely be changed. There are plenty of men who would be eager to take over the largest and most prestigious amphitheatre in the empire and be known by name to the Emperor himself. I lean my head against his shoulder. All will be well.

"I am sure you will find a way," Julia says. "But you will not be gone from here until the spring, I hope."

"It would be better to take possession of the farm in springtime," he says. "It would be a hard life to begin in wintertime, with the roof full of holes and no food stores in place. We will be here till spring."

When I see Maria and tell her she nods approvingly. "Bona Dea send her blessings over you," she says. She turns serious. "I will miss the boy," she confesses.

"He will miss you," I say. Karbo is all but a grandson to Maria. "But I can't leave him here all alone, he's my son and too young to live by himself. Farm life will be good for him."

"You hear that, scamp?" calls Maria to Karbo. "You'll be a farm boy. None of your city softness. Farm boys know the true meaning of hard work."

Karbo grins at her. "I could always stay here and live with you and be a charioteer," he suggests.

"You are not going to be a charioteer," I say. "It's much too dangerous."

"Celer says I'm gifted with horses." Karbo pouts. "He says I'm touched by Neptune."

"Well, if Neptune cares about you at all he won't make you a charioteer," I say. "He'll keep you out of danger."

Fabia's face lights up when she hears the news. "Oh Althea! I am so happy for you."

"I should have followed your advice and spoken up sooner," I say.

"All things come in their own time," Fabia says. "Venus and Juno were watching over you, ready to make you a bride. But I will miss you all so much!"

"If you wish to be a country physician, come with us," I say.

She laughs. "Too late, I have a taste for wounds, just like my father. I would be bored giving out herbs for low fevers and tending to the odd small cut, attending upon women in childbirth. Rome is the place for me."

"Then we must spend more time together this winter, before we leave in the Spring."

"That, I will willingly agree to. We shall have the best Saturnalia in Rome, a huge feast. And I will help you prepare for the country. It will be such a different life!"

"Marcus thinks I am a good farmer only because I grew some beans and peas and flowers. I have never lived on a farm."

"Ah, you will have Marcus by you and it can't be a harder life than running the Flavian Amphitheatre."

"That much is true," I say. "I'll be grateful not to be overseen by the Emperor himself."

"Tomorrow we're spending the whole morning at the baths," says Fabia, pulling my hand. "We'll get a massage and you can tell me every word Marcus said when he asked you to marry him."

When I return from the baths the next day, loose-limbed and sweet-smelling, I climb to the rooftop and find Adah looking after the bees. Singing softly under her breath she lifts the lids of the hives and pokes about within them with her bare hands, while Karbo clutches Letitia to stop her trying to chase the displaced bees and watches from a safe distance, anxious not to miss the golden treasure about to be excavated.

"How are you, Adah?" I ask.

"Aching," she replies, mid-croon. "My back, child, my back."

"Is there no remedy for it?" I ask.

"Dying," she says.

"Adah!" I say reprovingly. "You're not dying."

"It comes to us all eventually, as the Lord commands," she says, extracting a chunk of honeycomb and holding it out to Karbo, who approaches tentatively, cat tucked under one arm, takes the honeycomb and hastily retreats.

"You're not to die any time soon," I say. "Who would look after the bees?"

She smiles up at me. "Not clever enough, child," she says. "You could look after them by yourself."

"I wouldn't know where to begin," I tell her. "And I'm not going to learn, either, so you'll just have to stay alive."

She gives a small laugh. "A little more clever," she concedes.

"Marcus and I are going to be married soon," I say shyly.

"A good man," she says approvingly. "Though he shouldn't work in that cursed place."

"We're going to go and live on his family's old farm instead."

"Much better."

"I had a – a request to make of you."

She pauses in what she is doing, looks curiously at me.

"Would you give me away? On my wedding day?"

Her shoulders hunch up further. "I don't believe in your gods, child," she says, but there is a sadness in her refusal.

"Please," I say. "I would like you to place my hand in Marcus'. That's all you have to do."

She looks away. "Because you ask it," she says. "Only because you ask, child."

"Thank you," I say, not sure whether she is happy or not to be asked. I stand uncertain for a moment, wondering whether I have done the right thing, whether I have offended her, which was not my intention, but then Adah leaves the hives and shuffles over to me, pats my arm and holds out a broken chunk of honeycomb with her other hand, poking it into my mouth. My mouth full of sweetness, I smile down at her. When she tilts her face up, her eyes are full of tears.

"Good child," she says, her voice tremulous. She turns away before I can embrace her, back to the hives, surrounded by the bees, singing her old song again.

I look at Karbo, and we grin at each other, our mouths full of honey. I never knew happiness tasted so sweet, nor that there could be so much of it to look forward to in the days ahead.

I hope you have enjoyed this third book in the Colosseum series. If you have, I would really appreciate it if you would leave a rating or brief review, so that new readers can find *On Bloodied Ground*. I read all reviews and am always grateful for your time in writing them and touched by your kind words.

THE FLIGHT OF BIRDS

A loving wedding. A happy future. A dangerous Emperor...

Rome, 83AD. At last the Colosseum receives its promised awning, rippling in the air high above the spectators. Marcus and Althea are to be wed. All is well.

But Emperor Domitian's behaviour is giving the backstage team cause for concern. Is he just strange, or is he going mad? And is he dangerous? The bird omens don't look good and when Marcus is forced to arrange one last terrifying event, it seems the time has come to take flight from Rome... but who will escape and who will be left behind?

The fourth and final book in the Colosseum series. Coming winter 2023.

Have you read the Forbidden City series? Pick up the first in the series FREE on your local Amazon website.

Lonely. Used as a pawn. One last bid for love.

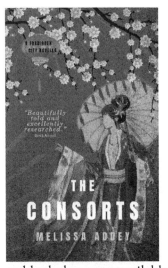

18th century China. Imperial concubine Qing yearns for love and friendship. Neglected by the Emperor, passed over for more ambitious women, Qing lives a lonely existence. But when a new concubine comes to court, friendship blooms, bringing with it a taste of happiness.

For the first time in her life, Qing has a friend and perhaps even a chance at loving and being loved. But when the Empress' throne suddenly becomes available, Qing finds herself being used as a pawn by the highest ranked women of the court. Caught up in their power games, on one devastating night everything she holds dear is put at risk.

As the power players of the Forbidden City make their moves, can Qing find the courage to make one last bid for love? Can an insignificant pawn snatch victory from the jaws of defeat?

The Consorts is the captivating prequel novella to the Forbidden City historical fiction series. If you enjoy slow-burn romance, courtly intrigues and the intricately researched legends of real women, then you'll be swept away by Melissa Addey's enchanting novella.

Enter the exquisite and stifling world of China's Forbidden City. Download *The Consorts* for free today.

AUTHOR'S NOTE
ON HISTORY

THIS IS THE THIRD BOOK in a series that started as the simple question I asked myself: who were people who made up the 'backstage team' for the Colosseum? There is hardly any mention whatsoever of them and yet Games on such an immense scale could not possibly have been put on without a very large and permanent team in place. *On Bloodied Ground* focuses on the element of earth, from the creation of an extraordinary under-arena area (the hypogeum) and a vast building programme across Rome, to the legend of the Minotaur and its labyrinth, earthquakes and a Vestal Virgin entombed alive. The other three books in this series focus on the same team through the themes of fire (*From the Ashes*), water (*Beneath the Waves*) and air (*The Flight of Birds*).

One of the ideas I have used in this book is that Emperor Domitian might have been on the autistic spectrum. This was first suggested to me by my historical consultant Steven Cockings, who is himself autistic, and is based on the preliminary work of Jen Cresswell, *Domitian and Asperger's Syndrome – a retrospective diagnosis*, which draws attention to Domitian exhibiting certain characteristics linked to autism, including a preference for solitude, some difficulty engaging with people, obsessions (including a huge building programme and the gladiatorial Games/chariot racing), and a love of routine. There can also be obsessive attention to detail leading to a tendency to micro-manage, as well as a rigid adherence to the rules, which results in a certain amount of inflexibility when applying the law (given this last point, it was actually more generous than it sounds for Domitian to have allowed the first two Vestals their choice of how to die). As my own son is autistic, and I found the historical evidence interesting and compelling, I have built in this concept and used examples of behaviour from people I know who are on the spectrum. The interest in wild animals and the vast patience in approaching them comes from my son. Domitian seems to have been judged overly harshly by historians in comparison to other emperors and I thought perhaps he lacked some of the social skills required to endear himself to people generally or to explain and promote his actions and choices. I also thought that the more positive aspects of his reign (such as the vast public building programme he undertook) might have made people nervous because of Nero's similar interests. Nero's madness would still have been very much in living memory and I thought that any odd behaviour at all coupled to a similar building programme would have made people around Domitian wary of history repeating itself and therefore quick to judge him.

I have used one of those irresistible tiny historical mentions you find from time to time during research, but brought it into my own era, even though the era it is from was more dissolute than Domitian's. In 197 AD Septimius Severus addressed the Senate in Rome and said:

> "*For if it was disgraceful for him (Emperor Commodus) with his own hands to slay wild beasts, yet at Ostia only the*

other day one of your number, an old man who had been consul, was publicly sporting with a prostitute who imitated a leopard".

Domitian had an architect named Rabirius, who probably undertook most of Domitian's many building works. Very little is known about him, although he is mentioned with praise by the poet Martial.

The two sister Vestal Virgins put to death were approximately in 82AD, so the timing of this is correct. But I have used poetic licence to bring forward the death of the Vestal Virgin Cornelia, as her entombment alive was such a close fit to the earth theme of this book. She was in fact put to death in approximately 90AD, so about 8 years later. Pliny the Younger felt strongly that she was innocent and gives this description of her last moments before the burial:

"... when she was let down into the subterranean chamber, and her robe had caught in descending, she turned round and gathered it up. And when the executioner offered her his hand, she shrank from it, and turned away with disgust; spurning the foul contact from her person, chaste, pure, and holy: And with all the deportment of modest grace, she scrupulously endeavoured to perish with propriety and decorum."

The Kingdom of Kush, where Funis's mother is originally from, was located in modern Northern Sudan and Southern Egypt.

People often ask whether I base characters on people I know and the answer is very seldom, but past pets often seem to worm their way in. It was only after I'd named Karbo's cat Letitia that I thought about our pet cat in Rome having been called Titi...

Recent scientific research has discovered that the Romans had actually worked out how to make buildings earthquake proof, by creating holes in their foundations and structures, which meant that the seismic waves could not travel on to the next piece of the building because there was a gap. This created a sort of 'invisibility cloak'. We are not sure if this was applied to all buildings, but it has been confirmed in the Colosseum (perhaps contributing to its longevity in a very earthquake-prone country) and other amphitheatres. Perhaps it was used in very large public buildings which would have been difficult to rebuild, or perhaps a large size was required in order to leave enough of the gaps. Earthquakes are very common in Italy, especially in spring and autumn, when the weather changes.

Archaeologists found a baby's bottle with gladiators on it, an irresistible piece to mention... I had to find a baby to use it and so Emilia arrived and brought Quintus with her! Unwanted babies were often simply abandoned. Some died, the luckier ones were adopted.

In approximately 64 AD, so about twenty years before the events of this book, Seneca wrote about a gladiator who committed suicide:

> *"In a training academy for gladiators who work with wild beasts, a German slave, while preparing for the morning exhibition, withdrew in order to relieve himself – the only thing he was allowed to do in secret and without the presence of a guard. While so engaged, he seized the stick of wood tipped with a sponge, devoted to the vilest uses, and stuffed it down his throat. Thus he blocked up his windpipe and*

choked the breath from his body... What a brave fellow. He surely deserved to be allowed to choose his fate."

While many of the gladiators I have depicted in this series were professionals (whether slaves or free) and lived many years in their line of work quite happily and if very successful were lauded as celebrities, like Carpophorus the bestiarius, there were others who were forced to fight and would have been unhappy and so I used Billica as one of these examples and gave her the fate of the unnamed gladiator mentioned by Seneca.

Many of the specific Games I have written about actually happened. Those that I have invented were based on very similar approaches, such as the regular re-enacting of myths and legends of the Greeks and Romans. The legend of the Minotaur was one of my favourite stories as a child (I was genuinely afraid of the dark because there might be a minotaur lurking about) and so I took this chance to build a story around it.

GLOSSARY

Aedile   A senator in charge of commissioning the gladiatorial games.

Bestiarius Gladiator specialising in fighting animals (plural bestiarii).

Bulla   Protective amulet worn by boys. Girls wore an equivalent pendant in the form of a crescent moon.

Cithara   Roman precursor to the guitar.

Cosmetes   Beautician (plural cosmetae).

Domina   Mistress.

Dominus   Master.

Fullery   A laundry which washed, dried and also dyed garments. Human urine (collected on street corners) was used as a cleaning and bleaching aid.

Garum   Fish sauce, a very popular condiment.

Imperial Palace   The place indicated on the map is an approximate location of Nero's Golden House (which Titus might have continued to use for official receptions) and also, later, the building started by Domitian at the beginning of his reign and completed in 92AD. There were additional locations, both official and residential, where the emperors would have been located in Rome.

Insula   Block of apartments/individual rooms, often built around a central courtyard.

Lararium   Household shrine.

Naumachia   Water-based spectacle often featuring re-enactments of sea-battles, held on lakes or in flooded man-made structures such as the Colosseum.

Nereids   Sea-nymphs (goddesses of the sea).

Ornatrix   Hairdresser.

Palantine   One of the hills of Rome, used by many as an expression to suggest the Emperor's residence.

Palla   A large rectangular outer garment of wool or linen, worn predominantly by married women, draped around the whole body, a fold of which could be placed over the head for protection and as a sign of propriety.

Popina   Streetside café (most poor Romans did not have cooking facilities, so street food outlets were very common and popular).

Tablet   A wooden 'book' of two or three 'pages', filled with wax, on which notes could be made using a metal pen called a stylus, then erased when no longer required. More formal, permanent writing could be done with ink and a reed/quill pen onto scrolls of papyrus.

Tullianum   One of the very few prisons in Rome, used for high status prisoners or those to be made an example of, as prison sentences were not used as punishment, only as brief holding places.

Venator   Performer who hunted animals for the morning hunt (technically not gladiators or bestiarii as it was hunting, not combat).

THANKS

Thank you to Jessica Bell for seeing my books in a new light and to Streetlight Graphics, making my writing life so much easier since day one.

Thank you to my beta readers for this book: Helen, Etain, Martin. Your comments and ideas are always insightful. Thank you to my editor Debi Alper for patiently improving my craft and seeing the bigger picture.

Many scholars and historians were helpful during my research. My thanks for all their fascinating work and always, of course, to my historical consultant for this series, Steven Cockings. You are far nicer and more approachable than the character I have given you! Your key as murder weapon idea is included here, as you'll see. Also thank you to the real Secundus and all his jokes and stories (the twins story is true!) which amused me during a lovely and memorable Saturnalia dinner hosted by Steven.

Professor Donald G Kyle's considerable body of work on Roman spectacles and especially on the disposal of bodies (human and animal) from the arena, was invaluable. Professor Christopher Ellett very helpfully provided me with his work on beast-hunts and executions. Professor Kathleen Coleman of Harvard University helped me to access her research on gladiators and naval shows.

All errors and fictional choices are of course mine.

**Chosen for imperial service, some concubines
rise to power. Others fall to madness.**

The Forbidden City series. 18th century China. An
extraordinary lost world of exquisite beauty, hard-
won power and deeply emotional choices.

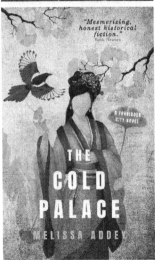

**Why did a Muslim emperor pick the son
of a Christian slave as his heir?**

The Moroccan Empire series. 11th century Morocco
and Spain. An epic journey of complex choices and
opposing faiths told by the voices of forgotten women.

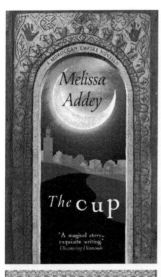

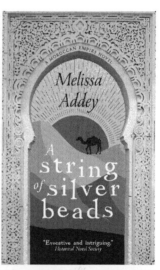

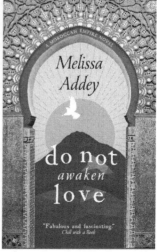

CURRENT AND FORTHCOMING BOOKS INCLUDE:

Historical Fiction

China

The Consorts (novella, free on Amazon)
The Fragrant Concubine
The Garden of Perfect Brightness
The Cold Palace

Morocco

The Cup (novella, free on my website)
A String of Silver Beads
None Such as She
Do Not Awaken Love

Rome

From the Ashes
Beneath the Waves

On Bloodied Ground
The Flight of Birds

Picture Books for Children

Kameko and the Monkey-King

Non-Fiction

The Storytelling Entrepreneur
Merchandise for Authors
The Happy Commuter
100 Things to Do while Breastfeeding

BIOGRAPHY

I LOVE WRITING HISTORICAL FICTION AND exploring a new era with each series I write. So far I've written The Forbidden City series set in 18th century China which explores the lives of the imperial concubines, as well as The Moroccan Empire series which follows the rise of a Moroccan empire through the eyes of four very different women. My current series follows the lives of the 'backstage team' of the Colosseum starting in 79AD in Ancient Rome. I've been the Leverhulme Trust Writer in Residence at the British Library and won the inaugural Novel London and Page to Podcast awards. I have a PhD in Creative Writing from the University of Surrey. I run regular workshops at the British Library and enjoy speaking at writing festivals during the year. I live in London with my husband and two children.

For more information on me and my books, as well as a free novella, visit my website www.MelissaAddey.com

Printed in Great Britain
by Amazon